CARPENTRY AND COCKTAILS

GREEN VALLEY LIBRARY BOOK #5

NORA EVERLY

WWW.SMARTYPANTSROMANCE.COM

COPYRIGHT

This book is a work of fiction. Names, characters, places, rants, facts, contrivances, and incidents are either the product of the author's questionable imagination or are used factitiously. Any resemblance to actual persons, living or dead or undead, events, locales is entirely coincidental if not somewhat disturbing/concerning.

Made in the United States of America

Print Edition
ISBN: 978-1-949202-49-6

CHAPTER ONE

WILLA

"'Til death do us part. That means something to me, Willa."

— *TOMMY*

Bang, Bam, Smash

Unfortunately, I was not a character in a comic book. Nor was I leisurely reading one while loafing around in bed. No, I had buried myself under my covers with a pillow wrapped around my ears, trying not to wake all the way up as the incessant pounding of the hammer outside my tiny basement apartment hit the crap out of something nearby.

Bam, Crash, Bang

Gritting my teeth, I snarled into the pillow. He was at it *again*. Blindly reaching out, I grabbed another pillow, added it to the pile atop my head, then rolled to my stomach. My head had hit this pillow at four a.m. I was not ready to get out of bed and be a fully functioning human. Or even a semi-functional one, which was my usual baseline.

Early birds were fine with me—I had nothing against them as a general life rule—but as a bartender/waitress I was up late almost every night. Therefore, this noisy, pounding bullshit going on outside my window when I was trying to sleep was unacceptable. I mean, he should know better. I reached an arm out and fumbled around for my cell phone to check the time.

It was dead.

I tossed it away, the useless piece of crap. It bounced off the mattress to land on the carpeted floor with an unsatisfying soft thump. I would have thrown it harder, but I was too broke to buy another one.

I flopped over onto my back and threw the pillow across the room. It was no use; between the banging hammer and the stupid daylight shining in my windows to assault me through my eyelids I'd never get back to sleep.

I sat up and looked around for my phone to plug it in. Freaking dead phone, freaking stupid daylight, and freaking Everett, who was outside building something or fixing something. He was probably out there being all hot and industrious and useful—and shirtless, which seemed to be his preference—while he worked on stuff around his house. His huge, beautiful old Colonial fixer-upper where I rented a furnished apartment in his walk-out basement. Damn him and his stupid, sexy handyman schtick.

Everett Monroe.

My landlord. My friend? My complication I did not need at this messed up juncture in my screwed-up disaster of a life. With a snarl I tossed the covers back.

Shower.

Coffee.

Attitude adjustment?

I got out of bed just in time to hear a knock on my door. Shoving my crazy blonde curls out of my eyes, I scowled at that door, then stuck my tongue out at it. He was probably about to tell me he had made more of his delicious coffee and had doughnuts from Daisy's Nut House waiting on the kitchen table upstairs. Freaking friendly Everett, always inviting me to breakfast and making it so hard to resist him.

Men are a complication I refused to need, or even want. I'd had enough of that crap to last a lifetime. Running away from home at age seventeen and marrying your twenty-two-year-old boyfriend could do that to a girl. I no longer trusted myself to do the right thing. And I wanted to *do* Everett, real bad.

Maybe *he* could be the right thing... *NOPE.*

"Willard are you up?" he called as he knocked. Everett never called me Willa. Or honey, sweetie, darlin', or even babe. He was too cute and funny for that kind of basic bull-crap. He made up ridiculous variations of my name and almost charmed me out of my panties every single time he came up with a new one.

"Yeah, I'm up. Someone was bangin' around on something outside and *woke* me up." I shouted at the closed door.

"Sorry about that. There's coffee and doughnuts upstairs. And, it's noon. Rise and shine Willie Bean, it's time to get *up*." He tapped my door once more and laughed. I heard his footsteps retreating and stuck my tongue out at the door again.

I ran over to my window to sneak a peek.

Yep, just as I'd thought. No shirt.

Damn.

He was in low-slung jeans with a T-shirt sticking out of his back pocket. His tanned skin was shiny with sweat as his back muscles bunched and unbunched, flexing with glorious rippling waves as he swung a huge ax over his head. Everett was splitting logs out there. He had dragged out his fire pit last weekend to place in the rear of his property, near the forest. I may have peeped on him then too; don't judge. Why couldn't he just go out and buy firewood like a normal person?

Rude.

I gulped and stepped back before he could catch me staring at him like a creepy, horny pervert.

Oh, eff it. Who was I trying to kid? I was totally a creepy, horny pervert.

I ran to the other window so I could catch a view from the front. I could sell tickets to this shit and probably make enough money to quit my job. Then I could sleep at night like everybody else and not feel like a cranky bitch all the time.

The front of Everett was just as good as the back. Debatably better because of his face and beard. Not to mention his perfectly not-too-hairy chest with its happy trail that led straight down through his magnificent abs into those low-slung jeans and toward what I liked to imagine was a very good time. In fact, I frequently imagined it. And it *was* very good.

He lifted an arm to swipe across his brow, flexing that huge bicep as his arm bent. It was almost as if he knew I was watching him. This was like something out of a commercial for after-shave or energy drinks or male strippers. Bending over, he grabbed a bottle of water from the ground, uncapped it, took a sip, then tilted his head back and poured it over his head, letting the water run down his gorgeously glistening broad chest.

Huh?

He shook his head, drops of water flew to the sides as he waved and blew a kiss at me.

"Ahhhhh!" I screamed and ran for the bathroom. I swear I could hear him laughing at me from outside.

Shit, crap, damn.

Busted.

Well, it wasn't the first time, and I doubted it would be the last. I stopped running and started stomping. Who did he think he was, anyway? The big, hot, wannabe lumberjack buttweasel. I sailed through my shower and getting-ready routine on righteous winds of indignation. So I'd been peeping at him. So what?

I'd caught him checking me out more than one time too. I pursed my lips and added some pink lip balm, giving myself a kissy face in the mirror. Yeah, he totally wanted a piece of old Willard. And as an old great song once said, he was "Never Gonna Get It."

I slipped into my flip-flops and cautiously ventured out my front door, peering left and right and across the backyard, on the lookout for Everett and his gorgeous bare chest. One sighting of that per day was all I could take. I was only human, dang it. I was in pretty serious danger of tackling him and riding him like a bull at the rodeo for Pete's sake.

I inhaled deeply. The unseasonably cool spring air made me want to blow off work, head upstairs with some of his freshly chopped wood and build a fire in that huge brick fireplace he'd just finished restoring. Toasted marshmallows and some warm and cozy ambiance would be awesome right about now. Brisk spring days in Green Valley, Tennessee, were one of the things I had missed when I was gone.

I had been away for too long...

I sighed and made my way to Everett's back door. A doughnut hit-and-run and a cup of coffee would have to do. My fantasy-filled thoughts of getting snuggly with Everett, his wood, a fire, and some cocoa were becoming way too tempting—because on top of all that sexiness, he was a sweetheart too. Nice guys like Everett were dangerous. Every girl knows that men like him were the most trouble, because they'd steal your heart all stealthy-like and before you knew it, you'd be sitting on his couch, watching TV while he cooked you a nice dinner. Then there goes your heart, right along with your undies, and *boom*, you're done for. Goodness like that was not meant for the likes of me. I would never risk my heart like that ever again. My divorce was barely final anyway. I needed time to...to...*to what?*

I just needed time to be alone. Probably forever. I was bad at love. And even worse at making good choices.

I climbed the steps and stopped on the covered brick back porch that ran the length of the house. He'd just finished rebuilding it, and it was beautiful. Made by a man who built things instead of tearing them apart. I blew out a sigh as I turned in a slow circle to admire his handiwork. The brick was original; he'd cleaned it and replaced the broken ones. But it was the woodwork that stole the show. Everett was a carpenter, but it went beyond that—he was an artsy-fartsy carpenter. The columns had leaves and vines carved in winding, meandering trails up and around the wood and along the little arches that lined the covered part of the porch. He'd stained it so the leaves

5

and vines were darker and stood out. It was the prettiest porch I'd ever seen.

"Coffee's still hot." His deep voice startled me.

I jumped and spun around with a gasp.

He stood, hips against the corner of the kitchen counter, sipping coffee and watching me through the open window. A white T-shirt stretched across his broad sculpted chest, which was easier to handle than when he was shirtless. Except that it almost *wasn't*. It clung in all the right places, like highlighter over your favorite parts of a book. I took a deep breath and headed for the gorgeous new French doors to let myself inside.

"Hey," I said and tried to prevent my elevator eyes from running up and down his tall form. And I meant *tall*. I'd hit six feet when I was twelve. Everett topped me by at least five inches, but I was not about to get close enough to him to get an exact measurement.

"Hey." His honey colored brown eyes crinkled at the corners as he unleashed a gorgeous white smile on me. Complete with not just one, but two adorable, kissable—fuckable?—dimples.

Gah! Why did he have to be so hot? And nice? And make such great coffee? And always invite me to freaking share it with him? But more importantly, why did I keep saying yes?

My nose scrunched up.

"You're a like a ray of midnight, Willard. How many shades of black are you wearing today?" His smile shifted sideways as he teased me and his frickin' beautiful eyes twinkled in the sunlight shining through the window.

"I'll change my color palette when I find something darker," I shot back along with my best don't-mess-with-me smirk.

He gestured to my black "Genie's Bar" tank top, under my open black cardigan, atop my black leggings. "Working early?" he asked, unaffected by the power of my smirk armor.

"Not until later. Saturday night is the best night for tips."

Saturday nights were always crazy at Genie's, a country western bar in town. It was the place to be for your wholesome line dancing and friendly-hookup needs. Those that wanted to skip the dancing and head straight for the hooking up headed to The Wooden Plank. And those with a taste for venereal diseases and hostile bikers headed to The Dragon Biker Bar, home of the Iron Wraith's biker club, located right outside of town. When I got back to Green Valley, I headed straight to Genie's to apply for a job. I'd been working in bars since the age of twenty-one and I'd learned the hard way which kind to avoid. Plus, Genie was my aunt and I was not above using family connections to land a job.

Everett gestured to the coffeepot and the container of hazelnut creamer sitting next to it—my favorite. "Help yourself."

"Thank you. You make the best coffee." I poured a cup, added a healthy splash of the creamer and took a sip, closing my eyes involuntarily. *Yum.*

I opened them to find his eyes burning into mine. I had caught him looking at me like that a few times before—eyes heated, hooded, full of sex—but the look always disappeared just as fast as I caught it. I was probably projecting my own dirty thoughts onto him.

Quit imagining things.

My eyebrows raised over my mug as he quickly turned away and placed his own mug in the sink.

He cleared his throat, but his voice still came out low and husky, "So, uh—there are doughnuts on the table. Help yourself. I'm going to shower." He opened his mouth again as if to say something else. The silence hung in the air between us like invisible strings pulling us closer. But then he closed his mouth and looked away. And I refused to let myself say anything more to him, so whatever that moment was, it ended.

I loved listening to his smoky, sexy voice. I wished I could talk to him all day just to hear the sound of it. But the more I talked to him, the more I fell into like with him and I couldn't have that. So, I kept quiet and watched him walk away instead.

"Bye..." I whispered to his back as he turned and headed up the kitchen staircase. I *would not* imagine him all naked and slippery with soap in the shower...

I should have just stayed in my camper van at the Walmart

parking lot in Maryville. Being semi-homeless was almost easier. With a twist of the key I could drive away from my problems. *Escape.* Sometimes I wanted to do just that. But my family and my best friend were here in Green Valley, and I wanted them to trust me. But mostly, I wanted somewhere to belong again. Plus, I had a job I actually liked for a change. Running away is what got me into this mess. It was time to rediscover the roots I'd left behind and attempt to start over.

No more running.

CHAPTER TWO

EVERETT

"You only have one life, Everett. Follow your heart, but make sure to take your brain along for the ride."

— *PAPAW JOE*

With a smile, I shoved open the door to the dusty old retail space I'd just taken over on Main Street. Finally, it was all mine. It was almost too big, but it would suit my purposes just fine.

"So, what do you think?" I gestured grandly to the room as I crossed the wood floor. I turned in a wide circle to take it all in. My youngest brother, Garrett, had followed me inside only to stop and stare out the front window into Stripped, Suzie Samuels' dance studio across the street. Back in high school I'd had a huge crush on her, but before I got up the nerve to do something about it, she'd hooked up with Jethro Winston. She was just the first of many in a long line of women who weren't interested in what I had to offer. A geek was a geek, no matter what the outside looked like.

"I know I'm not the smoothest guy. But what do you think my chances are? With that brunette? Or that one? Or any of them—damn." Garrett still hadn't removed his eyes from the candy in the

9

window across the street. He was full of crap. He was smoother than the sidewalk in January—meaning he was cool as ice and slick as anything—and ladies loved him.

"Slim to none," I answered with a light smack to the back of his head. "Show some respect, man. You're not at the Pink Pony. Pole fitness is not the same as pole dancing in a strip club. And even then, you can't assume. Don't be that guy, Garrett. We hate that guy."

"I was just looking. Mom would have my ass if I went across the street and acted a fool. And shit, don't tell her I was at the Pink Pony." His look of horror made me laugh until my head swung to the window to follow his gaze across the street. My body swung with it and I froze at the window, staring like a creeper, just like Garrett had been doing. My laughter stuck in my throat as I gulped.

It took me a second to process the fact that my gorgeous tenant was one of the girls spinning on a pole in the window. But before I could tell myself, *don't look, she's your tenant, dumbass,* it was too fucking late. My baser thoughts took over, and I couldn't look away. The same black leggings from earlier today hugged her long legs and curvy hips, but the baggy sweater and "Genie's Bar" tank were gone, leaving her with nothing but a little black sports bra on top—*holy hell.* Her pale blond curls bounced behind her back in a low ponytail, almost touching her tiny waist. She was nothing but lithe, sexy grace as she moved. The sway of her hips and the shimmy in her shoulders mesmerized me, making me realize exactly how much trouble I was in. It was already hard enough to be around her without *actually being hard* around her. The blood that fed my brain steadily flowed out of my head on a southern trajectory as my jeans grew tight at the front. I slammed my eyes shut to gain control. Damn it, I wasn't just in trouble anymore; I was completely fucked. Willa Faye Hill was like the *Death Star* and I was all caught up in her tractor beam. It was only a matter of time before my heart ended up in the trash compactor and smashed to bits—a.k.a. the usual ending of my romantic relationships.

"I guess everything will fit. There's room for the tables, at least,"

Garrett's voice wrenched me out of my dirty thoughts about Willa and I jumped.

"Huh?" I turned from the window to focus on Garrett.

"Don't be that guy, Ev. Show some respect." He smirked at me.

Flipping him the bird, I stepped away from the window and added blinds to my mental list of things to buy for my shop. With the business I was opening, it would be necessary to block that view. Or it could be a draw. I was opening a gamer shop, after all. We're talking *Dungeons and Dragons*, comic books, dice, and collectible figurines—tabletop roleplay gamer heaven. In other words, it would be geek central over here and having a dance studio full of hot women across the street could either be the best or the worst thing that could happen for my business.

Opening Twenty Sides and Sundry was my dream. Well, it was one of them. If life could be as simple as a game, then *that* would be a dream come true. Character sheets and dice made the unexpected somehow become expected. If only people in the real world were so easy to figure out. Games had rules. Life had no rules, and that had always been a problem for me. Scrubbing my hand down my beard, I sighed. I needed to get her out of my mind. *Fucking impossible.*

"You got it bad for her. I don't blame you." The slap on my shoulder made me jump again. "Caffeine jitters?" Garrett laughed at me. Yes, I'd been drinking a second cup of coffee every day at noon just to spend a few moments with her. So what? Garrett was just nosy enough to notice my change in lunchtime habits. Instead of meeting him at Daisy's Nut House to eat lunch together, I'd been picking up doughnuts and rushing home to feed Willa breakfast. Yeah, I probably had it bad, but I couldn't seem to stop myself. The pricklier she was, the more I liked her. Clearly, I was a glutton for punishment.

Town lore told me I probably had little chance of ever getting a date with her anyway. Everyone knew all about those wild Hill sisters, living with their momma up in the hills above town. Their reputations preceded them wherever they went—heartbreakers and hell raisers each one. I'd gone to school with the oldest two Hill girls, Sadie and Clara, but Willa hadn't gone to Green Valley High School. She'd attended the private all-girls school in Maryville. I knew nothing of her reputation other than she had run away from home to marry her boyfriend when she was seventeen and only came back to town a few months ago. She was also best friends with my brother Wyatt's new wife, Sabrina. Truthfully, I didn't know that much about Willa's past. The conversations we shared consisted of small talk, where she would be adorable and cagey while letting irresistible glimpses of her personality and sense of humor out for me to fall for. Either that or superficial landlord and tenant stuff, along with the occasional flirty interlude or hot look to keep me dangling on her line, where I suspected I'd be forever.

I shot Garrett a grin. "You should reconsider the shit you're shoveling. Don't forget I know things about you too." I said his latest ex-girlfriend's name through a fake cough, and he laughed.

"Touché, ya douche." I smiled at his mispronunciation and smacked his outstretched hand. Of all my brothers, Garrett was the worst about minding his own business. Barrett, the oldest, was a vault. I was pretty sure he still had leftover secrets from our middle school years buried somewhere inside his subconscious right alongside the secret location of wherever he had hidden the original set of X-Men action figures we had collected over the years. But I was always closest to Wyatt, both in age and in temperament. We were stuck in the middle of our group of four and remained close even when he was off living in Nashville with his evil ex-wife and two adorable daughters.

"All kidding aside, thank you. Your help means a lot."

"Don't get all mushy. I'm here to help you clean up, then kick some ass when we finish the overhaul and get those gaming tables set up. I need to level up my Paladin."

"Let's get to it. The shelves and furniture will be here in a few hours." The exposed brick was ideal for the vibe I wanted to create here, so there was no need to paint. I had enough of that left to do at home, anyway. Hours passed; we dusted, swept, mopped, and polished until the place was shiny.

"You should put the collectibles in that alcove," Garrett suggested, indicating an arched inset in the wall to the side of the long wooden counter where I would place my cash register.

"Great idea." The collectibles were my carvings, or "pointless wastes of time" as my father used to call them when I was a kid. Tiny dragons, wizards, fantasy creatures—little things I would create to escape the world around me—would be up for sale here. My father didn't think whittling wood was a worthwhile way to spend my extra time. Not like making the furniture, custom cabinets, or any of the other stuff I did for Monroe & Sons, the construction company he owned and where I worked as a carpenter. I loved my job. I loved creating something out of nothing—whatever form it took—which was why I would not quit working for my father completely. I'd just switch to part-time.

Monroe boys always joined Monroe & Sons, generation after generation for over sixty years. The only exception was my brother Wyatt, a deputy sheriff here in Green Valley. My father had been the only boy born in his generation of Monroes. He inherited all of it—the business, the sterling reputation, and the massive Victorian house in the middle of town where he lived with my mother. He worked there too; the office took up the downstairs parlor. He was an old-fashioned hard ass, but deep inside his heart was gold.

"Yoo-hoo!" We spun around in comic unison at our mother's voice in the doorway, just like when we were kids getting busted for doing something stupid. "I brought you boys dinner." She entered, carrying bags of takeout from Daisy's Nut House.

"You mean, you came to be nosy. I'm surprised you didn't go to Genie's to scope out Everett's lady." Garrett teased her. He was the only one of us with the guts to mess with our mother. Probably because he was her "baby."

"Oh, pish. I'm not nosy, I'm just a momma who loves her boys." With a flick of her wrist, she checked the time. "Willa never works this early at Genie's anyway. It's only six o'clock," she said primly. She passed me the takeout bag with an expectant smile. "So, how is Willa?"

I huffed out a laugh combined with a sigh. "Fine." My mother officially met Willa a few months back on Halloween when we joined Willa, Sabrina, Sabrina's nephew Harry and Wyatt's girls while trick-or-treating. Ever since, my mother had been asking questions, matchmaking and meddling, and trying to boss me into asking Willa out on a date. What she didn't know was that ever since meeting Willa, I'd been slowly and steadily—but most of all, hopelessly—falling for her. I couldn't ask her out until I knew she would say yes, which would probably be never. Willa was divorced and from what I could glean, it hadn't been pretty. Wyatt knew the details; they were friends when they'd both lived in Nashville. Willa's ex-husband had been Wyatt's partner on the police force. Plus, her ex, Tommy, was from Maryville. I'd played basketball against him back in high school, and he'd been an asshole. But Wyatt had yet to give me any real information, and Willa would never confide in me about that.

"Hey, y'all." The delivery guy stood in the doorway. Parked behind him on the curb was a truck full of my dreams finally coming true. I grinned and took the electronic clipboard to sign my name. He grinned back and congratulated me with a hearty slap on the shoulder. This was Green Valley, so of course we'd gone to school together. Everybody knew everybody in this town. Which was why it drove me so crazy that I didn't know Willa's story—yet.

"Okay, boys, this is where I take my leave. I have no interest in unloading, building, assembling, or anything other than a nice hot cup of tea and the *Downton Abbey* marathon tonight on the television. Kiss your mother goodbye." I exchanged a look with Garrett. We knew she would really watch *The Real Housewives* of somewhere and fix herself a huge martini, but we were both too smart to mention it.

Garrett kissed her cheek. "Bye, Ma."

She patted my cheek on the way out of the shop. "I'll stop by tomorrow, sweetie pie."

"Okay…bye," I answered distractedly. I headed to the delivery truck to make sure everything was there. This was like Christmas morning, but even better. This was a Christmas morning that would never end.

"Yo!" I glanced around the truck to see Wyatt and Frederick Boone, or just Boone as he preferred, headed up the sidewalk. Boone and I had been friends since our kindergarten days. He played football with Wyatt in high school, was a deputy sheriff, and not too long ago helped save his cousin Simone Payton and her man, Roscoe Winston, from being shot to death by the dickbag racist Sheriff Strickland. The Sheriff had lost his damn mind and shot up Daisy's Nut House while they'd been inside. Boone had fired the kill shot and was still having a hard time with it. Sometimes, doing the right thing could leave a person shaken up, even when the action was rightly deserved it and it was done to save lives.

"Hey, y'all." I patted the side of the delivery truck. "It's here, and you're just in time to help me put it all together."

"As long as we can hit up Genie's when we're done and have a round. On you." Boone laughed and slapped my shoulder as he passed by me to enter the shop.

"You got it," I affirmed. I had always been a semi-regular at Genie's. Shoot, most people over twenty-one in Green Valley were. I'd go with my brothers for dinner and darts, maybe a beer or two. However, since Willa started working there, I had become a constant fixture. It was only a matter of time before she figured out why I was there so often. I was taking a subtle approach with her—so subtle it was almost nonexistent. I had the feeling that a balls-to-the-wall approach would scare her away for good, and I didn't want to lose my shot. However, we'd shared enough hot looks to keep hope alive and I was hoping tonight would turn the tide.

CHAPTER THREE

WILLA

*"If you decide to run away from this house, Willa-girl, there will be
hell to pay when you come back. You hear?"*

— *MOMMA*

"Have you seen your momma yet?" I finished making the
margarita for my customer, passed it across the bar, steeled
my spine, then turned to my Aunt Genie—my mother's somewhat-
estranged sister, and my port in every storm I'd ever faced in my life.
I loved Aunt Genie with all my heart, but I did not want to talk about
it. However, I knew I should get ready to face the music. There was
only so long I could avoid talking about my mother, and I would
have to go see her eventually. It surprised me she'd roped Aunt
Genie into being her messenger. Genie and Momma butted heads
over a lot of things, the main one being my mother's method of child
rearing.

"Momma, leave her alone." I spun around to see my cousin Patty,
ready as ever to take up my defense. I grinned at her and she bumped
my shoulder with hers as she walked behind me to grab a beer from
the refrigerator beneath the long wooden bar. Uncapping it with a

flourish, she slid it, along with a wink, toward the hapless man hopelessly caught up in her spell. Patty was a looker: cute as a button with a brunette bob and athletic figure.

"Thank you," I mouthed as she went around the bar to head back out front, where I would join her soon enough. We took turns covering the bar when one of Genie's regular bartenders went on break.

With a salute, she disappeared, submerging herself into the crowd to dance her way across the wood floor toward the booths that lined the perimeter.

Genie's Bar was crazy busy tonight, just as it was every Saturday. I hoped I would earn enough in tips to go toward my rent this month. It was busy here and tips were good, but it was nothing like what I used to make when I lived in Nashville. This would be a tight month after I paid my attorney. Divorces were not cheap, especially when one party fought it every step of the damn way like my no-good, dumbass, dirtbag, dickhead, finally ex-husband had done.

Aunt Genie sighed as she filled a pitcher of beer from the tap and smiled sympathetically. "Darlin', your momma wants to see you," she shouted over the pulsing country music rippling through the air. It pounded in my chest almost as hard as the dread that beat through it whenever I thought of going home to see my mother.

I huffed out a sigh as I uncapped another beer. "Okay, I'll go up there tomorrow. Probably—"

Her eyebrows raised as her grin shifted sideways "I'm not here to push you, honey. But better you go there, rather than—shoot." Her eyes widened on whoever had approached behind me on the other side of the bar before her hands hit her hips. "Girls, I don't want any trouble."

I spun around to follow her gaze and froze when I saw my two older sisters standing at the bar. Both looked gorgeous and were dressed up to the country-nines in their tight jeans, boots, and skimpy tank tops.

"I ain't here to cause trouble, Aunt Genie," Sadie, the oldest, said as she took a seat on a barstool. "Momma is keepin' the boys tonight.

I'm here to get drunk. Make me whatever will fuck me up fastest, Willa. I ain't been out drinkin' in years." She smiled at me with a chin lift and a little wave before plopping her tiny purse on the bar and checking her lipstick in her cell phone camera.

Sadie had boys—I had nephews. Sadness washed through me at the realization that I'd missed being here for all of it. Years of family memories had happened without me because, like a fool, I chose my ex-husband over my own family. A nervous laugh escaped me as I started mixing a Long Island iced tea. Surely, they had something to say. I hadn't seen either of them in almost ten years. Should I apologize for being gone so long? Should I hug them? I'd missed them so much; hadn't they missed me?

"Well, that's good to hear," Aunt Genie said with a grin. "And what about you, sunshine?" She nodded to Clara, second in our sister quartet. I was third at almost twenty-eight. Our little sister was way too young to be here on a Saturday night. Gracie would be about sixteen now.

Clara tossed her long blond curls that looked just like mine over her shoulder and laughed. "I'm on the hunt tonight, Aunt Genie. Trouble with y'all is the last thing I'm fixin' to cause." She smirked and took the stool next to Sadie. "Hey, Willa."

"Hey, Clara. Sadie," I said, trying to keep my expression neutral. I loved them to death, but no matter what they said to Aunt Genie, I didn't trust that they were here for any other reason than to start something. It used to be their reason for living.

Sadie rolled her eyes at me. "Clara's on a man hunt tonight. I keep telling her men ain't worth a shit, but she won't listen." I finished making her Long Island and placed it on the coaster in front of her. She picked it up and sucked half of it back with one long drag on the straw. Holy crap. Sadie had always liked to party. Momma had to stop keeping alcohol in the house back then because of her.

Clara laughed. "Sadie is divorced. Her no-good husband left her and the boys and now she's livin' with Momma up at the farm. Her hootenanny is about to shrivel up and fall off, so she's bitter." She narrowed her eyes and gestured for me to come closer. I leaned in.

19

"All the girls we went to school with are gettin' divorces," she stated in a loud conspiratorial whisper. "I'm about to find me one of their ex-husbands. All the good ones got snapped up and married straight out of high school and now it's my turn to get a piece of one of those hotties. Have you seen Beau or Duane Winston since you've been home? Those two were always so cute. I haven't seen them since I moved to Knoxville after graduation. A red-headed Winston brother sandwich sounds good right about now."

"All the Winston boys are taken, you hussy!" Sadie yelled at Clara before smacking her arm. "Tequila shooters, Willa—I'm thinking three of them, if you please." She slid her empty glass across the bar. Genie took the glass with a wink for me, then headed down the bar to help some customers. I lined up the trio of shot glasses, served up the salt and limes with a flourish, and got Sadie set up.

Clara stole one of Sadie's shots. "Even Cletus?" she asked. Sadie nodded right before licking her hand for the salt. I guess it was time for her to catch up on gossip since she was in town. "Shoot, that boy always was hiding a lot of hot behind that scruffy exterior," Clara continued. "I saw him at the Donner Bakery a few months back when I was visiting Momma up at the house. Dang, I wanted to shave that beard off and climb on his face. Or maybe just climb on his face without shaving it off." She shrugged like it was all the same to her. "Who's the lucky bitch who landed him? I missed that bit of gossip when I was here last."

"Jennifer Sylvester," I told Clara. Sadie was too busy with her tequila shooters to answer.

"The banana cake queen? Good for her! I freakin' love her cake!" Clara yelled, then swiped Sadie's last shot and threw it back.

"Hey, you're supposed to be driving us home, dummy!" Sadie cried. "Willa! She's stealin' my shots." Her pout was comical. She'd skipped over tipsy and was well on her way to plastered.

"We got plenty of alcohol, don't worry." I poured two more shots and wondered if they had anything to say about me being back in Green Valley.

"I'm done drinking. Get me a Dr. Pepper, Willa, please." Clara requested. "What about Hank Weller? Is he taken too?" I shrugged. I wasn't up on all the Green Valley gossip. I was only familiar with the bakery gossip since I spent so much time there. Those banana cakes were like crack; I had torn through at least five of them with my friend Sabrina since I'd been home. I'd attended the private all-girls school in Maryville, so I'd missed out on some of the wealth of memories and connections one made when growing up in the same town with people. I'd earned a scholarship on account of having a genius IQ and learning to read when I was three. The school district had to bus me over there because they didn't offer a class advanced enough to contain my brain. Fat lot of good my supposedly gifted intelligence did me though. Being book smart didn't mean I made good life choices.

"I don't know about Hank," Sadie answered with a sigh. "I haven't seen him in years. He sure used to be fun though. I should have tried harder with him..."

"Sadie Lynn! I liked Hank back then, not you," Clara stated. I braced because every southern girl knows when a middle name gets dropped, shit's about to become serious.

"Uh-uh, no, it was me. Sometimes we would go to Cooper's field after Friday night football games. He was sweet to me. So good with his hands..." Sadie sighed, safe in her happy drunk bubble and oblivious to Clara's rising ire and the fact that apparently, they'd both slept with Hank Weller in high school. I held back a snicker, but it was hard. This would not end well. I did not want to be stuck in the middle of one of their bickering catfights again.

Clara flounced off her stool. "I used to hang out with Hank at his daddy's house up at Bandit Lake whenever his parents were out of town. And yes, he was very good with his damn hands." She had her hand on her hitched hip, leg out, foot a-tapping on the floor. The signs were all present—she was about to go on a tear. "Little Red Wagon" by Miranda Lambert blasted through the speakers, and I hoped it would not set the tone for what was about to come.

I shot a nervous smile to Aunt Genie, who was back on my end of the bar again. She grinned and shrugged. "Take your dinner break, Willa. Talk your sisters down from this decade-old business before the hair pullin' starts." She winked at me then headed down the bar again.

Shit. I needed to step in and get them off the potentially destructive path they were walking. Their fights were never malicious or hateful. But they used to get physical from time to time, with hair pulling and girl slapping. They were ridiculous. Occasionally they would knock over some furniture, break some dishes, then wind up collapsed together in a giggling heap with whatever made them angry having been forgotten. I was in no mood for their kind of antics tonight. Sweeping up broken glass after a bar fight sucked, thank you very much, no matter how funny the fight was. "So, how's Momma?" I asked to distract them.

"Huh? Oh, Momma wants to see you," Clara said, her hand now off her hip. With her foot no longer tapping out her anger, she turned to me. "You're hurting her feelings, Willa. And when Momma's feelings get hurt, ain't nobody happy. She's been blowing up my cell phone non-stop since she heard you came back to town." She took my hand and held it, forgetting about Hank Weller for the time being. "I'm so glad you came home, Willa. I missed you."

"I'm glad you're home too." Sadie took my other hand then picked up her last shot of tequila. "Let's have a toast to Willa! And fuck you, Hank Weller!" She tipped it back, then slammed her glass on the bar.

"To fucking Hank Weller!" Clara shouted with a huge smile. "And to our little sister finally being home. I missed you, Butterbean."

"I missed y'all too." I couldn't help but tear up. I was so happy they'd missed me that her use of my old, dreaded nickname didn't even bother me.

"Well, come around this bar then and give us a hug." Clara stood up and held her arms out. "Let's get this reunion done right, before we have to hold that one up for it." She tilted her head to Sadie. I headed around the bar and walked into Clara's hug. She squeezed me tight before Sadie joined us, wrapping both of us up. As we stood there hugging, relief filled me, warming my heart.

"Don't think we didn't notice that scar your pretty mermaid tattoo is hiding, little sister," Sadie whispered in my ear before she pulled back and sat down.

"Oh. Well..." I looked at my boots and clutched my arm self-consciously. My mermaid tattoo—in shades of blue, violet, and aqua —began with her tail wrapped around my wrist. She wound all the way up my arm to end with her face turned to the side on my shoulder, red hair billowing behind in her wake. Black waves tried to hold her back, but she swam through everything to break the surface. My scars were not quite hidden within her form.

"Is Tommy the cause of it? I could swear I saw his stupid, gaslighting ass in the parking lot. You're not with him anymore, right?" Clara asked with a face made of stone.

"No, we're divorced, and he's gone." *In prison...* "Why would you think that?" I tried to deflect.

"He was always a bossy little shit. That gets old after a while, doesn't it, Willa?" Sadie said knowingly.

Yeah, Tommy was a bossy shit and it did, in fact, get old. "This isn't the place to get into any of this—"

"Hey, Willa." My eyes shot to the voice, and I froze where I stood. Everett was looking hot as ever in blue jeans and cowboy boots, wearing a red plaid shirt with the sleeves rolled up. He had such nice forearms. They were strong and muscled, and dusted with exactly the right amount of dark hair to set off the delicious looking veins running up and down. His dark, nearly-shoulder length hair was tied back in a short ponytail just waiting for a woman to grab hold of it and—*Gah!* I wanted to get my hands in that hair so badly I could almost feel those soft waves caressing my palms as I—*stop it, Willa.* Sucking in a deep breath, I tried to calm my pounding heart and quell the dirty, racing thoughts chugging through my mind like a perverted freight train packed full of lust. Choo freaking choo.

"Well, hey there, Everett Monroe. You're lookin' less nerdy since I saw you last. Time has been kind to you and that is a fact," Clara greeted him before I could. "Wanna dance?" she asked and reached for his hand. I was pleased to see him avoid her touch by sticking his hands in his pockets with a half step back. Even though he didn't take her bait, a surge of jealousy shot through me. I felt myself arch up inside, like a pissed off cat. Maybe I would be the one to start a brawl tonight.

"Oh, honey, no. Everett has always been a cutie pie—all the Monroe boys are. Oh! How is Barrett? I haven't seen him around town since I've been back. We had gym together, back in school. I used to watch him in those tight gym shorts, running around the track. I made sure to always be behind him, yes I sure did—" Sadie slurred with a hiccup and spun around on her barstool. Her eyes narrowed on Everett as she wobbled on her stool. "Wyatt's the cop and you're the one openin' up that…that…store for—" She snapped her fingers as she struggled to remember Everett's gamer shop before getting distracted by—"Booooooooone!" she shouted and threw her hands in the air to wave him closer. "You're a hero, Boone!" She beamed up at him and almost fell out of her stool. He caught her before she could hit the floor.

"Long time, no see, Sadie. I see you haven't changed much." Boone laughed.

"You mean, I'm drunk and feisty, just like the old days." A wistful laugh escaped her as Boone grinned and sat down. "My momma has my boys and I'm getting wasted. I'm no fun anymore," she confessed.

"Wanna dance?" he asked.

Her head shook, blonde curls bouncing side to side. "I ain't dancing tonight, Boone. No more dancing for Sadie. Men ain't worth a shit. 'Cept you, of course." She slapped her hand on the bar for emphasis, making Boone laugh.

"How about I buy you a Coke then?" he offered her with an adorably sympathetic grin.

"Sure thing, as long as it has a whole lotta rum in it. Aunt Genie, c'mere," she hollered. "Me and Boone need some drinks."

"That girl…" Clara said with an eye roll. "So, I see what's

happening here." Her grin was wicked as her eyes bounced from me to Everett. "I'm gonna go dance. You two should shake a tail feather together." She shoved me in the back as she darted behind me on her way to the dance floor. I went flying into Everett, who caught me with a grin. *I was in trouble now.*

CHAPTER FOUR

EVERETT

"Everett, you'll know she's the one when she feels like everything. And everything else becomes just everything else."

— *PAPAW JOE*

We had danced together before, the night I'd first met her. Months ago, I'd been at Genie's with Wyatt to have a few beers and shake off the day. Instead, I'd danced all evening with the most beautiful woman I'd ever seen. Every time I remembered holding her close, I had to fight against getting hard. Since that night, I had been half in love with her. The physical half was all in—I was attracted to her something fierce. The mental half didn't know enough to start the fall, even though everything I learned about her drew me in and each day made me fall a little further. She was skittish with a fiercely sharp wit; she had been hurt. I could tell she was protecting a soft spot and it made me want to discover it so I could be the one to keep her safe.

But she had kept her distance from me—well, as much as she possibly could while living in the apartment in my basement—and we hadn't touched again, not once. Having her crash into my arms just now was heady stuff. Her scent, the feel of her body, the warm press of her against me—she made me feel intoxicated, and I had yet to order a single drink. My heart was in danger, but I couldn't make myself stay away.

"My sister...I'm sorry—" she stammered as she started to step back.

I tugged her closer instead of letting her get away. "Don't apologize. Dance with me?" My hands drifted around her waist as I started moving us backward toward the dance floor.

"Oh, I don't know if we should." Hesitation flashed briefly in her eyes, but she acquiesced and followed me across the floor as I turned to hold her hand, giving it a gentle tug of encouragement.

Leaning to the side, I whispered in her ear as we walked. "It's just a dance, Willard." I pulled back and grinned down at her with a wink. Her gorgeous eyes—big and light blue like the summer sky—widened as she opened her mouth to say something, but I twirled her under my arm instead of letting her speak. Country music blasted through the bar, fast and wild. It left no room for hesitation. I yanked her into my arms. "Okay?" I shouted over the music.

My mother loved to dance; she taught all us boys how. *A gentleman always takes his lady dancing. And maintains a respectful distance.* I took a small step back, placing my hand on Willa's upper back as our fingers linked together. With a step forward, she closed that distance to press against me once more. My lips curled up in a grin as her hand tightened in mine and her arm slid around my neck, hand drifting through the back of my tied-back hair. She wasn't as immune to me as she pretended to be and I wouldn't dare test that by stepping away from her again, even if it wasn't gentlemanly. If she wanted me close, then that's where I'd be.

Her gorgeous eyes twinkled in the lights as she smiled up at me and her body relaxed in my arms. "Okay, Everett. I'll dance with you," she breathed. Her voice was much too quiet to hear over the blaring music, but my focus on her gorgeous mouth allowed me to understand her words.

Quick, quick, slow—our easy Texas two-step was the same as

everyone else's on the floor but with her in my arms, this felt like so much more than a simple dance. I led her across the floor, spinning her out and pulling her back. I wanted to make her laugh again, like I did during our last dance so many months ago. I wanted her to want me as much as I wanted her. We had almost shared a kiss that night but were interrupted before anything could happen. She had the prettiest lips; full and soft and always pink. If I never kissed Willa before I died, it would be one of my greatest regrets. I had faith the right moment would present itself. As the song came to an end, I took both of her hands to spin her under my arms before dipping her low over my knee. Her ponytail brushed the floor as her neck arched back. She laughed, lifted her head and my heart skipped a beat as her eyes shone into mine with unbridled delight. Her sexy laugh tickled over my skin like I wished her hands would do and I felt the fall I was so afraid of coming even closer.

"God, you're such a good dancer. Where'd you learn to dance like this, Everett?" she asked, slightly breathless and totally adorable as she beamed up at me. It seemed that dancing with Willa was one of the keys to get her to respond to me. I filed that fact away for future contemplation as I pulled her up and into my hold once again.

My smile turned sideways as I was about to admit my nerdy momma's-boy truth to her. "From my mother," I shouted over the music. "She loves to dance. My father tries, but he isn't very good at it, so she taught all us boys how. We used to take turns two-stepping with her all over the living room."

"That's the sweetest thing ever," she said. *Score one for the nerds!*

"One more?" I didn't want to let her go yet.

"Sure, I have time for one more before I have to get back to work."

With its slower beat and romantic lyrics, Lady Antebellum's "I Run to You" changed the energy between us. The rise and fall of her chest as she sighed against me filled me with need as her forehead briefly rested on my shoulder and our fingers linked. I loved it that she was so tall. At six-foot-six I towered over most women, but

Willa fit me just right. My need grew urgent as I wrapped my arm around her waist and my hand met the soft swipe of her skin, bared by the tied hem of her Genie's tank top. Smooth and warm, it tempted me into thoughts inappropriate for our location. I inhaled a sharp breath to regain control. Dipping my head low, I took in her sweet scent as my cheek rested against hers—so soft. Her curly hair tickled my chin as my senses filled with nothing but her. Having her next to me felt right and I didn't understand why. My heart raced out of control and I wondered just what it was about her that made me react so intensely.

She reminded me of a Palomino horse; all long legs, flowing light blond hair, and pale skin kissed with adorable freckles. Willa was some kind of wild, and totally free. I shut my eyes and pictured her running across her momma's land up in the hills above town with her gorgeous hair flying behind her like a gold cloud, her laughter trailing through the air. God, she was the most beautiful woman I'd ever seen. I grit my teeth as my control started slipping away again. I was in danger of making a fool of myself. I was in danger of a lot of things, and a broken heart was at the top of that list.

"I love this song…" she whispered in my ear as she pulled away. Her head lifted from my shoulder as her hand trailed down my arm. She linked our fingers and I resumed leading her around the floor, rather than the slow sway we'd fallen into when the song started.

"Mm hmm," I muttered as I gazed into her eyes and smiled faintly, at a loss for words.

She studied my face. "Everett, why do I always feel like when you're looking at me, you really see me?" she murmured.

"I do see you. Sometimes you're all I see," I confessed, hoping it wasn't too much, too soon.

Lowering her head, she tucked her blushing cheek into the side of my neck and sighed against my skin, leaving goosebumps in the wake of her breath. I continued leading her across the dance floor with my heart beating like crashing thunder bolts in my chest. I should be careful; I didn't want her to end up being just another girl I fell for who didn't want me back. Story of my life.

The song came to an end and I let her go. The disappointment on her face as she reluctantly stepped out of my arms buoyed my spirits. "I have to get back to work. Thank you for the dance," she said.

I followed behind as she headed back to the bar. My eyes shot to Genie as she called for Willa. "Honey, you didn't eat dinner?" she asked as Willa darted around the bar and snagged her apron, tying it back around her narrow waist.

"Oh, no. I have food at home. I'll eat later," Willa said with a grin. My eyebrows shot up—I knew she *didn't* have food at home. I'd just finished repairing her empty refrigerator before meeting Boone and Garrett here. And from what I could tell, there wasn't much food in her kitchen at all. Was the doughnut from earlier the only thing she'd eaten today? I took a seat at the bar and ordered a beer from Genie. Boone had managed to convince Sadie to dance. I saw them out of the corner of my eye laughing and chatting at the edge of the crowded dance floor. Garrett was nowhere to be seen.

"Okay, Willa. Patty's divvying up y'all's tips before she leaves for the night," Genie informed Willa before sliding me a beer with a smile.

"Thanks, Miss Genie," I said.

"You're welcome, honey." She smiled at me. I sipped my beer and slid my eyes to the side to catch a view of what was going on with Willa.

Patty walked out from the swinging doors behind the bar, apron off, purse across her shoulder and ready to go. "Willa, here's your tips. I'm out of here." She hurried around the bar to leave.

Willa took the money. She frowned at the she flipped through the stack of bills. "Something's not right. You gave me too much. Patty, what are you up to?" I glanced at Genie, frozen near the cash register with a guilty look on her face.

"What's going on?" Clara asked as she sidled up to the bar and took a seat. She was breathless from dancing and followed closely behind by an equally breathless Garrett. I shot him a look, but he just grinned at me and sat next to Clara.

31

"Patty made a mistake is all," Willa insisted, thrusting her cash filled hand toward Patty.

Patty sighed and held her hands up, refusing to take the money. "I can add and subtract just fine, Willa Faye."

Willa turned to Genie. "Aunt Genie?"

"Attorneys are expensive," Genie replied. "If Patty wants to share her tips with you, I'm not gonna stop her." Her face softened. "We heard you on the phone, honey—making arrangements to pay her. There is nothing wrong with needing a little help now and then. Family helps family and you needed to be rid of that jackass you married. We'll help when we can." Genie's soft look turned pointed as she laid it out for Willa.

Willa's eyes shot to me, then quickly away. Her gaze bounced back to Patty. "I can't take your money. You need it too."

"Oh, Willa. Not as much as you do right now." She took the money from Willa, folded the bills in half and tucked it into Willa's apron pocket. "I know you'd have my back if I needed it. Right?"

"Yeah..." Willa whispered and looked away. The hit to her pride was obvious as her red face turned toward the floor. "But I won't take your money," she insisted.

"Well, too bad. I'm not taking it back." Patty turned and stomped off, dodging dancers across the floor until she was gone.

"You need help, Willa?" Clara asked, voice full of sympathy. I kept my face turned away from Willa. It was clear she was embarrassed, and I didn't want to add to it. But it wouldn't stop me from listening to every word and figuring out a way to help her.

"Thank you, Clara. But no. I don't need any help. I'll be just fine. Aunt Genie, I'm going to head in the back real quick and put the extra money in your office. Will you give it to Patty for me?"

Genie rolled her eyes with an impatient look. "Yes, you stubborn thing. I'll see she gets it."

"Thank you," she whispered and slunk through the swinging doors to the back.

"That girl—always was hard-headed." Genie muttered before heading off down the bar.

Everything I'd learned about Willa since meeting her told me she was obstinate. Or maybe she was just determined to be on her own after her divorce. Either way, she would not accept help from me. I already knew her enough to know better than to offer it flat out. I'd talk to Wyatt. He knew the details about her ex-husband, and it was time I did too. "Y'all, I'm calling it a night." I announced. Garrett lifted his chin in response.

"Leaving so soon? Want me to tell Willa goodbye for you?" Clara smirked.

"Yeah, thanks, Clara." I left. I had to get to the Piggly Wiggly before it closed for the night.

CHAPTER FIVE

WILLA

"I can't stand it when other men look at you. You're only for my eyes to see, my beautiful Willa. No more dancing."

— *TOMMY*

I blinked up at the ceiling and sighed as memories from the night before brought a reluctant smile to my face. Everett could *dance,* and he didn't ruin the fun by getting jealous. Not that I was his, or he was mine. We weren't together—yet.

Gah! There couldn't be a yet. No *yet* allowed.

But Everett was so sweet and fun and didn't wreck everything by stopping to glare threats at other men. Everett didn't seem to have the urge to mark me like territory the way Tommy always had. I shoved the unpleasant memories of my ex out of my mind. Thoughts of Tommy didn't belong in my new life—he had no place with me in Green Valley. I'd fought hard in the two years since we'd split to move on from him.

I flipped to my stomach and pulled the covers over my head. I needed more sleep. Waking up still tired sucked but waking up hungry was worse. My attorney was sucking up all my leftover cash, obliterating my food budget. I couldn't quit paying her. I owed my freedom to her. She worked tirelessly to get my divorce finalized; to set me free. But I also could not subsist on Everett's doughnuts and a cup of coffee for an entire day. My stomach growled loudly, vibrating the mattress beneath me. I hated mooching off Everett, but I was constantly hangry and in danger of losing my temper over every little thing. I mean, I ran out of ramen two days ago and could actually picture myself stabbing someone for a cracker crumb.

I was so hungry that my apprehension over visiting my mother had been shoved to the backburner at the thought of one of her home cooked meals. As a result, last night, I had let my sisters convince me to head up to my mother's house for dinner this evening. I wasn't even that nervous about it anymore. All I could think about was her Sunday pot roast. *Please let it be pot roast.* And please don't let her interrogate me about Tommy. I dreaded talking about my divorce and hearing how right she was about him. Yeah, so I'd made the biggest mistake of my life by running away with him. I didn't need that fact shoved in my face. The only thing I wanted to shove in my face was a huge plate of food. The very thought of it kept me hanging on. I stared longingly at my phone but resisted the urge to text one of my sisters and cancel our family dinner/reunion tonight. No more waffling. I had to get it over with and face my mother. Samantha Wilson-Hill was as tough as nails, mean as a snake, believed in absolute freedom, and would reem me out seven ways to Sunday the split second I stepped foot into her house.

Heaving out a sigh, I got out of bed. I'd showered when I'd gotten home so all I needed to do was start a load of laundry and sneak upstairs to steal a doughnut. So far Everett hadn't let me down with the sweet treats from Daisy's. Hopefully today would not be the exception—my stomach was about to eat itself. "Shut up," I whispered as it growled again.

I grabbed my basket and headed out my back door, which led to the laundry room in the part of the basement I shared with Everett. When the door hit the doorstop, he jumped and spun around. My lips shifted to the side as his booming laughter filled the room. I had startled him. Once more thoughts of my ex filled my mind; where Everett laughed, Tommy would have been angry. I sighed. Everett was standing at the long table in the middle of the space folding his clothes. Slamming my eyes shut, I clutched the basket to my chest. He was wearing a huge smile and nothing but a pair of gray sweatpants. I had caught a glimpse of his ass in those pants before he turned around and the sight made my mouth water. I wanted to take a bite out of it. I wanted to pet it, maybe cuddle up with it, and become best friends with it. I groaned, then covered the sound with a cough.

"Wilhelmina! You startled me." He chuckled. "I'm almost done with these clothes, and you're just in time for breakfast. I have pancake batter mixed and bacon ready to go into the oven. Scrambled or over-easy?"

"All your shirts were dirty?" I smirked, avoiding his tempting breakfast question. There was no way I could run off with a plate of food like he was offering. I would have to sit and eat with him. That was dangerous—to his bitable ass, as well as to my heart. My heart that filled with the realization that he'd most likely overheard Patty trying to give me her tips. He was cooking a pity breakfast. Yeah, no thank you.

He winked and slipped a shirt over his head. "Better?" he asked.

His biceps strained the limits of his T-shirt sleeves and my eyeballs were about to pop out of their sockets like one of those old pervy cartoon characters. "I guess so. I can't eat breakfast with you. I have things to do." My stomach protested—loudly. I puffed out a breath, blew an errant curl out of my eye, twisted my lips, and studied the ceiling.

"Your stomach doesn't seem to agree with you." With a shake of his head, he asked again, "Scrambled or over-easy? I'm headed up, so start your laundry and join me. Coffee is ready. I can't drink a whole pot by myself, Silly Willy." He touched my nose with his index finger, grabbed his basket of laundry and headed upstairs leaving me no opportunity to start an argument.

"Over-easy!" I shouted at his retreating back. "Thanks. Uh, I'll do the dishes."

With my stomach growling and my mouth watering, I started my clothes. In too much of a rush to sort them, I stuffed them in the washer and hit start. Not that I sorted much anyway. Almost everything I owned was black.

I trudged up the stairs, fully conscious of the fact that my hair was a wild mess and I was still wearing just black sleep shorts and a matching tank, no bra. I wasn't too worried. I didn't have much up top to ogle. I had been tempted to throw a party when I filled out a B cup back in my junior year. *Why was I thinking about my boobs?*

After climbing the wooden basement stairs, I shoved open the heavy door that led to the kitchen. My embarrassment over Everett's pity breakfast vanished as the delicious smells of bacon and coffee washed over me like a freaking benediction. This breakfast was about to become a religious experience. My stomach was singing the "Hallelujah" chorus, and I was about to sink to my knees in gratitude. My mouth watered. Drooling was a real concern. With a swipe of my hand I checked. No drool—yet.

"You're just in time, Willard." Everett was at the stove. His booty in those gray sweats plus those big arms in that T-shirt, that gorgeous bearded face and his tousled-up bed-head—all of it battled for my attention. My lack of sleep, lack of food, and overall sense of exhaustion had eliminated my self-preservation instincts. Everett was a hot piece of ass and I wanted to tap it, hard. I swear right now, if he was sweet to me, I would throw my shirt at him.

He gestured to the barstool on the other side of the counter where I stood, then turned to the island in the middle of the kitchen to grab a plate of cut up fruit. My mouth's waterworks started again in earnest when he set it on the bar. I popped a grape into my mouth and admired Everett's dishes. They were a manly, dark gray pottery style, heavy and shiny with a black edge. The bar top was ready for breakfast. The cutlery was in perfect restaurant order beside the plates and rolled up napkins were centered in in the middle of each one, complete with napkin rings—was that the Millennium Falcon on the napkin rings? I picked one up and grinned. It was! Holy heckarino, he was the cutest.

"Can I help?" I asked as I eyed the goodness he was cooking up.

"No worries, I've got it all under control. It's early for you. Couldn't sleep?" he asked. The smile in his voice forced me to smile back at him.

I plopped into the stool and put my head on my hand as I rested my arm on the countertop. "I never sleep well anymore," I muttered as the smile left my face and I looked out the window.

"Want to talk about it?" He slid me a mug full of coffee, a spoon, and my favorite hazelnut creamer. His expression was full of sympathy. I had the feeling he would probably understand if I dumped my troubles on him—he seemed like the type—but I had a bit of a crush on him and I didn't want him to think less of me once he found out I'd married a dirt-bag, controlling asshole at age seventeen and was in debt up to my eyeballs to my attorney from the divorce.

Heaving out a sigh, I poured creamer in my coffee and swirled it around with my spoon. The cream dissipated into the coffee like so many clouds. I wished it were that easy to lose my problems. "Nah, I don't want to dump on you, Everett. You'll get sick of it and have to find a new tenant."

After flipping a pancake, he turned away from the stove to study my face. "Never, Willard. I'm used to your grumpy ass. I'd miss you." He gifted me with another wink, and I shivered under his hot gaze before he turned around to slide the pancakes onto a platter. He had enough food to feed a family of four over there.

"You like to cook?" I asked. I glanced at my mug, adorned with Princess Leia and her famous "I love you" quote, from *The Empire Strikes Back*. I grinned and took another sip of coffee as I searched the counter for Everett's mug. There it was, featuring Han Solo and his famous reply, "I know". Could he be any cuter? Not even if he tried. *Damn*.

"I love cooking. I hardly ever have anyone to cook for though. Thank you for coming over." He placed the pancakes on the island, turned, then bent to open the oven—that ass! *Gah*!

Between the smell of the bacon that wafted from the open oven and the sight of Everett's ass as he bent over to retrieve it, I was about to orgasm right here on this barstool. I shut my eyes and gulped my coffee in an effort to regain control. I opened my eyes only to watch as he poured the fat from the bacon filled baking sheet into a frying pan, then cracked four eggs right into it. I swear I fell in love. All pretense of cool control vanished as my stomach growled, I squirmed in my seat, and allowed myself to avidly watch him cook the rest of our breakfast like a teenage boy watching a dirty movie. Holy shit—eggs fried in bacon fat? Everett was a god in the kitchen. I wondered how he was in the bedroom. Food and sex were my two favorite things in the world, and I had been without both for way too long.

"Are you ready to eat?" he asked. His deep voice poured over me like honey, and I wanted him to lick it off.

Heck yes, I'm ready to eat. Let's go upstairs to your bedroom and I'll eat whatever you put into my mouth—

"Uh...yeah. I'm ready. Everything looks great." That's what I actually said, thankfully. I picked up my napkin and fanned my face with it. Holy potatoes, I was about to make an ass of myself all over his ass.

My eyes got big on the bar in front of me as he placed the bacon, pancakes, syrup, and other breakfast necessities down. With a twist to the side that did delicious things to his muscles, he grabbed the frying pan and served two eggs to each of our plates before placing the pan in the deep double sink.

As I looked at the food I wanted to cry. How had I let this happen to my life? After my divorce I had spent two years driving aimlessly all over the country, living off my savings and my portion of the money from selling our house in Nashville and working short stints in bars here and there. I came home to Green Valley and my Aunt Genie had graciously hired me, but I had been living in my camper van at the Maryville Walmart parking lot as I searched for an apartment, for crap's sake. Then I had spent a few weeks parked near the barn at my best friend Sabrina's ranch. And it didn't get better from there; it got worse. I didn't have enough money for food, and I would barely make rent this month. I couldn't go on this way—this would have to be my last month here. Maybe I could park at Sabrina's again. The humiliation would never end. I couldn't see a way out. I sipped my coffee. Despite my hunger, my appetite had disappeared.

"Dig in." Everett stepped around the bar and sat next to me—close. He smelled like clean laundry and coffee. The feeling that he was everything I needed and would never deserve washed over me along with the ever-present melancholy I had managed to kick away for a few minutes when I was too busy lusting over him and sniffing the bacon to pay attention to it.

"Sure. It looks delicious, Everett," I murmured and helped myself to a pancake.

He raised an eyebrow and flopped a second pancake onto my plate. "You're too skinny. You need to eat." He rolled his eyes and laughed. "Oh man, I sounded just like my mother."

I cracked a grin and reached for the syrup. "If I were my mother right now, I'd be asking you if this were organically grown whole grain you used in your pancakes and if the answer was yes, I'd demand to know if it was locally sourced. Not to mention the fact that I would have to refuse to eat the bacon. And are those eggs from free range chickens?" I snagged a piece of bacon and folded the whole thing into my mouth with a grin.

His eyes got huge in mock horror. "She sounds fun." He took a huge bite of pancake with a twinkly, crinkle-cornered eye smile.

"I'm supposed to drive up and see her tonight. Dinner with the family." I sighed and dipped a bite of pancake into the perfectly-runny egg yolk. With every bite I took, my apprehension about seeing my family came back.

"You'll be okay. Get it over with quick, like ripping off a Band-Aid."

"Oh, it won't go quick. I've been back in town for months and haven't gone up to see her yet. My sisters weren't at Genie's last night solely for shits and giggles; they were her messengers. My mother is gonna have a fit and there is nothing I can do but take it. I mean, I deserve it, don't I?"

His eyes softened on me over the rim of his mug. He set it on the bar and studied me with a thoughtful expression. "I don't know. Something besides your ex made you run away all those years ago, right? Maybe she deserves some of the blame. And for the sake of full disclosure, I knew Tommy back in high school. He was on the Maryville High basketball team and we used to play against each other. Maryville and Green Valley are huge rivals. I didn't like him back then, and based on the little I've heard from Wyatt, I don't like him now."

It was slightly disconcerting that Everett seemed to know my story. Or some of it, at least. I guess I couldn't affect an air of mystery when it came to him. Of course, I was fooling myself to think that in a town like Green Valley I could keep anything a secret in the first place. No matter how low a profile I tried to keep, people were slowly realizing I was back—hence the visit from my sisters at my mother's demand. I grimaced at the thought of Wyatt filling Everett in on everything that happened in Nashville. "There was a lot I didn't know about Tommy when we were together. Uh, a lot of stuff came up as the years went by and I—"

Everett shook his head. "He hid himself from you. I can totally see him doing shit like that. He was always kind of a bully."

Bully—yeah, that fit Tommy. With a noncommittal shrug, I shoved another piece of bacon in my mouth, wishing he would drop the subject. I was beginning to care way too much what Everett thought of me. The idea of him losing interest once he found out about my sordid, teen-runaway past was heartbreaking no matter how determined I was to keep him out of my heart. And if he ever found out what happened on the day I left Tommy? It would all be over. Wyatt had promised it would stay between the two of us. But where did brotherly loyalty fit into that promise?

He gestured to the last pancake and I shook my head, so he took it. "Pancakes are like my kryptonite," he confessed.

"With these pancakes, I could see that. You're a good cook."

"Thanks." He beamed at me, then tugged one of my curls, straightening it then watching it spring back into place. I grinned as it tickled my nose. "I like your hair when it's down, when it flies everywhere. You have happy hair, Willard."

"Happy hair?" I giggled at the strangely irresistible compliment.

With a decisive nod he answered, "Yeah, it's curly and bouncy and wild. It makes me happy when I look at it. Or maybe it's just you that makes me smile." The warmth in his eyes shot straight through my body to land in my heart.

My giggle vanished as I fought the urge to jump in his lap. Or, throw my shirt at him. Or both. "Everett…" I breathed.

"So, I…uh…have sort of a proposition for you," he finally said.

I raised my eyebrows. All he had to do was ask and I'd be his. Right now.

CHAPTER SIX

EVERETT

"Always take care of your woman, Everett. And she'll be sure to take care of you."

— *PAPAW JOE*

"I'll cut your rent in half if you help me paint the house," I blurted before thinking of a way to make the offer more palatable to her skittish nature. Her fork clattered to her plate and her head drew back as she studied me with suspicion. She reminded me of that scared little fawn I rescued last year in the back yard, near the forest. Maybe I should have offered her an apple first. My lips quirked up at the corner as she glared at me.

Then her glare vanished as disappointment clouded her features. "Do you feel sorry for me, Everett?" she demanded. Her southern accent became more pronounced whenever she was worked up over something. During my nights spent at Genie's Bar, I'd often notice her getting annoyed with male customers attempting to chat her up— several times I'd almost waded in—but she was adept at sidestepping, avoiding, and just flat-out stopping their advances with a well-timed glare and a good old verbal dressing-down, thick with her irresistible southern sass. Genie also employed several large busboy/bouncer types and a few of her bartenders were constantly on the lookout for trouble while they mixed drinks. Willa could handle herself just fine. She could probably handle me too, if she had a mind to. Plus, I got the feeling that me stepping in at Genie's would piss her off.

Making Willa angry was the last thing I wanted to do, and pity was so far from what I felt for her it was ridiculous that she'd even think it. I wanted to take care of her. I wanted things I had no business wanting from her yet—like her body, her soul, her every waking thought, and every secret she had ever kept.

I slid my plate to the side and cleared my throat. "No. I don't feel sorry for you. I need help around here. I'm busy with my shop, busy working for my father, and this place is falling through the cracks. I thought you might be interested. And since you already live here, you could keep your own hours, no rush on anything." I attempted a casual approach. My real motivation would send her running.

"Bull crap," she said. Her plate joined mine as she slid it across the counter then folded her arms across her chest. I eyed her chest then quickly looked back to her face. She wasn't wearing a bra. I saw, uh, things. Nipples. I saw her nipples poking out above her crossed arms. The thin fabric of her tank top did nothing to hide them. I slammed my eyes shut and tried to find my train of thought. It had left the station without me, leaving me stranded in Perky Poky Nipple Town, population: Everett, who was about to get smacked across the face. "Everett! You don't need my help. You overheard Patty tryin' to give me her tips. Didn't you?"

"Um, yeah. I heard that. I'll admit I did. But, that's not why I'm asking." With a shove of my stool, I stood up. "Come with me. I'll show you what I need done and you can tell me if you're interested. Okay?"

I gestured to the big double doors to the rear of the large kitchen space that went through the dining room and into a formal living room—or parlor, as my mother called it. She scowled with suspicion as she crossed in front of me to open the door. Her arm swept over the wall inside, looking for the light switch. I reached around her and flipped it on.

With a jump back she crashed into my chest. "Oh, god. Is it haunted? Because I feel like it is. All those sheets on the furniture remind me of an old episode of *Scooby-Doo*. That chandelier is creepy! There are holes in the walls, Everett!" She backed into me and I held her arms to steady her. Soft skin met my hands while her sweet scent filled my lungs. I wanted to run my hands over every square inch of her body and see if she was soft everywhere. I wanted to bury my face in her hair and breathe her in, but I resisted the urge.

"No, it isn't haunted," I whispered in her ear. "This was my Grandfather's house, on my mother's side. He lived in the basement apartment, where you live now. He was kind of a hermit and none of us ever went inside the main part of the house. He wouldn't let us. He'd always come to us at my parents' house, or we'd barbecue out in the yard, or sit with him in the apartment. Everything looked fine from the outside."

She turned in my arms. "He isn't okay?" she asked, her expression full of sympathy.

I shook my head. "Alzheimer's. He wasn't the same person I knew growing up. This place bore the brunt of his illness. I want to fix it."

Stepping out of my arms, she wandered over to the front window, slid the heavy drape aside and looked outside. "This house is kind of symbolic then?" she mused as she looked out at the front yard below.

I hadn't thought of it that way before, but she was right. "I guess so. This place is something I can fix, unlike him. Nothing could fix him. This old house is full of lost memories. I just wish—"

She turned from the window. "I'll help you, Everett." Her sympathetic eyes held mine as she smiled at me. Her heart was right there, I could see it. She knew what this meant to me. Maybe she understood it better than I did.

I grinned at her. "You will?"

"Yes. It's a mess, you weren't lying about that." She chuckled as her eyes swept the room. "I'm sorry that I thought—"

"I know, it's okay. I'm sorry my timing was bad. I was never great at...talking. Communicating, or whatever."

"You do just fine, Everett. But I can't start today. I have to get my family reunion over with. But we'll start real soon. Deal?" She held her hand out for me to shake.

With two long strides, I clasped her small hand in mine and wished...I wished so many things when it came to her that I had no idea where to even begin to sort through my rapidly growing feelings. "Deal. And thank you, Willard."

"Oh, don't thank me. I should be thanking you. The half rent thing will help me out," she admitted somewhat sheepishly.

"Good, then it's win-win." I stuck my other hand out. She took it with a bemused smile. We held hands and I fought the almost irresistible urge to sweep her into my arms and carry her to my bed.

"So, uh. Thank you for breakfast. It was delicious," she whispered. Her upturned face and luscious, pouty lips were a temptation I could barely resist. Adorable freckles covered her face and I wanted to kiss each one of them. With a fingertip, I traced the trio of freckles that formed a tiny little heart next to her lip. Her breath caught as her tongue darted out to wet that full lower lip and I almost groaned out loud.

"You're welcome. I'm glad you liked it." I managed to say. My heart raced. It pounded in my ears like a drumbeat urging me to do something foolish—something we weren't ready for—and yet, my head lowered toward hers just the same. I forgot myself whenever I was with her, forgot my manners, my restraint, the gentlemanly behavior my mother had drilled into us boys since birth. I forgot everything and just *yearned.* Willa made me want her, she made me burn for her, and it hurt. It tore at my soul that she wasn't mine. I couldn't understand why I felt this way, why I had seemingly fallen for her so fast and couldn't stop the descent no matter how hard I fought against it. Or how much she refused to acknowledge it.

In my grasp, her hand tightened and tugged at mine, urging me closer. I bowed forward without thought, seeking that undefinable connection we shared. She felt it too; she was losing control just as I was. Her body arched up into mine as my body sought to surround her, fill her, make her mine. Dark lashes drifted against her freckled cheeks as her lips parted. Only inches apart, my lips tingled in anticipation as her warm breath whispered against my mouth.

"Open up, Everett!" The knocker on the front door clattered against its brass plate and the doorbell sounded throughout the house like a warning bell.

We flew apart. She stumbled back, and I caught her by her upper arms before she hit the floor. A hysterical giggle escaped as she steadied herself and I stood there, chest heaving, and mind muddled with confusion and regret. I had almost taken what I wanted. Would it have ruined everything? Or would it have been the spark necessary to make her mine?

"Sounds like Wyatt," she murmured.

"It is," I ground out through the tight clench of my jaw.

"Let us in, Uncle Everett." My eyes slammed shut as I struggled to subdue my racing heart, reckless thoughts, and out of control body.

She scrambled backward out of my hold and darted for the kitchen door. "I'll go clean up the dishes before I get ready to go. Answer the door, Everett." I watched as she slammed the kitchen door behind her and disappeared. I had never seen her in so few clothes; her long smooth legs were dotted with freckles just like her arms, face, and upper chest. I couldn't help but wonder what the parts of her not kissed by the sun looked like. The doorbell rang again, and I cursed it. A rush of breath escaped me as I struggled to get a grip on myself.

I required a minute for the sake of decency—probably more, but a minute would have to do. I was not in control, not yet. Images of her still burned in my mind. Her gorgeous face was constantly in my sight no matter if my eyes were opened or shut. I scrubbed my hands through my hair, digging my palms into my eyes to escape the visions of her, of us together, that haunted me and wouldn't let me be.

I stalked through the archway opposite the doors that led to the kitchen and headed through the parlor to the front door. I threw it open with a disgruntled sigh.

"Uncle Everett!" A smile escaped at the sight of my adorable red-headed nieces. Mak and Mel, ages nine and five, stood there along with my brother, Wyatt, and his new wife, Sabrina—who, coincidentally, was Willa's best friend.

"We're on the way to Daisy's Nut House for breakfast," Wyatt informed me. "Want to come with?"

"Doughnuts!" Mel screamed and threw herself at me. I scooped her up and blew kisses into her neck, making her giggle. Mak hugged me around the waist and I wrapped my free arm around her. I loved these girls with all my heart. I'd been overjoyed when Wyatt decided to move back to Green Valley.

"Hey, Sabrina," I greeted my brother's shy wife. An assistant librarian at the Green Valley Public Library, Sabrina was an unexpected and sweet blessing to our family. She couldn't be more opposite Willa if she tried, which made their friendship a mystery to me. "Where's Harry?" Harry was her ten-year-old nephew, and her newly adopted son. He was adorable and quickly becoming my favorite fishing buddy.

"Hi, Everett," she answered with a smile. "Harry is at the senior center with my dad. Is Willa around? We tried her door first, but she didn't answer, and her camper is here…"

"Uh, yeah. She's in the kitchen. You can go on back." I answered. Sabrina walked around me with big eyes full of questions. I smirked. I felt glad Willa would be getting those questions and not me—until I faced Wyatt and saw the same questioning look on his face.

His cell phone pinged with a text. He flipped it up to check and we both saw the message was from Willa.

Willa: Keep your mouth shut about Tommy.

.   .   .

My eyebrows hit my hairline as I set Mel down. She and Mak ran after Sabrina into the kitchen. The questioning look was mine now, while Wyatt was left to stand there avoiding my eyes. "What's that supposed to mean?" I asked.

"Exactly what it said. I can't tell you." He heaved out a huge put-upon sigh. "Her ex-husband, my ex-partner, current hateful douchebag doing a nickel in prison. Tommy Ferris. You remember him, don't you? I sure did when they partnered me with his dumb ass."

"What's he in prison for?" I demanded.

"Google it," he shot back with a stone face. Wyatt always was a stubborn little turd.

"Why are you keeping her secrets?"

"She's my friend, and she trusts me. She's like a little sister to me."

"She ain't my sister," I muttered.

"That's a good thing. I see how you look at her." He smacked my arm. "It would be sick if she were." Wyatt chuckled and headed to the doorway that led into my living room. It was one of the few rooms I'd managed to finish before starting the work to open my shop. He plopped onto my couch and dug around in the cushions for the remote.

"Can I really Google it?" I asked as I sat on the opposite end of my dark blue sectional couch. My living room was decorated in mid-century man-cave—comfort was my only concern. Yeah, I had toss pillows, only because they were good to shove behind your head while playing video games. I glanced around the room—at my framed *Gone with the Wind* version *Empire Strikes Back* poster hanging above the fireplace, the mantel covered with my Marvel superhero Funko Pop collection, and the lightsabers sitting amongst the fireplace tools in the holder. My replicas of the *Serenity,* from *Firefly,* the *Enterprise,* from *Star Trek,* and the *Millennium Falcon* decorated the top of my coffee table. I sank back into the cushions with a groan as I took in the shelves beneath my 75-inch HD 4K television where my video game consoles were housed, along with my

X-Men action figures on their little plastic display stands. What was I thinking asking Willa to help me out around here? Once she found out what I was planning to do with the formal dining room, any interest she possibly could have had in me would die. My house was not quite on par with Steve Carell's apartment in *The 40-Year Old Virgin,* but it was too damn close.

"Why the face? What's wrong?" Wyatt asked as he held up the remote with a victorious grin. "Found it!"

I shook my head. "Look at this place. What kind of woman would ever want anything to do with a guy like me?" A rare moment of vulnerability washed over me as I confided my fears to Wyatt.

"You're a great guy, Ev. Quit that talk."

"Look at this place, my shop. My entire life..." I snatched the remote from Wyatt and flicked the TV on.

Wyatt carefully put his feet on the coffee table and eyed me from the corner of the sectional. "If you're worried about Willa, don't. She's not the type to judge you, even if she looks like she would be."

"What's that supposed to mean?"

"I mean, with the way she looks, people make assumptions about her. None of which are true."

"How do you know so much?" I felt like he owed it to me to tell me. He was my brother for fuck's sake.

With a quick look behind him at the kitchen door, he leaned toward me. "Tommy has been in prison for almost two years, Everett. Since the day he got locked up, Willa has been driving all over the place in that camper van of hers trying to find a place to be. For almost two years I've been telling her to just go home—to come back here, to her family. She only listened to my advice after *I* came back here. I already told you, she's like a little sister to me. And you have nothing to worry about when it comes to superficial things, like your *Star Wars* obsession, or your *Dungeons and Dragons* game-playing schedule, or your shop, okay? Trust me, and don't ask me anymore questions. Willa needs friends, and I don't want to hurt her by breaking her trust."

"Okay. I won't ask any more questions." I absentmindedly

agreed as my mind raced through the hidden meaning of what he'd just told me.

"And yeah, you can google Tommy. But wouldn't you rather she tell you about it herself?"

I let my cell phone—with Google ready to go—drop from my hands to land on the couch cushion. Yeah, damn it, I would rather she confide in me herself.

Wyatt was right. She needed friends more than she needed me and my pathetic, ill-timed crush.

CHAPTER SEVEN

WILLA

"I'll die without you, Willa, and your family will tear us apart if we go back.

Stay with me, baby, please..."

— *TOMMY*

The temptation to drive out of Green Valley was real. While I was washing the breakfast dishes, Sabrina, my bestie, and her stepdaughters paid me a visit in the kitchen. They were full of questions about me and Everett—had we eaten breakfast together? Was Everett my boyfriend? Would I be their aunt someday? Sure, Sabrina had shushed the "aunt" questions from Wyatt's girls, but I could tell she was wondering the same thing. The chemistry between me and Everett was obvious and the more I fought it, the more tangible it became. I didn't want him to become just another person to disappoint. I had to stay away.

Thus far, my life consisted of a sad series of bad decisions all of which culminated in my eventual running away from the consequences. The repercussions from everything I'd ever done had worn me down so much that the pressure to just *be here*—be home in Green Valley, near all the people I cared about, was becoming overwhelming. I was going to let them all down and the anticipation of that inevitability was making me twitchy. Bolting was an enticing possibility that I couldn't stop thinking about.

I turned the key in my camper van—if you could even call it that. It wasn't really a van; my home away from everything was a 1989 flat-nosed Bluebird short school bus with a 5.9 liter Cummins and an automatic transmission. I'd bought it when I was still married to Tommy, thinking we could convert it and use it for camping. He thought it was a stupid waste of money, but I had fun rebuilding the engine, gutting and redesigning the inside, then eventually decorating it. The transformation from short school bus to the glamping extravaganza I had created was extraordinary; it was all me, and I was proud of it. To spite Tommy, I'd painted her a matte, creamy, pale pink and named her *The Rambling Rose.* I stenciled her name on the side, along with a rose covered dream catcher. I decorated her in pastel shabby chic—lace and flowers, wicker and white-washed wood, broken-tile-mosaic trim and fluffy pillows everywhere. I had a tiny kitchen, bathroom, and convertible bed, plus plenty of storage for all my things. It made being semi-homeless bearable, even almost fun, like an adventure. It was the escape I had so desperately needed after the end of my marriage.

With a sigh, I backed out of Everett's driveway, promising myself I'd go to my mother's house and not, well, anywhere else. I *would* come back here when dinner with my family was over and not run off. I pinky swore to no one and laughed at my reflection in the review mirror.

The narrow road wound up and up as I left Green Valley proper and drove into the foothills above town, toward home. My momma's land was technically part of Green Valley, but it felt like a different world up here. The creepy quiet of the hills started to freak me out so I flipped on my CD player. I had Bluetooth, WIFI capabilities, and a satellite dish, but some places didn't accommodate the needs of techy stuff that required signals. Since off the beaten path was my favorite place to be, oftentimes CDs were all I had to keep the quiet away. And it was quiet up here, except for the sound of the light breeze rustling through the tree branches and blowing the shrubs around outside. Miranda Lambert was much preferable to the eerie sound of the hills.

I tried to decide if I had missed my mother or not. We weren't ever that close. I'd been closer to my daddy and his side of the family before he'd gone and run off on us soon after my baby sister, Gracie, was born. Maybe I got the urge to wander from him. Hill family stories always said there would be a black sheep in every generation. Maybe I was the one in mine?

With a turn off the main road, I headed into the misty sunlight. Squinting my eyes against the brightness, I drove down the narrow gravel-covered road. Purple signs decorated with white arrows proclaimed that I was indeed headed toward my mother's place.

I inhaled a huge breath as I passed beneath the scrolled-iron sign arched delicately over the road. My hands trembled on the steering wheel as I tried to regain my composure. Lavender Hills, my mother's farm, was named for the rolling lavender fields on either side of the narrow road. She sure as heck didn't name it after the Hill side of the family. She cut us off from all of them after Daddy left. Lined with white-washed farm fence, the road curved gently before widening into a large parking area with her farm stand on the left. Since it was Sunday, it was closed. Herbs, planted in neat rows, filled up the land on the right. I rolled to a stop and looked out the window. Green houses sat in the distance alongside the elderberry bushes she had trained to grow like trees. Straight ahead, on the private road, was the long, winding driveway that led to the house. You couldn't see them from here, but beehives filled the rear of the property. Momma was a farmer, a beekeeper, and an herbalist. She sold honey, soaps, herbs, and various lavender products in the Lavender Hills Farm Stand as well as at the Green Valley Farmers' Market in town, and on her online shop. Momma was an entrepreneur, always hustling to take care of us girls. As for my Daddy, he was a "good-for-nothing" Hill, according to Momma.

When I was a little girl, he worked for the Payton Mill, but now he was just gone.

Finished with my lollygagging, I drove on. The long meandering driveway led through green grass and abundant trees with patches full of wildflowers dotted here and there. Momma's green thumb and desire to make everything pretty was obvious as I admired the beauty of this place. Memories crashed into my mind, while a sharp bolt of sorrow pierced my heart. I had missed this place. I missed my sisters and found myself wishing I'd never left. The beauty that filled my eyesight seemed to eclipse the bad memories that had kept me away for so long. Blinking back tears as the white clapboard farmhouse rose in the distance, I wondered how I would ever make them forgive me.

Two little boys kicked a ball back and forth in the grass across the white picket fenced-in front yard. They stopped and stared as I drove slowly toward the huge detached garage with its steeply pitched roof line. I smiled and waved to them. They had to be Sadie's boys. My heart swelled at the thought of meeting them. They looked adorable. Would they like me? Did they even know about me?

"Flynn! Rider! Boys! Y'all come on inside and wash up for dinner. Your Auntie Willa is here." Sadie's head popped out the front door and she waved to me with a big smile. I pulled to a stop next to a white minivan, shaking my head at the change from the wild party girl Sadie used to be to the minivan-driving mother she was now. The boys waved, faces full of curious smiles, before gathering their ball and darting into the house.

With a hop, my feet hit the gravel driveway. I stared at the house with a pounding heart, my shallow breath escaping to the beat in panting puffs.

"Oh. It's just you. Don't expect a hug or nuthin'," a snide voice called from the swing on the back porch. She sat sideways, glaring at me over the railing, blue eyes flashing fire, and upper lip curled in a snarl.

"Gracie?" She was beautiful, grown up, and probably as tall as me.

"Who else would it be? Did you forget I existed?" She got up and stomped off into the house, through the back door. Yikes, that couldn't have gone worse. Gracie had been a tiny kindergartener when I'd run off. She had been such a sweet little thing, constantly after me to read her stories and play *My Little Pony*. Obviously, I'd broken her heart. There was no trace of that sweet girl left from what I could see. If her hostile, black-lined eyes didn't already tell the story, her ripped jeans and red plaid Doc Marten's would have done the trick. Sadie was a sullen teen, direct from central casting.

"Never mind Gracie and her bad attitude. Are you done bein' controlled by your man, little miss?" I whirled to find my mother standing behind me, eyebrows up with a faint smile drifting across her face. Her tall, slim figure was dressed in a bright yellow sundress with matching Birkenstocks on her feet. My eyes roved over her features. She had hardly changed at all. Her silvered blond hair was in a long, twisty braid over her shoulder and her face remained almost untouched by the years that had passed by.

"Yes, ma'am. And he's not my man anymore," I replied. Promptly and with respect, just like Momma liked.

"I'm glad to hear it. Come and give me a hug, darlin'. I've missed your pretty face 'round here." *That's it?*

"I missed you too," I whispered as I returned her hug. Apprehension kept me tense in her arms, and my heart fluttered nervously in my chest. I didn't know what to expect from her. None of us ever did; Momma was always unpredictable and moody. Her stress levels had determined the entire mood of our household, and that was even before Daddy left. Maybe that was why he left.

My eyes burned as I looked over her shoulder. Tears threatened to spill over as my gaze wandered over the perfectly landscaped yard behind Momma's back, then drifted over the huge old-fashioned farmhouse that was always a crisp, freshly-painted white. It was always clean here. Immaculate, even. Nothing was ever allowed to sully this place—no sticky little fingers, no dusty work boots lying around, and no toys to clutter up the yard. Everything around here looked the same. And in her arms, I *felt* the same—

hesitant and longing for her to just love me as I was. Why was that so hard?

Momma let me go, and both our heads turned as tires crunched through the gravel driveway. A shiny, white BMW pulled to a stop and Clara got out with a big smile. "Hey, y'all." She wrapped me in her arms. "I'm so glad you came," she whispered.

"Make sure you show Willa your new car, Clara," Momma sniped. "Waste of dang money..." was muttered under her breath.

"Everything will be okay," Clara murmured before letting me go. "I like nice things and I work hard, Momma. There is nothing wrong with that. Let's go inside. I could use some Flynn and Rider hugs. You could too, Willa. Those boys are good for lifting the spirits up around here." She grabbed her purse from the front seat, took my hand and tugged me toward the house. Momma followed behind.

"We're in the dining room, y'all," Sadie called after the heavy screen door slammed shut behind us. Clara kept hold of my hand and pulled me along. I wasn't planning on running off, not yet anyway, but the way she held on to me made me feel good. It was the welcome I didn't completely feel from Momma. My mother's affection came with strings attached. We'd all felt them as we grew up, tugging us around, leading us in the directions she wanted us to go.

My flip flops slapped across the wide wooden planks of the floor. Lemon floor wax and the scent of fresh cut lavender filled my nostrils as we crossed through the spacious living room toward the closed double pocket doors of the formal dining room.

"Can we meet her now? Will she have presents for us?" I heard tiny voices coming from the dining room. *Shit! I should have brought presents.*

"Oh!" Clara let my hand drop and pulled the huge—Louis Vuitton?—purse from her shoulder to rummage around in it. She pulled out two small gift bags and passed them to me with a wink.

"Oh sure, you can buy their affection Willa. Just like Clara does. Never mind that the very roof over their heads comes from me since their no-good daddy up and left." Momma stomped around us to enter the kitchen off to the right of the stairs.

"Ignore her. You know I always do." Clara rolled her eyes, then flipped the bird to Momma's back. That gesture snapped me back to the past. Clara would always hug my neck and smuggle cookies in her pockets whenever I was stuck in the time-out spot underneath the stairs. She taught me to flip the bird to Momma's back instead of cry over her words. It was a lesson I'd never fully learned since the tears came no matter how hard I tried to be defiant instead of heartbroken.

I peeked inside the bags. "Clara, I don't know what to say. Thank you."

"Those two boys are spoiled by their Auntie Clara. I've set a precedent." She pulled two more gift bags out of her purse for herself to give. Her eyes twinkled as her grin turned sideways. "Now we're both prepared. And girl, don't ever cry over presents that aren't even for you." She smacked my arm. "Buck up, Butterbean. This is just the beginning of what should be a long, largely unpleasant evening."

My head bobbed up and down in a nervous nod and I clutched the bags to my chest. "Please tell me it's pot roast, at least."

"Is it Sunday? Nothing ever changes around here. You'll see."

"Oh, man." My feet stuttered to a stop as I considered heading for the hills. As if she had a sixth sense, Sadie slid the dining room doors aside, grabbed my arms and walked backward as she pulled me inside, thwarting my almost-mad dash out the front door.

"Boys, this is your Auntie Willa." She beamed at me, pride shining in her eyes, then stepped aside with a flourish to reveal her adorable sons standing behind her. All blond hair, mischievous blue eyes, and freckled faces. I couldn't help but grin at them.

"I'm Flynn. I'm in second grade." He held his hand out in a grown-up gesture of greeting. I shook it, he tilted his head to his brother. "This is Rider. He's in second grade too." He lowered his voice. "We're identical twins, but I feel compelled to add that our intellect is vastly different. I'm studying astrophysics—"

Rider pushed past and took my hand, guiding me through a complicated secret handshake that involved a high five and a hand swipe through our hair. "Yeah, astrophysics—Flynn wants to be a fleet commander. You know, from *Star Trek*?"

"No, I do not. I want to be an astronaut for NASA," Flynn protested indignantly.

"He totally does," Rider whispered as an aside. The aside paired with the eye roll reminded me so much of Sadie that I almost burst into tears. Instead I handed him his gift bag.

He pulled out the small toy version of an X-wing starfighter from *Star Wars*. A smile crossed my face as I thought of Everett. "Sweet, Auntie Willa! I don't have this one. Thank you." He rushed forward to hug me around my hips. My heart rapidly turned to mush in my chest as I hugged him back. Clara nudged me with a wink.

"You're welcome. Here you go, Flynn." He took his gift with a small smile.

"Whatever. Well, I wish I could stay but I have to go to work." With a shove of her chair and a glare aimed my way, Gracie stood up. Her eyes were shiny; was she about to cry? I started to take a step toward her, but her glare froze me in my tracks.

"But dinner hasn't even started." Sadie smiled nervously at me then turned to Gracie to hiss, "You promised, Gracie."

Collectively we turned to the kitchen archway as Momma entered with a huge platter full of pot roast and veggies. "Run and grab the mashed potatoes, Clara. Sit down, Gracie, you aren't going anywhere." Clara darted around Momma and into the kitchen while Gracie plopped sullenly back into her chair.

"I'll stay for a few minutes," Gracie said to her plate.

"It's not like you have a real job, sugar pie. You won't get fired," Momma said as she placed the platter down and took her seat.

"What do you do, Gracie?" I asked. She rolled her eyes then stared at the wall behind my head in answer.

Clara entered with the mashed potatoes and an explanation for Gracie. "You remember the old Pizza Hut in town?" I nodded. "Well, they still don't deliver. Gracie sits down there in her car, people text her what they want, she gets a table, orders, has them box it up, and then she delivers it. Never underestimate what people will pay when they have the munchies." I grinned at Gracie, impressed with her ingenuity. I also contemplated taking her place at the Pizza Hut while she was at school.

"Gracie May, I don't know why you waste your time doing that when you could work for me part-time after school," Momma complained.

"I make more money delivering pizzas, Momma. I make more than Sadie does working for you." She plunked a pile of mashed potatoes on her plate and avoided everyone's eyes.

"Hey!" Sadie protested. "Really?"

Gracie looked up. "Yeah, but money won't be a problem for you anymore. Ain't you going to work for Bill Monroe next week?" she replied with a shit-eating grin.

"What?" Momma's hands hit the table. Clara gulped her glass of wine with big eyes and I turned my head back and forth between all of them, so I wouldn't miss anything. Clara was right; some things never changed. Hill family dinnertime drama was one of them.

"Gracie!" Sadie exclaimed.

"I gotta go to work." Gracie snagged a dinner roll out of the basket then ran for the door. The bomb was dropped, the detonation a success, and her escape plan was brilliant. I aimed my grin at my lap so no one would see. She reminded me of myself of that age.

"Explain yourself, missy." Momma's angry eyes shifted to Sadie who heaved out a huge sigh.

"Boys, go on in the living room with your plates and turn on the TV, and make it as loud as you want it. Grandma and Mommy have to talk." Flynn hesitated and looked concerned, but Rider shoved him toward the door with a shake of his head, grabbed their plates and then took off, returning to close the pocket doors. Those poor boys. Meanwhile, I could see Sadie bracing herself for a fight.

"You're going to work for Bill Monroe instead of your own mother. The woman who took you in after your useless, no-good husband up and left you? Bill Monroe has a reputation for being a hard taskmaster. Do you really think he will put up with your flighty nature? And what about Barrett Monroe? I know you had a crush on him back in high school. He knew better back then to get involved with the likes of you, and he'll know better now too. Don't think you can weasel your way into his bed and into that big house of his in town. Do you think any man wants to deal with another man's castoffs? News flash, Sadie—they do not. You're best off staying put."

Sadie sucked in a huge breath as tears filled her eyes. "I don't care if Bill Monroe is a hard-ass or a grouch or a complete bastard. He can be whatever he wants because he is going to pay me enough to live on. And furthermore, I still live here because you pay me minimum wage, Momma. You can't get mad that I'm quitting to work somewhere else!" Sadie shouted. "You're bossy and mean and you won't pay anyone enough to live. You like having people under your thumb so you can be in control, don't you? I'll put up with Bill or Barrett Monroe or anyone else's shit, since they're paying me what I'm worth. I went to design school and that ain't nothing! I can afford to support my boys on my own with what they'll pay me." Tears filled her eyes as she shoved her chair back and stood up. "I can't believe you sometimes. You wonder why everyone leaves. This. This shit is why. Is it so hard to just be nice? To have some sympathy? To be proud of me for once? Call me, Clara. I'm so sorry, Willa." She returned Clara's *The Hunger Games* District Eleven salute then stormed out of the dining room. I heard her feet stomp up the stairs followed by the slam of the door, the echo of which was right above my head—she was in her old bedroom. *Déjà vu.*

"And now she'll expect me to get the boys to bed. Unbelievable! I raised you girls to depend on no man. And look at all of you— dumped, broken, and used up—every single one of you. Nothing but disappointments, the lot of you." Momma shook her head as she filled a plate and passed it to Clara.

Clara silently took the plate, shut her eyes, and held my hand. We knew what was coming. I was always after Sadie.

"And as for you, Willa. Is your divorce final? Or did you run away from him without a word too? Don't expect anyone in this town to welcome an irresponsible flight risk like you back with open arms. I cannot believe Genie hired you after the damage you've done to this family and our reputation in town. Sadie might have been an idiot to marry the man she chose, but at least she was of proper age. You've embarrassed us all with your sordid ways, young lady. Like I've always said, that IQ you were blessed with was wasted on you. Your choices will always be foolhardy and reckless."

"I'm sorry, Momma," I whispered, transported back to the past where I used to try so hard to win her approval—and always failed.

CHAPTER EIGHT

EVERETT

"Ev, if you're determined to be a loner, you may as well enjoy the company."

— *PAPAW JOE*

A frustrated scream filled the air, followed by two hits to the wall. I froze with the sledgehammer in my hand and listened for a second before rushing over to Willa's door to knock. "Everything okay in there, Willard?" I shouted.

"No!" The locks clicked in rapid succession before the door swung open to bounce off the spring stopper and hit her in the side. She flinched as she stood there, eyes flashing pale blue fire, face twisted with—well, I couldn't tell what she was feeling. Pain? Rage? Whatever it was, was bad. With trembling lips, she spoke. "My shoes smudged the wall when I threw them." Her hand swiped beneath her eyes, glassy with tears that I knew were about to fall. "I'll clean it up. I'll repaint if it won't come off—"

"Hey, hey, don't worry about that. What happened? Wanna talk?" I wanted more than talking. I wanted to hug her, hold her, let her work that painful rage out with me and make her smile again.

"I've had enough of talking. I'm all talked out right now, Everett. No thanks," her voice squeaked over the words as she stared somewhere beyond the back of my head.

"Okay, no talking. Wanna break shit?" I offered her my sledgehammer.

A startled laugh escaped her. "I thought you were fixing shit around here. Not breaking it."

"Sometimes the best part of building something new is tearing down what stood in its place." I held out the sledgehammer as an offering.

She took it from me with a twisted smile that fell somewhere between about to laugh and glaring at me. She gasped as her arm fell under the weight and the sledgehammer dropped to the floor still held in her hand. "Real funny, Everett." I chuckled at her shocked expression, causing her to scowl at me.

"I have a lighter one, no worries. Do you have steel toed boots?"

"Oh yeah, sure, I'll go put them on right now. No, I don't have steel toed boots." Sarcasm dripped from her tone, but it was better than the pain that had filled her voice before. So, I'd take it.

"You can wear some of mine." I gestured to the shelf next to the laundry area where I kept my work things.

"Thanks." She eyed me and headed over to the shelf to peruse my stuff.

"Grab some coveralls, and protective glasses too. You don't want to get that pretty white shirt all dusty."

"Okay…" I watched as she slipped on a pair of coveralls, laughing at how big they were on her.

"Sit on the bench, Willard." She sat. I knelt in front of her to roll up the hems. As I moved to adjust the shoulder straps, our eyes met and held. Her breath caught as my fingertips grazed her arms. "The boots will be big on you, but it's better than breaking a toe, right?" She nodded, eyes never leaving mine, as I slipped a boot on one foot, then the other. I stood and took a step back. "Better?"

She stood up and giggled when she stepped right out of the boots.

I caught her arms as she stumbled toward me. "Dang, Everett, your feet are huge."

"I'm six foot six. If my feet were smaller, I'd fall over."

"True enough. I'll just put them on when we get—wait, what shit are we gonna break?" Her eyes were lit with amusement instead of unshed tears. Proving that demo day could cure whatever ailed a person.

"We're going to knock down a wall in the dining room." I couldn't stop myself from winking at her.

Her eyes grew big with excitement as her lips quirked to the side. "Cool."

"Yeah, cool." I grinned. "Come on." Grabbing a lighter weight sledgehammer along with my own, I gestured for her to precede me up the stairs to the main part of the house.

"I still think that room is haunted," she said with an exaggerated shudder as we passed the entrance to the formal living room.

"Well, we're about to knock the wall down. If there are any ghosts, we'll find out."

She turned back to face me, and the laughter in her expression made my heart pound hard in my chest. Improving her mood had become essential to me. "Ha ha, make your fun, but when we're run out of here by angry spirits, I'll be the last one laughing." Her teasing voice only added intensity to my heart's pounding reaction to her.

"Sure, from behind me, from where you'll be hiding while I battle the crazed demons from the underworld that were living in my walls. *Muahhahaha*." I laughed ominously and led her into the dining room where white sheet-covered furniture dominated the center of the room.

Her laughter trailed behind her as she stepped around me to go through the arched entrance and fully into the room. Spinning around with a smile, her blue eyes twinkled at me beneath the light of the chandelier. She was so fucking beautiful. The fact that I'd been the one to light her up pierced my heart with a bolt of—*stop it, Monroe*.

"What's under the sheets?" she questioned.

"Oh, just a table, chairs…" Damn, the thought of her witnessing the true depth of my geekery had me a bit nervous. I flinched when she flung the sheet from the table. Her wide eyes snapped to mine, and her mouth dropped halfway open.

"Is this a gaming table? I knew you were opening a shop. I didn't know you really played. I thought you were just trying to make a quick buck off the nerds in town. Dungeons and Dragons and that kind of stuff is very popular lately—"

"Why would you think that?"

"Look at you!" her voice was accusatory, like I'd done something wrong.

"What do you mean—look at me?"

"Duh, you're gorgeous, Everett. Hot guys like you don't play games, or at least not the kinds of games I want to play."

"Well, do you play?" I asked. Her smirk was her answer, her raised eyebrows and laughing eyes were a challenge. "I mean, look at you," I accused right back. She rolled her eyes. "You look like a supermodel—you don't play," I scoffed, throwing down the gauntlet.

Her eyes twinkled into mine as she held her hand out. "Ceto, my surname is dependent upon who's asking for it. Chaotic neutral, half-elf rogue. I used to play back in high school with Sabrina and a few other girls. It's been a long time.

Fucking marry me right now. I shook her hand before whipping the sheet from one of the chairs to hold in front of myself. I was hard as a fucking rock. She looked like a wet dream, had the smartest mouth I'd ever encountered, a tender heart I was pretty certain I'd die to protect *and* she played Dungeons and Dragons. I was in serious danger of making a giant ass of myself over her. "Well, what do you play, Everett?"

"Uh, usually I DM; but when I play, I'm Ulfric Heartgrave, Neutral good, human ranger."

She threw her head back and laughed. "Of course! Of course that's what you'd be. You big hero, you." The shadows moved back in her eyes as the smile left her face. "I'm ready to break shit. Let me at it."

I pointed to the wall in front of her. "Take a swing."

"Straight in? Just swing at it?" She hesitated.

"Watch me first." I wound up like I was swinging a baseball bat and sunk my sledgehammer into the old drywall with a soft crunch. Dust puffed out to coat the floor and my coveralls. I pulled it out, dragging a large piece of the wall to the floor. I tilted my head toward her, and she stepped up with a determined look. Imitating me, she swung and hit the wall, laughing as she tried to pull the stuck sledgehammer out.

I stepped close and reached around her to grasp her hands and help her pull. Her back brushing my front put me in danger of another hard-on, but I managed to act like a grown-up and not regress to my teenage reactions. "You have to wiggle it sometimes," I explained as I shifted her arms side to side.

"Like this?" she breathed, turning her head to face me.

"Yeah." With a fingertip, I pushed the safety goggles up the bridge of her nose, breathing in her sweet scent and trying once more to regain control over my body's raging response to being this close to her.

"Thanks," she murmured. Black eyelashes fanned over her freckled cheeks as her eyes drifted to half-mast and the goggles slid adorably down her nose. Then her stomach rumbled loudly, and she shook her head side to side as her eyes slammed the rest of the way shut and a blush rose over her neck to color her face.

I chuckled, her rumbly stomach and I were becoming well acquainted. "Is that your stomach again, Willard? I thought you went to dinner with your family?" I straightened and set her sledge-hammer next to mine on the floor.

Her chest rose with a huge sigh as she met my eyes. "I decided to skip dinner since it came with a heaping side of my mother's bull-shit. I don't need that anymore. It's why I ran—I mean, I left. Who needs that? Right?" Shutters slammed down behind her eyes, attempting to hide her hurt feelings, and probably her past, from me.

"Right, life is too short to put up with bullshit. Anyway, my mother was doing her canning today and she brought over a few jars of her spaghetti sauce. I'll cook, and you can pick something to watch. We can eat in there." I gestured to the living room and paused before entering the kitchen. "Willard, you'll be okay—promise." I headed behind the counter to open the fridge. I took out two beers and tossed her one. She caught it, her face relaxing into a smile. The best way to take care of her was to just do it without the option for her to accept it. Took me awhile, but I'd figured that out, at least.

"Okay. What do you want to watch?" she asked, cracking open her beer. "Movie or a binge watch?"

"Binge watch." I peeked over the refrigerator door to grin at her. "I just got the limited-edition DVD set of the greatest show of all time. Put that on."

Her laugh was obnoxious, like seals at the beach. It was adorable and unexpected from someone who looked as if dainty tinkling bells should be the sound to express her joy. "Ohhh, is this a test?" She snorted and I grinned broadly at her from behind the counter. "Do I have to figure out what the greatest show of all time is?" she asked.

"Yeah, we'll see if you can get it right." I reached high for a pot hanging over the stove, smiling inside when I noticed her checking out my abs. She slid onto a barstool and sipped her beer as I filled the pot with water for the noodles.

Her eyes were gentle as she searched my face. "You like to take care of people, don't you, Everett? Just so you know, I usually don't need this much taking care of—"

"Stop. It's just spaghetti, Willard." I downplayed my feelings, sure that she would run off if I let out even the slightest clue to what I was really beginning to feel for her.

"It's more than spaghetti…" she whispered. And it *was* more than spaghetti. I found myself wanting to fall for her right now—but it wasn't safe. So, for now, I'd settle for wanting her to let me in, just a little bit. I smiled my encouragement for her to keep talking. "I don't want to be that girl ever again, Everett. The girl begging to be loved and accepted without having to change everything about myself. I won't do it."

"Real love takes you for who you are," I declared.

"Real love doesn't exist," she countered.

"Look at Wyatt and Sabrina. Are they real?" Her lips pursed as she looked away, out the window. "They wouldn't change a thing about each other," I said as she avoided my eyes.

"Maybe they're the exception. Maybe after everything Sabrina went through as a kid, she deserves it—"

"And you don't?"

"I didn't say that—"

"You didn't have to," I murmured. Abruptly, she stood and snatched up her beer.

"I'm going to put the show on. I bet I can figure it out," she teased as a too-bright smile that didn't quite reach her eyes crossed her face. She turned away and I realized I had pushed too far. I needed to be careful not to scare her off.

I heard her rummaging through the cabinet full of my DVD collection, muttering to herself, but I was too far away to hear what she said until, "Ah-ha! I'm on to you, Everett," she called.

"We'll see about that," I called back. I stirred the sauce and dropped the noodles into the water, grinning to myself like a sap. She had me all wound up with lust and curiosity. It was the strangest feeling; I wanted to know everything about her just as much as I wanted to take her to bed. I'd never had both desires at the same time. I grabbed a bagged Caesar salad, dumped the contents into a serving bowl, tossed some frozen garlic bread into the oven and set the timer.

"Here we go," she popped her head through the archway with grin on her face, brandishing the remote control over her head like it was prize she had won. My eyebrows went up as she tilted her head and pressed play. The theme song from *Firefly* filled my surround sound speakers. I was glad to be behind the kitchen counter because my almost ever-present Willa-induced boner decided to make his presence known at that very moment, making me cringe inside because—*really? Come on.* My heart surged because I felt like maybe she did know me—even just a little bit—and it was thrilling.

The grin that split my face was huge as I took her in—heading my direction with her huge smile, tight jeans, and tiny white T-shirt —but it was more than that. I saw her spirit shining in her eyes.

She'd fought her melancholy mood and won, at least for now. I felt a curious pride at her strength. "You win, Willa," I conceded her victory.

"I saw the *Serenity* on your coffee table," she admitted. "It gave you away. But I agree, *Firefly* is the best—Captain Tight Pants for life."

She made me laugh. The expression she wore was adorable, and her grin was irresistible. Each new side of her personality became another reason to like her more. "How old were you when that show came out? A toddler?" I teased.

"Sabrina and I got into it years after it was on TV. But that doesn't mean we didn't appreciate the finer things about it—like Nathan Fillion's ass in those brown pants."

"Gotcha." I chuckled as I grabbed dishes from the cabinet. "Time to eat." I heaped a huge serving of spaghetti onto her plate, chuckling again as her eyes widened at the never-ending pile of parmesan cheese I began grating over the top. "It's all about the cheese." I winked at her and noted that her cheeks grew pink and her smile softened after I did it.

"That's too much." Her words contradicted the nodding of her head each time the grater passed over the cheese.

"There's no such thing as too much when it comes to parm." She laughed, and we finished filling our plates and brought them to the couch, grinning at each other like kids as the episode started.

We ate and we watched. I was surprised that I was able to relax with her just like I would with any one of my friends. I did not have to hide the geek that lived within, and it was a breath of fresh air. Women I had dated in the past never seemed to want me to be…myself.

"Curse your sudden but inevitable betrayal!" We recited in unison, then roared with laughter before collapsing together back against the cushions with my arm around her shoulder. She stiffened briefly, then relaxed into my side to watch the rest of the episode.

CHAPTER NINE

WILLA

"Men tell you what they think is true. Then you spend the rest of your life figuring out that they're wrong. You can only depend on yourself."

— *MOMMA*

B elatedly, I realized my mistake.

Here I was, like a stupid, clueless ingenue, watching TV with him, on his freaking couch, after he'd cooked a nice dinner. I had warned myself about this very thing and just look at me.

He got me here—stealth mode—like all the good guys did, and now I was sprawled against his deliciously hard body watching the best show ever with a satisfied stomach and a heart filled with…I didn't even know what it was filled with, but it needed to get lost. I couldn't fall for Everett. That went against my whole lone wolf, no men allowed life plan. I heaved out a huge sigh, which only served to press me closer into him. *God, he smells good.*

Despite the rules I had set for myself—and the fact that I was breaking them—I was smiling. He'd made me feel better tonight, and it had been effortless. His heart was kind and he could cook the heck out of spaghetti. Plus, we shared the same life philosophy: *no such thing as too much parm*. He was becoming the best part of my days—and it had to stop.

Did I play it smart and move to the other side of the couch? Of course not. I rarely played things smart; I was the queen of bad choices. And in that spirit, I made an inevitable decision and pulled his face down to mine to kiss the hell out of him. Pressing my lips to his, breathing him in, running my hands into that gorgeous soft hair I'd been dying to touch—*Gah*! I flicked the band that held his hair back and let it spill over my palms, giving a tug to bring him closer to my open mouth and seeking tongue. I wanted some part of him in me and I wanted it now. His hands gripped my waist as he hauled me closer. We didn't speak. Words wouldn't be adequate to express the way I felt right now, and his eyes had done the talking for him. His gaze stripped me naked.

"Willa…" he breathed against my lips when I pulled back to look into his eyes. And didn't that just push every sexy button that existed in my body. *He said my name.* Heat flooded my veins as I moved to straddle him, gasping when I discovered he was already hard for me. Crazed with lust and mesmerized by the sound of my name on his beautiful full lips, I ground down against his lap as he wrapped his arms around me and took my mouth in a searing kiss. I felt a change in me as he touched me. Something shifted as a spark of trust joined the lust and lit me up inside. I had the feeling that all I had to do was say the word and he would stop without anger or recrimination.

He had already taken care of me enough in the last few months for my defenses to lower, but the feel of his gentle hands running up my spine to sift through my hair and cup my cheeks as we kissed, combined with his hard body beneath me…

It was the opposing nature of him, the dichotomy—soft inside, so sweet and kind, yet all hard, brutal strength on the outside—that drove me insane. Reckless want surged through my system. I needed him.

"Willa, is this—are you okay?" *I knew it…*

"Yes," I whispered. "Don't stop." He groaned against my lips and

I smiled against his. I allowed myself to sink into him, to feel the comfort and care he provided without even trying. Everett had been sneaking up on me for all these months, with his friendly eyes and constant smile. So, I let myself go and it made my heart soar.

I was drowning in him, absolutely going under, and I was not about to wave my arms or kick my legs because I didn't want to break the surface. This little world right here on his couch was where I wanted to be—surrounded by delicious spaghetti, *Firefly*, and held in the arms of the sweetest man I'd ever met—and I would stay here until I inevitably, unwittingly destroyed it. But for now, this fantasy was mine and I was going to keep it.

His shoulders were hard as I ran my hands around his upper back to pull at his T-shirt. With a shift of his body, he rocked us forward so I could gain better purchase and yank it over his head. With a grin, he slipped his hands beneath my shirt's hem and pulled up as I raised my arms to assist. "You are so fucking beautiful, Willa." My irrational heart burst at the words as I reached between my breasts to unhook my bra and let it slip down my arms to drift backward to the floor.

"So are you," I murmured as my eyes roved over his sculpted chest and abs, the fine, sharp line of his bearded jaw, and his gorgeous honey brown eyes that warmed on mine as I spoke to him. All those times I had watched him outside while he worked flitted through my mind like the wings of a butterfly, scrambling my thoughts and ramping up my desire for him. Beneath my palms, goosebumps rose over his flesh and he shivered. I had never felt like this—wild, powerful, *safe*. I felt like he sensed my need for control and as such, he gave it up to me.

I hovered over him on a precipice; if I jumped off, things would never be the same between us. But if I stayed on, I would live with the regret of missing out on something I knew would be beautiful. Every bone in my body screamed at me to take this chance, to lie back and let him have me. "Everett," I begged seconds before his mouth slammed to mine in a kiss that defied everything else I had ever experienced and probably ever would. Pieces clicked into place, things that I didn't know were missing were found, and I felt home for the first time since I'd returned to Green Valley. I gasped against his lips and pulled away.

His eyes burned into mine, just like all those secret looks he had given me from time to time—heated, hooded, full of sex—only this time I didn't look away. I let my secrets out and smiled at him, lifting my arms to wind around his neck as he yanked me closer with an arm banded around my hips.

Succumbing to the gravitational pull of his kisses, his body, his wonderful heart, I relaxed, giving over the control I had relished only moments before. His arms tightened around me, enveloping me in warmth as I melted against him. While tracing my jaw with kisses, his fingertips dipped below the back of my jeans and I arched back as he held my waist. The feel of his lips—on my skin, down my neck, over my breasts—was intoxicating. It rocked me on my axis, leaving me disoriented and full of need. Then he sucked a nipple into his mouth, and I lost all control. The precipice was no more as I fell into Everett.

"God, Willa…" he murmured against my breast. His breath over my skin caused goosebumps to rise in its path as he kissed and licked his way across my chest to the other nipple. "I want you so much. Can I? Are we…?"

"Yes. Please, Everett. Yes." *Snap* went the button on my jeans and *whoosh* went the zipper as his hand dove inside to touch me intimately. I writhed on his lap, pressing myself against his hard length as his fingers swirled tight circles against my burning skin. "I want you, too." I gasped against the top of his bent head as I held him to my breasts, where his lips and the softness of his beard worked magic over my sensitized nipples.

Warm hands on my waist lifted me up as he stood to shift my body to lie on the couch and tug my jeans and undies down my leg to toss them somewhere behind him on the floor. I opened my arms to welcome him as he rose above me, placing a knee high between my legs as his other leg bent to kneel on the floor, elbows on either side of my shoulders, fingers sifting through my hair as he kissed me deeply, completely. He was so tall and covered with hard muscles, the planes and angles of which fascinated me as they flexed and released beneath my wandering hands and eager mouth. He chuckled and I knew I'd found a ticklish spot, so I lifted upward to kiss it. "Come up here, there's room," I murmured. His couch was huge, and I wanted him up here with me, against me, inside me. I reached for his belt buckle and pulled.

He stood and I sat up to unbuckle that belt, licking my lips in blissed-out anticipation. But he had other ideas. His pants fell to the floor, but then he lifted me, wrapping his huge, beautiful arms around me like a groom carries a bride. The rooms in this old house passed by in a blur, our eyes only for each other as he swiftly carried me to his bed, peppering kisses over my lips, my cheeks, and the tip of my nose, cherishing me, keeping me close as he walked. Never, ever had I experienced anything like this. I was overwhelmed and lost in a way that left me feeling like I almost didn't want to be found.

Sinking to a knee on the mattress, he lowered me to lie beneath him. His body covering mine was all I could feel. Doubts, fears, insecurities, everything but him floated out of my mind as he *consumed me*. "Everett, Everett, Ev—please don't stop..." my voice was unfamiliar, full of wanton, wild pleasure, the likes of which I had never felt.

"My god, Willa. You feel so good," he groaned against my lips. I felt him, huge and hard, pressed against the inside of my thigh. "Sweetheart, I can't stop. Tell me you want me. Tell me you need me —tell me *yes*. Please, Willa. Let me inside."

"Yes, Ev. Yes, yes, yes," I chanted as he slipped inside. He filled me so deep I imagined I would feel him inside of me forever, branded by him for the rest of my life.

His forearm fit perfectly underneath my neck as he took me. Brushing the hair out of my eyes with his fingertips, he bent low but didn't kiss me. Our eyes met and held, our lips touched briefly only to press together and drift apart with each thrust he drove into me. And his eyes... God, the way he looked at me? He saw my soul and he understood it. He smoothed my edges and made me soft again.

But I couldn't afford to be soft. My eyes drifted shut as I fought against his irresistible pull. It would be so easy to lose myself again. Too easy.

"Willa..." he whispered. "Willa, Willa..." With each thrust, the gift of my name on his lips pushed me closer to the edge. I arched up, wrapping my legs around his waist to let him go deeper.

With a pleasure-tortured moan, I pulled myself up off the bed and into his hard body, clinging to his shoulders and burying my face into the side of his neck, biting down to taste the salt of his skin. Little explosions rocked me to my core, shooting sparks of delicious sensation throughout my body, taking me higher than I'd ever been. I was afraid to let myself go, scared I'd never come down from this.

"Give it to me," he murmured in my ear, his breath ruffling my hair, his words driving me crazy, guiding me to the brink. "I feel it happening, Willa. Let it go." His hand slipped between us to press against my clit. "I want to taste you here," he growled in my ear as his fingers rubbed and tapped lightly against my skin.

"Ohhh, god," I groaned, and it was loud, out of control. I let go of his neck and my back hit the bed, arching up as my body worked toward release. He rose to his knees and plunged into me deeply, moving hard inside of me as his fingers kept up their delicate torture. His eyes blazed into mine with a satisfied gleam as we came apart together. He collapsed forward to lie at my side and gathered me close, reaching down to grab his comforter to cover us.

"Stay with me tonight. Don't leave me." His voice was soft against my neck, where his face rested, pressing sweet kisses against me after every word.

"I'll stay. I want to be with you," I whispered with a kiss to the top of his head. His arms convulsed as he squeezed me tighter and we fell into sleep.

CHAPTER TEN

WILLA

"I'll kill any man who looks at you twice. Don't pretend you don't know what I'm capable of, Willa."

— TOMMY

I awoke to sweet kisses and a mug of Everett's yummy coffee sitting on the night table next to the bed. "I have to go to work, sweetheart. Stay as long as you like. What's mine is yours," he had whispered before grinning at me and closing the bedroom door behind himself. Now I was up with the midafternoon sun shining through the windows, a cold mug of coffee, and a big empty house to explore. Involuntarily my face morphed into a huge smile and for the first time in years—maybe even in my entire life—I felt hope.

After throwing the covers back I realized I had no clothes; they were somewhere on the living room floor. Delicious tingles ran through me as I recalled the night before. Everett had kept me close all night, his strong arms wrapped around me, never once letting go.

Absentmindedly I reached for my cell phone to call Sabrina, giggling when I remembered it was downstairs in the back pocket of my jeans instead of landing somewhere in my bed after I fell asleep.

With a reach to the ceiling, I stretched, glorying in the satiated feeling that spread throughout my body. Everett had a wide array of useful skills, and a huge dick that he knew how to use. I was dying to see what else he could do with it—maybe tonight? I spun around in a circle to take in his room—framed sci-fi movie prints decorated the walls while heavy wooden furniture dominated the space—and I let out another giggle when I noted that his king-sized bed had plain navy-blue sheets. *Not* Star Wars *sheets?*

Who was I? Giggling and spinning like a girl. Happy, relaxed, and looking forward to my day. It was all because of Everett. My heart was a Jell-O pudding cup, and my brain was a puddle of lusty, love drunk goop. I couldn't wait to see him later and I needed to get my phone so I could *squee* at Sabrina. I had never *squee*-ed in my life and I wanted to do it real bad right now. I found a folded pile of clean laundry stacked on a chair in the corner. I grabbed a T-shirt and slipped it over my head. "Comic-Con 2016," it said. I made a mental note to bring it back; it was probably a collectible T-shirt.

My feet flew down the stairs as my eyes searched for my jeans. After yanking out my phone I slipped on my undies and collapsed onto the couch while swiping to call Sabrina. I was a lucky girl that she forgave me for running away without a word all those years ago. Then again, she knew my life back then, and she had always understood me.

"Hey, Willa."

"Sabrina! I slept with Everett, he's—he's everything I don't deserve but I want him anyway," I blurted.

"Oh my god! And you deserve every good thing, including Everett if he's the one for you. I knew this would happen!" She squealed into my ear, making me laugh.

"Everett is nothing like Tommy," I stated.

"Of course not. Everett is a nice guy. Tommy was a—I feel like we can talk about this now, right?" Her voice was hesitant.

"Sure, I guess so." I was not sure I wanted to talk about Tommy, but clearly Sabrina needed to get it off her chest and maybe it was time I got it off mine too.

"With Tommy, it was all about him. Does *he* love me? Does *he* want to be with me? You were always worried about where you stood, and he liked it like that. Tommy told you enough of what you needed to hear so he could keep you around. He was obsessed with you, not in love with you. Love doesn't feel like a trap. Everett isn't that kind of guy. Tommy wanted to own you, and I'm pretty sure Everett will just want to love you—you know, someday."

"I think you're right. You know, Sabrina, the best times in my life were with you. Back then, I felt safe at your house, hanging out, talking to you and your sister. I'm starting to feel like that again, with Everett. He makes me feel like *me* and I don't want to lose this. But I have made so many mistakes and I don't want to make anymore."

"It was that way for me too, Willa, with you. Then life got real. You chose to run away with Tommy, and after you left and my sister died, I chose nothing. At least you made decisions to regret. You lived your life. If you've learned from what happened with Tommy, you won't make the same mistakes now."

"I think I learned. I mean, I wanted to get away from my mother so bad that I accepted Tommy's version of love like it was real, and then I fought to keep it even though it was worthless. It took me years to see what a manipulative liar he was. Everett isn't like that. He's a good man. He loves his family."

"He does. He's an awesome uncle. Oh! If you marry him, we'll be sisters in law!" she practically shrieked into the phone.

"Wow. I can't even imagine that right now," I lied. The split second he picked me up to carry me up the stairs it was all I'd been thinking about—but admitting it out loud was another story. Even though the thought of marriage was still a little bit scary, happy shivers ran through me whenever I thought of it with Everett. Shaking my head to clear it, I tried to get control over my out-of-control, racing thoughts. Jumping to conclusions, reacting too quickly, and *not thinking* were all the things that led up to this moment. Even though this moment was awesome, most of the stuff leading up to it was not.

"I wish we could go to lunch or that I could come over to talk to you more, but I have to get to the library for my shift," she complained.

"It's okay, we'll talk soon. There's plenty of time."

"Yes, we'll make plans. Bye, Willa."

With the sudden urge to see Everett, I slipped into my jeans to head to my place for a shower and a change of clothes. The decision to head to his shop had me feeling—euphoric. Was this what falling in love *should* feel like? Safe and warm, like a hug or slipping into a hot bath? Rather than constantly feeling nervous and worried about what you should say? Could this be real? Oh, how I wanted this to be real.

I darted down Everett's kitchen stairs. My keys were somewhere in my apartment, wherever they'd landed after I threw them—along with my shoes—during my bid for best dramatic actress after having a bitchy-mother-induced temper tantrum. The backdoor to the basement was unlocked and I couldn't remember if I had locked the front door. Hopefully I wouldn't enter to find a bunch of hobos had taken up residence in my living room. With an anticipatory smile, I threw the door open and stepped inside. I rushed through my shower and getting-ready routine and with joy in my heart I slipped Everett's T-shirt back over my head.

After finding my keys and phone I opened the front door only to dash backward and slam it shut, locking it with panicked haste.

White roses. Bruised and battered, scattered all over my porch and down the stairs. My head darted rapidly from side to side taking in my empty apartment as I stood frozen against the door.

He couldn't have been here. Tommy was in prison. He'd always given me white roses to make up for some cruel thing he had said to upset me or for something he had done to someone else while "defending me"—a.k.a. pissing all over his property.

Everett would not have thrown roses against the door like this...

My chest heaved with labored breaths as thoughts shot through my mind like a spray of bullets being fired, tearing me up inside. Was he out? And why didn't I know?

In my hand, my cell phone vibrated and started ringing. At the same moment someone banged on the door. "Willa, it's Wyatt! Open up!" he called.

I spun around to open the door. "Tommy." I gasped as panic filled my heart.

"He's out. I just got the information. The roses? He was here." His worried eyes darted around the area as he gestured for me to let him inside.

"How?" I whispered and stepped back for Wyatt to enter. Cold dread filled my veins. And the only thought to enter my mind was *run.* "How is that possible? He had two more years left on his sentence."

"Good behavior." Wyatt snorted. "But he's on parole, if he tries to mess with you we'll arrest him."

"I have to get out of here." I ran to my bedroom and started stuffing my clothes into a duffel bag.

"No, you can't leave. You just got back home." His footsteps pounded across the floor as he followed me. "Willa, stop. Will you look at me?"

"Tell Sabrina goodbye for me, Wyatt. Please." I tossed the words over my shoulder as I frantically packed anything I could find.

"I will not tell her that. Stop it, Willa." With a gentle hand on my arm, he turned me. Tears burned in my eyes at the concern etched on his face.

"You were there when I needed you and I'll never forget it." A sob lodged in my throat as I choked on the words.

"Stop talking crazy, you aren't going anywhere—"

"For two years you were my only friend. The only constant thing in my life. You saved me, Wyatt. Talking with you every day on the phone kept me from losing myself completely after—you're the brother I never knew I wanted." His soft eyes were sympathetic on me and I couldn't take it. He was weakening my resolve to leave. And I had to leave. I may not completely know what I wanted from my life, but I knew what I didn't want. I spent two years driving all over the country in peaceful silence. It taught me that would rather be alone than with someone like Tommy. I refused

85

to subject anyone else to his horrible ways, especially someone sweet like Everett.

"I didn't save you. You saved yourself, Willa. I was just there to listen is all. Please don't go. You'll break her heart. And I suspect you'll break Everett's heart too. I see what you're wearing, Willa." He gestured to my shirt—Everett's shirt—that I had so giddily dressed in earlier this morning. I should have known better. I should have known that nothing as good as him was ever meant for someone like me.

I inhaled a huge sigh. I had to make him understand. "But I can't stay. I can't be around him anymore—"

"Which him?" he demanded.

"Both hims. I must not be meant to—"

"That's a load of crap and you know it."

"Tell them goodbye for me. Tell them, Wyatt."

"Willa, please don't do this. You're not alone. You have me and Sabrina. You have Everett—"

"No! I won't do this to him. To your family. You remember what Tommy was like—always in a fight, always throwing punches—and you know what he'll do to Everett if he finds out I was ever with someone else." A resigned look crossed his face. "Tell Sabrina I'll keep in touch this time. Please?"

"No. I'm here for you, Willa. And Everett can take care of himself," he insisted.

"He shouldn't have to! It wouldn't be fair to him. And think of your family, the girls!" I shouted as tears streamed down my face. "Please. Tell them all goodbye for me. Please, Wyatt."

"Fine, I'll tell them. But this isn't over. I know I can't stop you right now, but that doesn't mean I won't come after you. I'll be looking for him and I will arrest him the second he steps a toe out of line. Unfortunately, there's no way to prove he threw the roses at the door or that he was even here."

"This is where it starts again with him, isn't it?" I turned to grab another bag to fill it.

"Probably..." he sighed. "You call me every day, just like before. Promise me."

"I promise."

"And you'll come home the second I make it safe. Promise that, too."

"Fine, I promise." But there was no way Tommy would ever let me go. It was easier to just leave.

Wyatt took one of my bags—I didn't have much—and helped me haul it to my van. But he paused at the door after tossing it in. "No. I don't like this. There has to be a better way. Let's talk more. Let's get you calm and then figure this all out. You can get a restraining order, probably even an order of protection. Between that and the parole conditions, he'd be a fool to try anything. He reached for my bag in the van, but I shut the door before he could grab it. "Stop it, Willa. I can't let you leave. I won't do it. Come home with me. Stay at the ranch with me and Sabrina."

"Goodbye, Wyatt." He reached for my arm to stop me, but I side-stepped his hand and ran for the driver's door. "Thank you for everything." He followed close behind, his hand on the door stopped me from entering. I darted around to the back, jumped in, locked myself inside, and scrambled for the driver's seat. After turning the key, I waved to Wyatt and took off. I felt bad, but he wasn't going to let me go. And I had to get away.

CHAPTER ELEVEN

WILLA

"You know I can't stand it when you get upset. Stop that crying and kiss me, honey. Remember, there's nowhere you can go where I can't find you. You'll always be my Willa."

— *TOMMY*

The tears would not stop. My vision was so clouded I was almost too blind to drive. But still I kept on, determined to get as far from Tommy as I could. I wiped my eyes with the hem of Everett's T-shirt, my chest heaving with sobs as I drove slowly down the highway that led out of Green Valley. I should have known better. Being alone was better than being hopeful. Losing hope was worse than never having it in the first place.

My phone rang from the center console. Wyatt's name showed on the screen briefly before voicemail picked it up. I couldn't bear to talk to him right now, and I couldn't imagine facing him ever again. He'd been there the day my life exploded. He'd saved me in so many ways and I owed him too much—I refused to stick around and put him at risk. Tommy's temper was legendary, and I refused to put Wyatt in the crosshairs any more than he already was.

The phone rang again. Sabrina's name flashed on the screen before heading to voicemail. My van veered to the side as tears flowed like a river down my cheeks. This was worse than when I'd left Nashville. The cloud of black grief I had been in back then was nothing compared to what I felt right now. Back then my life had been so small. That grief still stayed with me, but now it had grown to include the people I would miss when I was gone. *Especially Everett.*

Spotting a parking lot ahead, I decided to pull over. I had lost all semblance of control; it was too dangerous to drive this way. I inhaled a deep shuddering breath and concentrated on the road as I made my way to the parking lot. My head crashed into the steering wheel as I shut the engine off, safely ensconced in a spot in the back of the lot. Turning my head to the side, I saw the flashing neon sign of The Wooden Plank, a biker hookup bar right outside of town.

Gathering my thoughts, I sat up to lean against the door and let my mind wander away from my troubles. Headlights flickered in the pre-dusk hour as cars pulled up and parked and customers crunched through the gravel lot to enter the bar.

My eyes squinted in the dim light and I could swear I saw my cousin Odin exit the front door of the bar. I hadn't seen him since we were kids. He was too old to play with me when we were young, but I remember him being close to Sadie and Clara. Then my father left, and Momma quit letting his side of the family come around.

I watched him turn around and gesture angrily for someone to follow him. With a gasp I shot out of my van when I realized it was Gracie he was ordering out of the bar. Sixteen-year-old Gracie! What the ever-loving hell was she doing here? My own troubles retreated to the back of my mind as I so clearly saw Gracie on the same path I had been walking at her age—willful, reckless, and looking for trouble—trying to find anything to get her mind off Momma's cruel neglect and our life at home. No way would I let that happen to her. I mean, just look at me. I was the definition of a tragic hot mess and I refused to let that her make those same mistakes.

Determination kept my stride fast as I jogged toward them, not even thinking of the fact I was in Everett's way too big T-shirt and a pair of leggings with my face a red, tear-streaked horror of a mess.

"Willa, honey. I heard you were back in town. Who died?" Odin greeted sardonically as I finally made it to where they stood under a tall lamp in the parking lot and he got a good look at my face. Gracie merely shot me a glare then looked away with a huff of her breath.

"No one died. I'm having a bad night, is all. What was she doing in there?" I asked Odin.

"Hustling pool and drinking beer. Got a call from an old friend that one of my kin was in here stirring up a ruckus. He knows about your momma's ways and thought it would be nicer if someone with a friendly face picked this one up. So, I swung by and there she was." His head jerked to the side to side while his shoulders shook with suppressed laughter. "She was winnin', too."

"I want my money, Odin." Gracie demanded at his side. "I earned it. Give it over."

"Listen here, you little troublemaker. I'll give you your money, but I don't want you coming here again. Don't make me tell your Momma. One, I don't want to talk to her. And two, bars are not safe for sixteen-year-old girls who look like you, you hear?"

"I hear you, Odin. Fine, I won't come back." She held her hand out for the money.

He sighed exasperatedly and shook his head as he handed it over. "Keep an eye on this one, Willa. She's lookin' for trouble in all the wrong places. Kind of like you used to do."

"Okay, I will. Thank you, Odin." He wrapped me up in a hug, patted the top of Gracie's head, then took off for his car with a wave.

"What the hell, Gracie?"

"None of your business, Willa." She darted around me and took off into the parking lot. *Yeah, no way.* I ran after her and, placing a hand on her arm, spun her around.

"Where do you think you're going?" She shrugged, not meeting my eyes. "How did you even get here?" I pushed.

"I hitched a ride. How else would I get way out here? I'm still waiting on the parts for my VW. I have no car right now."

"Jeez, are you trying to get yourself killed, or worse?"

"Oh yeah, totally. I have a death wish. No, dummy—I'm here to play pool and make money." She hitched her hip and rolled her eyes at me. It was like looking at a mirror in a time machine. Damn.

"You can't make money by getting drunk in a biker bar, genius." I stated facts.

"I'm wasn't in there drinking. I just had a few sips so they would think I was drunk. Girl who looks like me? If I smell like a beer they bet more—then I win more. Duh."

"Well, okay then." Maybe she wasn't like me. I used to sneak into this bar to get drunk. I met Tommy in this bar. I ruined my life in this freaking bar. Still, she wasn't on a good path and I was going to make it stop.

"Okay then," she mocked.

"Knock it off, smartass," I sniped back.

"Whatever." She turned to leave again, and I grabbed her arm. She shook me off and kept going.

"Gracie! Stop running off, dammit!" I shouted at her retreating back.

"I'll do what I want, Willa." She stopped short and turned to the side to shout at someone. "I see you, Devron Stokes! You owe me two-hundred and fifty dollars. Don't make me tell your wife!" she shouted.

"Why would Devron Stokes owe you money?" I asked.

"He sucks at pool and he's too stupid to know it."

"Okay. Okay, Gracie, my van is over there. Come with me." I offered, taking hold of her hand before she could dart away again.

She stopped walking and faced me. "Why would you care what I do?"

"Because you're my sister, that's why."

"It didn't stop you from leaving before," she accused. Her eyes were filled with a pain that I recognized. I felt it from my father after he left and I, like a fool, had been the one to put into Gracie's eyes.

"I'm sorry I left you, Gracie." I whispered. "It is the worst mistake I've made in my life, leaving y'all." Her hands went out to ward off my apology as she stood there shaking her head. "I mean it. I never should have left—"

"Quit it."

"Okay…" I took her hand again and started heading for my van. Reluctantly, she followed along. She was like a ticking bomb at my side. Her energy was unpredictable, and I was afraid I would say something to set her off.

"You can stay at my place tonight, if you want to." I offered.

"Really?" She seemed surprised.

"Sure. Maybe we can talk or something?" I opened the van door, forgetting that everything I owned was piled all over the back. Gracie turned to glare accusingly at me.

"You're leaving again! Why do you even care what I do when you're leaving! Again! Ugh!" She shouted. The tiny bit of progress I had made with her had vanished. *Shit.*

"I'm not leaving." So, yeah, I had everything I owned in the back and was halfway out of Dodge. I couldn't leave now. Not when Gracie clearly needed…me. Gracie needed what I never had—unconditional love and guidance. *Gah!* Who the hell was I to attempt to guide anyone? Damn. We were so screwed.

"All your shit's in the back. I'm not stupid, Willa."

"Well, I'm not going anywhere now. I've changed my mind."

"I don't care."

"You don't have to care."

"Good. Cause I don't care what you do."

"So, you've said."

"Yeah. I said it."

"Cut the crap, Gracie." She stuck her tongue out at me and flipped me off, reminding me of her age and the fact that I had to be the grown-up here.

"Go on and tell Momma. She won't care. This will just be another life lesson for me to learn. Such bullshit." Her arms crossed and her eyes grew glassy with unshed tears under the glow of the lamp light in the parking lot.

"You're right. It is bullshit."

Her head whipped around, and she studied me with narrowed eyes before shrugging and turning back to glare at the parking lot, still unwilling to meet my gaze. "Whatever."

"Yeah, whatever. I messed up my life, Gracie. I'm not going to let you do the same."

"You're not Momma. You can't tell me what to do. Momma doesn't even tell me what to do." She sneered in what I had come to suspect was a semi-permanent expression on her face.

"You should be glad about that, Gracie May." I loved her and I wanted to help her, but I also wanted to smack that smirk right off her face—right after I scrubbed the raccoon eyeliner off.

"Screw you."

"Yeah, screw it all."

"What?"

"Screw it. Fuck it. Move in with me. We'll get an apartment together. You're right about one thing—she'll let you do it."

She didn't face me, wouldn't even look at me. "You mean she won't give a shit if I leave. Just like she didn't try to find you after you left." Her words were harsh. Was she trying to hurt me?

I inhaled a sharp breath. Deep down I knew Momma didn't look for me, but hearing it spoken out loud hurt. Now I was the one to turn away. I saw Gracie turn toward me out of the corner of my eye. "I didn't mean to hurt your feelings, Willa," she whispered.

"I know you didn't. It is what it is. She'll never change." I sighed with defeat.

"Can I still go with you?" Gracie asked quietly. Now my head whipped to her. We were finally meeting eyes. I was surprised and pleased.

"Of course you can." She smiled at me. It was small, but it was real. I smiled back.

"Let's go." We got in my van, buckled up, and took off. I slowed down and pulled into the Piggly Wiggly parking lot. If I was staying in town, we needed food. And If Gracie was going to live with me, I needed…a second job, probably. Would Everett be okay with her staying with me for now? *Gah!* I couldn't keep living in his house after what we did last night, and we could never do it again because of Tommy. Putting Everett at risk like that would be horrible and selfish and wrong, wrong, wrong. Tommy had only hurt me once, but he would go after any man who dared to look at me twice. I heaved out a huge sigh. What was I doing?

"Why are we here?"

"Food. Come on. My cupboards are bare. We need groceries. But let's stick to the sales, cause I'm broke." Reality crashed into my mind the more I settled down from my earlier panic. How had I thought I could leave town with no money?

"I have lots of money. We can buy whatever we want. Can I really stay with you?"

I was pleased to see a tiny ray of hope shining from her eyes. "Yes and we can get your stuff from the farm tomorrow."

She grinned at me. "Thank you." I began to relax as we exited my van and headed for the row full of buggies in front of the store. One step at a time. My mind always turned into a muddled mess when I tried to figure everything out at once.

"We'll be okay, Gracie. I promise, somehow I am going to make it all okay."

"Well, I can help." She placed her hands next to mine on the cart and laughing together, we walked down the aisles, filling the cart as we went.

"How do you have so much money, anyway?" I asked her. "From hustling pool?"

"Nah, I only do that if owner isn't there, which is hardly ever."

"Oh. Okay…" She dug around in her pocket then handed me a business card. It read "What do you need?" with a phone number beneath and a website on the back:

www.youneedgracie.com

I grinned over at her. "This is yours?"

"Yeah, I do odd jobs. I deliver pizzas at the Pizza Hut and pick up groceries for some of the old people in town. They usually tip me pretty good, along with my fee. I mow lawns and I babysit. I made five-hundred bucks babysitting just from the Winstons last month. Sienna Diaz-Winston pays a lot, and she's nice too. I want my own place, soon as I turn eighteen. Clara helped me get a bank account and she helps me invest my money, so my money makes money, or something like that. Sometimes I don't always get what she says but I listen to her because she's so smart. You and Sadie should have listened to her too." The last part was whispered under her breath.

"You're probably right about that," I agreed.

Embarrassingly, Gracie paid for the groceries and we loaded up and left. Trepidation built up inside me the closer we got to Everett's house. What would I say? Had Wyatt already talked to him? How would I ever make him understand that I couldn't be with him?

I slowed to a stop in my spot in the driveway and we began to unload. I froze when light filled the back porch and Everett's tall silhouette filled the space as he headed our way. Shit, crap, damn, he was beautiful. And for one glorious night, he had been mine. Deep down I had always known that a man like that was not meant for the likes of me, and I was right. But I still couldn't help how my heart flew out of my chest at the sight of him. Gracie eyed me as I stood there with my arms full of groceries, watching Everett and frozen in place like a statue.

"Hey, Everett," she called. Giving me a look out of the corner of her eye as if waiting for me to react. "Do you have the new Smash-Girl comic yet?" As an aside, she explained to me. "I'm old-school. I like buying my comics from a shop and Everett said he would order them when he opens up. It's more fun to wait and anticipate. Isn't it?"

"Uh, yeah. I guess so," I muttered.

"Just got them in today," Everett answered her, eyes on me as he took the bags from my hand. "Willa. Hey, sweetness," he whispered. His gaze fell over my shoulder and he frowned as he took in my haphazardly packed bags sitting in the back of my van. "Going somewhere?"

"No. I'm not going anywhere," I murmured, lost in his eyes. I needed to get out of his eyes and back into reality, dammit.

"Do we need to talk?" he asked. I glanced at Gracie, who was making no secret of the fact that she was listening in.

"Yeah," I glanced pointedly at Gracie. "In a minute, okay?" He nodded then headed toward my apartment with the groceries. I watched him walk up the stairs and go inside. I turned around to see Gracie smirking at me. "Y'all totally boned," she whispered excitedly.

"Gracie May!"

"It's written all over his face." She studied my face then reached for my other duffel bag. "It's all over yours too. He wants you bad. Is that why you were runnin' away?"

"It's part of it, but don't say stuff like that."

She laughed. "You sound more like a mother than Momma does." I shook my head. "So, is that it? Is he the reason you were leaving?" she demanded quietly.

"Part of it. Tommy's out. I think he's here in Green Valley."

"Is he coming after you? Like, to hurt you? We can go get some of Momma's shotguns tomorrow. I can shoot. I shot the heads off all the black-eyed Susan's up the hill on the back forty. I can sure as hell shoot the head off your asshole ex-husband if he tries anything. Or his dick. I'll let you choose where I aim."

"You're not shooting anything. No one is going to do any shooting. Jeez, Gracie. And aren't you too young to go shooting back there?" I exclaimed.

She studied my face. "I'm not too young for anything. I hit every single thing I aim for, Willa. I don't think you're aiming for anything. I think you're just running away." Her eyes narrowed on me. "You'll end up telling me everything, you know. I might be sixteen, but deep inside I have the soul of a forty-five-year-old divorcée and I'll probably understand your problems better than you do." She was too perceptive and clearly way too smart for her own good. I scowled at her, grabbed my other bag, and went inside.

CHAPTER TWELVE

EVERETT

"If it's love, you'll feel it long after the kiss is over. Remember that, Everett."

— *PAPAW JOE*

I placed her bags on the kitchen counter while uncertainty and cold dread filtered through my thoughts. She had packed her stuff. Why? Her eyes had held no clues and I was left to stand here in a state of confusion, wondering if the best night of my life was about to turn into what would be the biggest heartbreak I would ever experience. If the hints she had dropped outside came true, it certainly would.

"Let's talk out there." She gestured to the door to the utility area after she tossed her duffel on the table. "Make yourself at home, Gracie. I'll be back in a minute." I followed behind, keeping my cool until she closed the door behind her. All pretense of cool was lost when she faced me, all tremulous smile and soft, shining eyes and looking more beautiful than I could believe. She wore my shirt and it unlocked something primal in me to see her clothed in something that belonged to me.

With a huge step forward I grabbed her—one arm behind her waist, the other behind her knees—sweeping her up and slamming my lips to hers as I carried her toward the worktable in the middle of the basement utility space. Her arms wound around my neck while the fingers of one hand drove into my hair to pull me closer. She was rough, needy, and just as desperate for me as I was for her. Her lips opened beneath mine and her soft moan went into my mouth and straight down to my cock, making me hard. Everything about her—every single thing—was magic. She tasted like heaven and she felt like a fucking dream come true in my arms. My head spun through every fantasy I'd ever had about her as my lips moved urgently over hers. Blindly, I found the table and lowered her to sit on it. Wrapping her legs around my waist, she forced us closer, keeping me tight against her soft heat. I rocked against her as she pressed herself against me in return. I couldn't think when I needed her like this—her body, her heart, her hands on me—and I knew I was made to be with her. She was mine to love and keep safe.

I pressed kisses to her forehead, her temple, her cheek, then finally once more to her lips. She kissed me back, then pulled away with a sigh. Why did it feel like she was about to slip away even though I held her so close? Her hand went to my chest, pushing slightly as she leaned back, avoiding my eyes.

"Everett—" Why did this feel like goodbye?

I cut her off with a whisper. "No, don't talk. I don't think I want to hear what you have to say." Denial forced my eyes shut as I took a step back to let her off the table.

"I'm so sorry. I can't do this with you. I just can't right now, I—" Tears shimmered on her lashes. She blinked once, and then they were gone. Just like the light in her eyes.

"You're breaking my heart, sweetness. Please don't." I was stuck in this terrible moment where fighting her words would get me nowhere and accepting them was my only choice.

"No. Oh, Everett, no, no, no. I don't want to break your heart." Her words were broken breath as her hands caressed over my chest to come to rest above my heart. She wouldn't meet my eyes as she shook her head softly from side to side while looking at the floor.

With a fingertip, I raised her face. Her eyes, soft and sorrowful, met mine. I couldn't understand how after everything we did and said and felt last night—and just now—why she would do this. I couldn't have been this wrong about her. We'd made a connection last night, talking together, then later in my bed. I *felt* her now in a way I didn't before. I sensed the untruth in her words by the way she gravitated toward me, staying near even though her words threatened to tear us apart. Touching me even though she was letting me go. My gaze roved over her face, taking in the heartbreak in her lowered eyes and the hopeless resignation that colored her expression. I needed to know what had put that look there. "Tell me what happened," I softly demanded.

"I can't," she choked on the words as her eyes finally met mine and screamed the truth she tried to hide from me. I was not wrong about her. She didn't want to do this, to pull away. Her tears fell like pieces of a puzzle. I wanted to put her back together, to discover the truth, but she wouldn't let me.

"Last night was no lie, sweetheart. This spark between us is real. When I was inside of you, your heart opened to me. I saw it in your eyes, and it was beautiful. It's still open—I see you, Willa—and I can see the truth in your eyes. So why are you lying to me?" I tried to hold her eyes, but they slid away to find the floor again. "Look at me, please." Her stricken gaze met mine, along with a determined expression. I braced.

"Because I have to," she cried. "Because it's the right thing to do. I'm not the kind of girl you should be with, Everett. I'll mess every-thing up. And if I don't ruin it myself, the baggage that comes with me will." With a rough swipe over her cheeks she brushed away her tears and steeled herself.

"What baggage? Tell me what happened. How can I help you?"

"You can't help me, no one can. I have to—"

"I'll do anything for you, anything you need—"

"I need you to let me go, Everett."

"No, please—"

"You said anything I need. I can't talk about this, and I need you to let me go." She was unwavering, resolute, and at this moment, *gone.*

My jaw was tense as I agreed. "Fine, we don't have to talk about it—now. It will be like this never happened until you are ready to talk to me." My heart fell apart with each word from my mouth, but what else could I do?

"Thank you..." Her whisper drifted over the air like one last touch. But I couldn't help myself, I needed one more. I placed a soft kiss to her lips and realized I was wrong before; this kiss was good-bye. But I didn't want a goodbye kiss. I wanted all her kisses—the hellos, the goodnights, the see you laters, and the ones that are given just because.

If all I ever got was one night to share with her—one night when I'd felt what love should truly be—then I guess I was still a lucky man. Maybe I should try to accept that, but I knew my impossible feelings for her would never allow it. I watched her enter her apartment and close the door. I ran upstairs to grab my jacket. It was time I got some answers. If she wouldn't give them to me, Wyatt would.

This was far from over.

* * *

I turned off the ignition to my truck and slammed the door before stalking toward the front door. Wyatt's new home with his new wife was on her family's horse ranch on the edge of town. Flipping my wrist, I checked the time. Since it wasn't that late, and I figured someone should be up. I knocked and waited. I pounded and waited some more. If Wyatt wasn't here, I decided I'd grill Sabrina.

The door flew open. Ruby, Sabrina's sixteen-year-old niece, and Wyatt's niece now too, stood there, eyebrows up and a grin on her face. "Hey, Everett. No one's home, they're all at Daisy's Nut House eating pie. Whatchu need?"

"Uh, I was hoping to talk to Wyatt or Sabrina—"

"Oh, about Willa? Am I right? Come on in, I just got all the information." I hesitated in the doorway.

"Well, what are you waiting for? Matchmaking is like, my hobby now." She glared at me impatiently, tapping her foot. "I mean, I guess we can talk here. Whatever. I'll just lay it out for you, okay?" She sat on the little bench perpendicular to the door, next to a huge pile of shoes. "So, Willa is real stubborn and her ex-husband is a giant douche bag. He was in prison, you know?" I nodded. I'd already known that much. "He threw her through the front window of their house after she told him she was leaving him—that's where that huge scar on her arm came from. Wyatt drove up right as it happened. He was the one to arrest him." Ruby watched me carefully after she dropped that bomb of information. I grabbed hold of the doorframe and flinched, upset that Willa had gone through something so horrific. The urge to hunt down her ex and hurt him was real. My anger was so palpable that Ruby eyed me knowingly and stood up with a smirk. "Well, come on in. I know you want to hear what I have to say. Don't try to deny it."

I followed her into the living room and sat on the couch. I needed to hear this, even if it broke my heart even more to know what Willa had gone through. "Go on. Tell me," I urged.

"Tommy, her ex, just got out a few days ago. I overheard Wyatt talking about it to Sabrina, all pissed off and upset that Willa was leaving town because of him. She's not leaving anymore though, you know that, right?" I nodded and gestured for her to continue. "Gracie texted me about a half hour ago and told me you two were talking in the basement. How'd that go? She dumped you, right? Don't worry, it won't stick. Gracie said you two were eye-boning all over the living room before you went to talk, and that Willa has it really bad for you."

"You know Gracie?"

"Duh, is this Green Valley? I've known Gracie since kinder-garten. We're in the same grade. Everybody in school always knew not to talk to her about Willa or she'd start crying so hard she'd have to go home. We started hanging out this year, after she joined the debate club. And I grew up knowing Willa until she ran away. I love Willa. She used to let me win at *Candyland* all the time, and sit on her lap, and twist up her hair—her curls are so boingy—and… *Gah!* So basically, I'll do anything for her, including piss her off by meddling in her business." A small smile crossed my face. All the stuff Wyatt had told me about this girl was not an exaggeration.

"Okay…"

"Shush, Everett. Okay, sooooo…" She looked at the ceiling, lost in thought, before her eyes snapped back to mine with a decisive gleam. "You just back off for now, and she'll come to you. I guarantee it. Just be all sexy and protective from afar. Trust me, she'll love it. All us girls do. Act broody and hovery, like Heathcliff in *Wuthering Heights*. But without the creeptastic qualities. And don't worry too much—I overheard Wyatt talking to Sabrina on the porch earlier and he said Boone and Jackson James and all the other deputies are helping keep an eye out for Tommy. Plus, I have my own contacts keeping an eye out too. No one effs with Cletus Winston in this town, and I called him first thing. I mean, after the roses on the porch? None of us are taking any chances—"

"What roses?"

"The smashed up white roses all over Willa's porch this morning. Wyatt cleaned them up. I overheard him telling Sabrina that it freaked the heck out of Willa. She packed up her stuff in a panic and he couldn't stop her from leaving. Then of course, she ran right into Gracie getting busted at The Wooden Plank. I mean, classic Gracie." She shook her head in amusement. "Anyway, Willa took Gracie home. Talk about perfect timing, right?"

"Right. Um—"

"It's a lot. I get it, Everett. But you almost ripping the frame out of the doorway told me you're totally in love with her—"

"I'm not in love—"

"You're not?" Our heads whipped to the side as Wyatt entered the living room followed by Sabrina. I waved to her and the kids as she hurriedly led them upstairs to let us talk.

"No, I haven't been with her long en—"

"You're so full of crap, Ev." Wyatt chuckled.

Ruby smirked. "Well, he is a man. Most of y'all are pretty dumb about love, right? Like, he's here taking advice from a teenage girl. I mean, it's good advice, but still. I'm going to go call Gracie. Later."

"But I didn't actually ask you for—" Wyatt smacked my arm to shut me up. "Uh, later. Thanks, Ruby." I called as she rushed upstairs. The vast amounts of information she had just imparted on me filtered through my mind but what stood out the most was that Willa was most likely in danger and I would do whatever it took to keep her safe.

"She tell you everything?" Wyatt asked.

"Yeah, I think so."

"Good. We tried to talk loud enough so she would hear."

"What?"

"I told you before—Willa is my friend, she trusts me. Sabrina and I didn't tell have to tell you anything. Yet, you still know what you need to know to be there for her."

I shook my head. "She told me to be sexy and protective." I chuckled.

"And don't forget to brood like Heathcliff. I heard that one from outside. We waited on the porch so she could finish telling you everything," Wyatt added.

"How the hell do I do that?"

"Ask Sabrina when she comes downstairs." I laughed and sank back into the couch.

I shook my head against the cushions. "This feels impossible. She was so determined to let me go. And love? It's too soon for that. I'm not in—"

"You're in love with her," he argued.

My head shot up in denial. "No, I'm not. I just never felt this way before, is all."

"Like what? How do you feel?" he prodded with a grin, goading me into an answer like he always used to do.

"Like, being with her last night was the right thing to do—the *only* thing to do. Like I was finally at home and I never wanted to leave."

"Yeah, that's love. You love her," Wyatt insisted.

"Fuck." I ran my hands into my hair, digging my palms into my eyes as I sat up, elbows to my knees. "I do love her. I am in love with her. Shit, how do I fix this?"

"You just will. You can rebuild anything, Everett. It's what you do. Look at your house, the shop…look at Willa. I've been her friend for years and *you* managed to fix her heart enough so it would open again. You can fix it, and you will."

"Right, okay. I'll just go home, be sexy and protective, and hover broodingly from afar, just like Heathcliff."

He shot me a grin. "Good plan."

I heaved out a sigh and stood up to leave. "No more secrets, Wyatt. You keep me informed so I can keep an eye on everything. Finishing the security system just got bumped up to the top of my to-do list."

"I will. Between the two of us and the sheriff department, nothing will happen to her."

CHAPTER THIRTEEN

"You know I don't mean the things I say when I get mad. Momma loves you, Willa. But you need to try harder to act right."

— *MOMMA*

I had to move—again. It wasn't right to stay here, with Everett, after I just broke his heart. I stared at the wall as I contemplated where to go. I mean, I had Gracie to think about now. I couldn't leave town again.

"Willa, are you going to stare at the freaking wall all night?" I jumped and refocused—on reality, I guess—to notice that Gracie was sprawled on my couch, cell phone in hand, furiously texting with someone. Her phone was going off like crazy. *Ping, ping, ping.* Jeez.

"No. Uh, are you hungry?" I asked, still in a broken-hearted daze, frozen against the closed door behind me. Kids needed food. Regular home cooked meals and stuff, right?

"Yeah, I could eat. Let's make sandwiches. Oh wait—are we eating a late dinner, or your feelings? I threw some pizza rolls into the cart at the Piggly Wiggly." She studied my face and stood up. "I'll preheat the oven. I also got some cookie dough ice cream and hot fudge—dessert for the win! Don't worry, Willa, I got you. Go sit down."

"Okay…" I whispered as I wandered to the couch. When I felt it behind my knees, I sat. Unconsciously, I rubbed my chest. I hurt. I was a little bit scared of seeing Tommy, and my heart was burning a hole in my chest. I missed Everett already. I felt Gracie's hands gently push me back into the cushions. Startled, I looked up at her, softly smiling at me.

"Relax, Willa," she whispered.

"Okay, thanks. I'm glad you're here, Gracie." She grinned and tugged the afghan from behind the couch to rest over my shoulders.

"Me too." Her grin shifted sideways before she bustled off to my tiny kitchen. I really liked this place. The thought of leaving made me sad. I shook my head against the cushions. It wasn't this place, it was Everett. The thought of leaving *him* made me sad. It was more than just sad; it felt unbearable, unimaginable. I quit thinking and let my eyes drift closed. Belatedly, I realized I was supposed to be at work right now. My eyes flew open as I sat upright with haste. Shit!

"I have to go." I stood up and spun crazily around, taking in my packed bags on the floor and the groceries that were still strewn all over the table and countertop.

"I called Aunt Genie for you. Patty is covering your shift. Go on, sit back down," Gracie said calmly as she opened the oven to shove in a tray of pizza rolls. Ooh, that looked good. My stomach growled as the scent started to fill the space. My eyes burned with hot tears as I remembered Everett's reactions to my growly stomach. I ran a fingertip underneath my eyes to catch the tears and turned away from Gracie so she wouldn't see.

"You did? Thank you," I murmured through the lump in my throat.

"I did. You're a mess, Willa. You can't go to work like this. And for the record, I heard everything you said to him." She held up an empty glass. "I listened at the door." No shame, this one. I chuckled despite myself.

"That actually works?" She nodded with a grin, then opened the pantry to continue putting the nonperishables away, tidying the kitchen as she went.

"Yep. Flawless. You didn't have to break up with him though. That was dumb." She tossed over her shoulder.

"It was the right thing to do," I argued as I sat in a chair at the tiny kitchen table to watch her gather plates and napkins for our late dinner.

"Oh yeah, sure it was. Incredibly hot, ripped AF, fine as hell man wants to protect you from your ex. He begs you to stay with him and practically cries over you to your face, and you dump him. You're a literal freaking genius, Willa. But your legendary IQ is wasted on you, just like Momma always says." She turned to me; face scrunched up in apology. "I'm sorry, that was mean. I went too far. Clara is paying for a therapist for me. I'm working on my 'anger issues.'" She added air quotes when she said anger issues, and I smiled at her.

"It's okay, don't worry about it. Momma is right about me. I make terrible choices. I have screwed my life up in every way that exists," I admitted.

"Haven't we all?" she said with a sardonic wisdom that a sixteen-year-old girl should not be capable of.

"We'll be okay, somehow," I told her, even though I didn't believe it.

"Sure. We're gonna be *just fine.*" Sarcasm dripped from her tone as she slid the plates on the table and popped open a root beer. She took a sip and sat across from me. "Want one? I also put wine into the cart. It's the pink kind. The bottle was pretty."

I chuckled. "No thanks on the wine. Wine and melancholy do not pair well with me. I'll get a root beer too." I stood up and headed to the fridge. I snagged a root beer and opened the freezer for the ice cream. A root beer float sounded good. Eating my feelings sounded even better.

"Good idea. Give me a scoop too." Gracie smiled at me from the table.

"Sure thing. Let's get food-wasted and watch a movie," I suggested.

"Just like real sisters," she murmured with a sad smile.

"Come here." I set my root beer down on the counter and opened my arms. She stood up, tears filling her eyes as she stepped into my hug. I pulled her head to my shoulder. "I love you Gracie, and I'm so sorry I left you," I whispered. Her shoulders shook against me as I held her. "I'm staying here in Green Valley, with you. No matter what happens. I will never leave again."

"Okay," she hiccupped. "I want you to stay. I missed you so much."

"I missed you too. I...I wish I knew what I was thinking all the years I was gone. But I still don't understand it," I confessed.

She pulled away and I wiped her tears with the hem of Everett's huge shirt. "We don't have the best perspective on things. Clara said it's because of Momma always being so mean and angry and Daddy leaving us. She wanted me to live with her, but my friends are all in Green Valley, so I said no."

"What about Sadie?" I asked.

"No way. Her husband is a dick. But he's gone now, and she's stuck with Momma until her job starts. I'll miss Flynn and Rider, but I don't want to stay there anymore." She shrugged like it was all the same to her. Sadness washed over me, while memories of my child-hood stabbed me in the heart. "Do you ever want kids, Willa?" I stiffened, unsure of what to say. How much did she need to know? The timer on the oven went off and she laughed. "Time to get food-wasted," she announced with a huge smile. I smiled back, my heart only halfway in it. I scooped ice cream into glasses, she plated the pizza rolls, and we headed for the couch to deposit our goodies onto the coffee table.

I found the remote tucked into the cushion next to my hip and turned the TV on. "Everett gave me his Netflix password," I said, offhand.

Nudging my shoulder with hers, she squealed, "Oh my god, Willa! Sharing a Netflix password is the new pre-engagement, everyone knows that." She giggled as she poured root beer over her ice cream and inserted a straw. I peered at her out of the corner of my eye, shaking my head.

"You're a bag full of nuts, Gracie," I said with an involuntary smile. My life no longer felt like a hopeless void, and I had her to thank for it. She made me feel like I had something to live for, because she needed me. "I love you, kid," I stated.

"I love you, too." She beamed at me. We watched *The Lego Movie*, pigged out on pizza rolls and root beer floats, and I allowed myself to relax into this moment with my little sister.

I shoved everything else out of my mind. I lost the panic, the heartbreak, and the angst that had dominated my life for so long and let my soul sigh. I was determined to get better, to do better, and for once I had hope that I could really do it.

I awoke early—and not early afternoon, like I usually woke up—to sunlight streaming through my windows and Gracie sprawled next to me like a starfish. Her arm rested over my neck and her leg was over mine. We were both six feet tall, and the two of us in a double bed was crazy. Still, I wouldn't make her move for the world. I grinned and got out of bed. Loss hit me when I realized I would not be going upstairs to join Everett for coffee and Daisy's doughnuts. I had taken that ritual for granted. I'd had months of coffee and doughnuts with Everett. Months of him taking care of me without me even realizing he was doing it until it was much too late. I heaved out a sigh and made my way to the kitchen, hoping Gracie had tossed some coffee into the cart last night.

Searching through the cabinets I unearthed a bag of coffee and a box of muffins. It was a poor substitution for Everett's, but it would have to do. While the coffee brewed in the pot, I found my phone and sent a text to Sabrina asking her to meet me for lunch. I had to work tonight, and I wanted to talk to her before she grew too upset over my attempted run away yesterday. Wyatt was sure to have told her, and I wanted to explain myself. I also wanted to make sure she didn't hate me.

Bang. Boom. Crash.

I choked back a sob as I recognized the sounds of Everett working outside. There would be no dash to the window to watch him this time. Because I had been right. Goodness like him was not meant for the likes of me. I poured a cup of sad coffee and headed to the table. It sloshed in my cup when I heard knocking on my door and I jumped. Cautiously, I snuck to the peephole to check. I frowned when I saw Everett standing there, box of doughnuts and takeout coffee in hand.

"What—" I opened the door and gaped at him.

"Mornin', Willard. You're up early today. I brought you and little sister some breakfast." He pushed passed me and placed the box on the table. He sipped the coffee with a wink. "This is for me, but I'll share if you ask me nicely."

"'Kay…" My heart busted apart in my chest into a million tiny pieces that all wanted the same thing—for him to call me *Willa*. I wanted it in the worst way. He stood there smiling at me just like nothing had ever happened between us. Meanwhile, I stood there ogling his bulging biceps and broad chest in his perfectly snug white T-shirt. He had a red flannel shirt tied around his waist, dark blue jeans, and work boots. He was lumberjack sexy and I wanted to climb him like a freaking tree and let him bang my brains out again. Brains were so overrated. Nothing good ever came of my decisions anyway, so why bother using it anymore? My head whipped to the side as Gracie entered the room, flinging the bedroom door aside to dramatically announce her presence. What was it with these people? Smiling and alert like mornings weren't meant for moping. And now, for pining and yearning like a sap.

"Ooooh, doughnuts!" Gracie squealed as she ran to the table. "I knew I overheard that word. Yes! Thank you, Everett!" She flipped the box open and took a chocolate-iced, pink-sprinkled extravaganza out, sinking her teeth in for a huge bite. "Mmmmmm," she groaned. My gaze turned toward her.

"You're welcome," he chuckled as he watched her antics. Then with a pointed look he glanced at me. "Eat up, Willie Bean. I'm going to be in and out of here all day finishing the alarm system and installing the fence."

Ah, so that's what it was. Obligation—the same sense of duty Wyatt felt. Those Monroe brothers were something else—always honorable and kind, just like their Momma raised them to be. Everyone in town knew about Becky Lee Monroe's pride in her boys. She was famous for it. It wasn't bragging; it mostly had to do with her graciously accepting compliments whenever she heard of something wonderful one of them had done.

"Thanks, Everett," I muttered. "Nice of you to think of us." His knowing look and sideways smirk hit me like a caress.

"You're welcome, Willard. Anything you need, anytime. Always," his voice grew dark and growly with promises as he finished his statement.

"Okay…" I murmured to his back as he walked toward the door and shut it behind himself as he left.

"Holy crap, Willa. You're so crazy. If I had someone like him, I'd be tapping that ass twenty-four seven."

I spun around to face her. "Gracie!" My shocked expression made her laugh.

"What?" She stuffed the rest of her doughnut into her mouth with a wicked grin. "Sorry if this disillusions you, but I ain't no virgin."

My eyes almost popped out of my head. "Uh, no. I mean—I—I wasn't a virgin when I was sixteen either," I confessed. Was honesty the best policy here? I lost my virginity to Tommy when I was fifteen and he was twenty-one. I thought my dreams had come true. He used to be so dreamy and treated me like—well exactly what Sabrina said the other day—like he was obsessed with me. What a foolish girl I had been.

"Don't worry, I'm on the pill and I use condoms. Clara told me everything." *Condoms*. My stomach sank down to my feet and came back up with a lurch.

Oh. My. God.

Last night Everett and I didn't use protection. And when he came —aside from it being the hottest thing I'd ever seen, all muscle-flexy and growly and intense—he did it inside of me, not anywhere else fun. *Gah!* I was not on the pill, or taking a shot, or sporting an IUD. Shit, shit, shit. I soooo did not need this right now.

"Dang, Willa, you turned all white. Did you see a ghost?" She thrust a doughnut at me. "Eat something. You'll feel better." I took the doughnut, but I would not feel better. I would *never* feel better. I was stuck in an eternal loop of stupidity and suffering the consequences of my bad choices.

My heart dropped as adrenaline shot through my system and I started worrying about Tommy again. The worry was mitigated a bit by the fact that Wyatt and the Green Valley Sheriff Department were keeping an eye on the situation, and therefore me. Still! What had I done to my life? Who was I right now with my flip-flopping emotions and crazy thoughts?

"Thanks, Gracie." My distracted whisper made Gracie laugh. She probably thought I was just pining over Everett instead of having the ultimate existential crisis. I broke the doughnut in half and bit half of that off. I chewed and I obsessed—tasting nothing but dread as I sank back into the kitchen chair, pushing my mug of coffee aside.

"I'm taking a shower, space-girl. Try not to freak out while I'm in there." Gracie patted my head and laughed at my vacant expression.

"I'm going to lunch with Sabrina, then to work. Want to come?" I offered.

"Can't. I have somewhere to be, then I'm off to school. It's nice being so close to town. And Ruby finally got her driver's license. She's going to drive me to the farm tonight to pack my stuff."

"Oh yeah, of course—school."

"You might want to get more sleep before you leave the house, Willa." She laughed at my blank expression, then darted toward the bathroom.

I stuffed the rest of my doughnut into my mouth and let my mind wander.

CHAPTER FOURTEEN

EVERETT

*"Everett, if you're going to like someone, love them. Don't just
stand up for yourself; fight for yourself, and if you're going to be
strong, you may as well aim for invincible."*

— *PAPAW JOE*

I flipped the closed sign around and propped my shop door open
before heading inside to get everything set up for Garrett. He
would be working the shop for me today while I finished installing
the security system at the house and started the new fence. Sunlight
filled the space as I yanked open the shades, sending the tiny dust
motes flying off into the light beams. I waved to Suzie Samuels
when I spotted her across the street doing the same thing I was. She
smiled and waved back until a man with a beard came up from
behind to sweep her into his arms. I grinned, happy for her.

Main Street was busy today, as it always was on a Saturday afternoon. People on the street bustled about as life went on, just like it
was supposed to. Like I should do but couldn't. Why did I keep
finding myself in impossible situations like this? Wanting things I
had little chance of getting? Falling for women who would never

want the real me? I sighed as I went behind the counter to ready the cash register for Garrett.

What I felt for Willa was so much more than falling. I was already gone for her in a way I had never experienced. She was under my skin, infiltrating my every thought, inside my heart in a way I would never get her out and it scared me. I saw the heartbreak coming from miles away, and even that didn't stop me from putting myself on the line for her. From the moment I'd met her, little by little, month by month, she'd taken over my heart without even trying.

"Hey, Everett." I looked up with a start to see Gracie, waving my 'help wanted' sign over her head as she approached the counter. "I can help," she stated with a smirk.

"Uh, hi, Gracie. Do you have any retail experience?"

"Yeah, I have loads of experience. I used to work for my mom. You can call her and ask her about how I tripled her honey sales at the Green Valley Farmers' Market. Or call Frankie. You know Frankie? And you should really be online, Everett. You need a website. I can help with that too."

"You can?"

"Yup." She pulled a business card from her pocket and slid it across the counter. I took it with a small grin.

"Look, I'll be honest with you. I don't really need the money and I prefer to make my own hours, but I think this could be a mutually beneficial set-up for the both of us. I want to see what a regular after school gig would be like, and you need my help with Willa. Plus, I need to work on my rogue—Ruby and Marianne and the rest of the girls from the debate team want to meet here after school on Fridays to play." My eyebrows shot up to my hairline as I tried to prevent my jaw from dropping. "Oh, and by the way, Willa put me in charge of making the list of apartments for us to call so we can move out—"

"What? You can't move—"

"Don't worry, I'm good at stalling and I usually get my way. So, about that job?"

"You're hired. Does tomorrow after school work for you?"

"Perfection. Thanks, Everett." She wadded up my help wanted sign and shot it into the garbage can at the side of the counter like a basketball. "Swish! Later."

"Yeah, you're welcome. Later." Just like her sister, Gracie had steamrolled me. I shook my head to clear it while wondering where all the girl gamers had been back when I was in high school. Sheesh.

"Yo, Ev." Garrett entered, ever present cup of coffee in hand and an easy smile on his face.

"Thanks for covering for me."

"No problem. I'd rather work here than work on that freaking house at Bandit Lake. Barrett is driving me crazy. 'Historical accuracy, structural integrity combined with an organic approach to the regional blah blah fucking blah.'" I laughed as he mocked our older brother. Barrett could be a stickler for details and a bit rigid in his ideals. In other words, he was a giant pain in the ass sometimes. "Dad hired Sadie Hill. Did you hear? Barrett lost his damn mind over that. Especially after Dad told him to get over old crushes and grow the fuck up. It was hilarious."

"Wow, Sadie Hill?"

"I know. Sisters, man—"

"Hello." Cowboy booted footsteps sounded through the doorway and we both turned toward the sound, only for me to lurch forward as black rage blinded me and Garrett shoved a hand into my chest to hold me back. Tommy Ferris stood in the doorway with a huge smile radiating out of his smug face.

"What do you want?" Garrett asked.

"I'm looking for Everett. Long time, no see, bud." he said to me, quirking one eyebrow up in amusement as he glanced at Garrett's hand on my chest. My curt nod only amused him even more as Garrett stepped in front of me to cage me in behind the counter with his body. "My wife rents a room from you—" I didn't even recognize the sound that came out of me after I heard the word, 'wife' come out of his mouth. Garrett shifted to lean back forcefully, shoving me into the wall behind the counter and holding me there with his body.

"Last I heard, Tommy, y'all were divorced," Garrett taunted. "Get the fuck out of here or I'll step away and let him have a go at you."

He held his hands out placatingly. "I just want to talk is all. I ain't looking for trouble. I'm just here to make sure you stay away from my wife. Little birds told me you have a thing for her. I have some stuff to discuss with her, things to make up for—that's true. But don't you worry. Willa will forgive me, like she always does. Then I'll take her off your hands as a tenant. Maybe I'll see if she's workin' tonight." He waved a dismissive hand and turned to leave. "Have a good day, now." He chuckled as he left the shop got into his truck and drove away.

"What the fuck was that?" Garrett stepped away from me and turned around, still blocking my way out from behind the counter— unless I wanted to vault over it. "I always hated that prick. He was such a dirty player back then. What an asshole."

"I'll fucking kill him." I couldn't think. Everything rational had flown right out of my head the second I saw him, the second he dared to utter her name with such a tone of ownership.

"Fucking kill who?" Once more, our heads shot to the side as Jackson James strolled into the shop. I'd gone to school since kindergarten with Jackson. He was a good guy and a good friend. His father, Jeffrey James, was the sheriff around here. He was well-respected and revered. Jackson was following in his footsteps as a deputy.

Garrett answered for me. "Tommy Ferris was just here. You missed the show."

"Huh. We've been looking for him. Supposedly he's staying with his folks over in Maryville, but we haven't managed to run into him yet. To talk, of course. Though Wyatt mentioned something about running him over with his cruiser." Jackson let out a laugh that met two stone faces. "Sorry. What did he have to say?"

"A bunch of shit about Willa being his wife and warning Everett to leave her alone." Garrett piped in. I was still stewing over the whole confrontation, remaining silent as the anger dissipated in my system to slowly be replaced with the cold calculation I usually felt when I was angry about something.

"Delusional prick," Jackson huffed. "Okay, I guess that tells us where his mind is. That's good, at least. I'm out. I'll talk to Wyatt and let him know." He stepped to the door to leave then turned back. "I almost forgot why I stopped by. Wanna grab a few beers later? Y'all, me, Boone? Over at Genie's?" I shook my head and he sighed with exasperation. "I'm trying to help you, man. Wyatt and Sabrina are planning to show up there tonight to keep an eye on Willa and get her mind off…well, everything."

"Oh, well, okay then. I'll meet y'all there."

"Later." He flicked two fingers out in goodbye and was off.

"Don't go looking for Tommy," Garrett warned.

"I won't. I'm going to do what I said and finish the alarm and the fence. I'm fine now."

"Sure, you are. I haven't seen you that pissed off since Wyatt used to get picked on back in elementary school. You used to kick everyone's ass back then. Then there was that time you decked Devron Stokes for yelling at Sara in the check-out lane at the Piggly Wiggly when she was trying to work. Oh! And remember when you helped Jackson beat up old what's his name for talking shit about Ashley Winston back in eighth grade? And those racist douchebags who got all up in Boone's face a few years back? Y'all two wiped the floor with those motherfuckers—"

"So basically, you're saying I'm violent with a bad temper?" I cut him off with a laugh.

"No, I'm saying if there is a friend in need or an underdog anywhere within a ten-foot radius of you, you'll be cracking some heads in their honor."

"I don't see Willa as an underdog," I protested.

"I know you don't. The way you see her is written all over your face. That's why I threw an arm out to stop you. She's yours. This is a fight you don't want to take on right now. It's not the time."

"I have a bad feeling that a time will be coming."

"I do too. I got your back when you need it. Always, man."

"All right. I'm going. That fence ain't gonna build itself."

"I guess it's safe to let you go," he joked and with a smirk, stepped aside to let me out from behind the counter.

I waved goodbye over my shoulder as I headed out of the shop to my truck parked at the curb. My mind whirred through all the things I had to accomplish today, and I wondered how I would be able to be around Willa when the huge step forward we'd taken together had turned into one giant step back. Could I find my footing and navigate this without fucking it up entirely?

Frustration dominated my thoughts. My temper was holding on by a thread, and I knew I was in for a series of sleepless nights until I could get her in my bed again. She was all I could think about—her body beneath mine, her soft skin, sweet smile, gorgeous face—and with an embittered growl, I shoved my hands through my hair, then twisted it up with a rubber band to get it out of my face. The way her eyes had melted on mine and she'd tightened around me when I'd said her name flashed into my memory, making me smile, making me fight against getting hard right here in my truck driving down fucking Main Street. I wanted that woman more than I'd ever wanted anything in my life. We'd only had one night, and I needed more. I needed all her nights, and her days too. I hadn't gotten to try everything I'd been fantasizing about, and that was just unacceptable. I'd never even gotten a taste of her. I always imagined she would be sweet, like honey, or maybe a little salty-sweet like a salted caramel Frappuccino...

Fuck, I was ridiculous. Wyatt was right. I was in love with her. I was desperate with it, sick with all these feelings that had nowhere to go. I knew she felt for me at least some of what I felt for her. There was no way she could have faked the emotions I saw in her last night. I was also pretty sure that once her fear of that dirt-bag ex-husband of hers was gone, our feelings would be equal. I knew her fear held her back, and it was understandable. I thought of Ruby's advice: *be sexy and protective from afar.* Shit, I really was about to take advice from a teenage girl. With a huge sigh, I pulled into my driveway, trying to think of a way to be sexy.

CHAPTER FIFTEEN

WILLA

"I need all your love and I won't share. All of it, Willa."

— *TOMMY*

Gracie left, and like the chicken-shit I was, I hurriedly dressed for work and left the apartment for the day so I could avoid seeing Everett when he came back. I wouldn't be able to face him coming in and out all day long to install the security system. Especially knowing he was moving that project up because of me. And also, *especially*, because of his tendency to work without his shirt. I had been up close and personal with each one of his magnificent abs and I missed them already. Not to mention all his other glorious parts. And his sweet disposition. Along with his big—uh, heart. I heaved out a sigh and continued driving. I'd been cruising aimlessly around town for the last half an hour trying to decide where to go.

I had lunch plans with Sabrina, but my entire morning was wide open. Normally I would be asleep at this time, but I'd slept uncharacteristically hard last night. And the night before, with Everett, I'd slept like a baby, wrapped up in his big, strong arms, pressed against his hard body, naked and warm. Safe, secure, and sincerely happy for probably the first time in my life. My stomach turned somersaults in my abdomen just thinking about it. The way he'd said my name…

I slowed to a crawl on Main Street and pulled over. I didn't want to see anyone, or talk to anyone, or find out that anyone knew my business with Tommy *or* Everett. If anyone knew about my sordid teenage runaway past, I didn't want to *know* they knew. I couldn't handle being judged. I judged myself enough for everybody, and my mother did enough of it for whoever I happened to miss. I wanted to go back home and crawl under my bed, but I'd lost that option when I broke things off with Everett. Just like before I came back to Green Valley—during those almost two years on the road—I had nowhere to be. Except now, it was miserable and empty instead of peaceful and quiet. I didn't want to be alone anymore, but I didn't know if I would ever be able to have anything else. I crossed my arms over the steering wheel and rested my head there, looking out the driver's side window as people passed by, living their lives, just like I should be doing. But every time I tried to live, I messed something up with my stupid choices.

Squinting my eyes against the sunlight, I studied the green truck parked close to Everett's shop. It reminded me of the truck Tommy used to have. Then I wondered if it really was his truck. I'd never sold it; one of his friends had picked it up and kept it for him for when he got out. I shoved that thought out of my mind, because why would he go to Everett's shop? There was no way he could know what happened between Everett and me—was there?

Tommy had only hurt me physically once. But that was enough to make me want to stay away forever. He was capable of vicious words when he was angry with me. And when pushed beyond the edge of his temper, violence was always his response. Luckily, that violence had never been directed toward me until the end of our relationship. If I refused to go back to him? I didn't want to imagine what he could be capable of.

My stomach growled, reminding me of Everett. Then it reminded me of the doughnut half I'd eaten earlier. I decided to go to Daisy's

Nut House for a quick breakfast. If anyone wanted to judge me, well, screw them. I had a right to live my damn life. It was time to take some control back. With a bravado I only half felt I pulled away from the curb and drove toward Daisy's. I could do this. People ate alone in restaurants all the time, and I could too.

As I accelerated, my van began to chug and vibrate, like maybe the spark plugs were misfiring—hopefully nothing worse than that. Of course, this would happen when I was totally broke. I mean, I could fix whatever was wrong myself, but I had no money for parts. I scanned the road ahead and pulled into the gas station on the corner, sputtering to a stop in the closest parking spot.

Just great. Lovely. Freaking perfect. Exactly what I needed right now.

My head bounced softly on the steering wheel as I let it drop. For a moment, I gave up. Shutting my eyes, I decided to—take a nap? I didn't have the heart to get out and see what was wrong yet. I didn't have a heart left at all. I'd left it somewhere in Everett's bed the other night and I doubted I'd ever get it back.

I had to work tonight and I had no ride. I guess I'd be hitching, just like I had told Gracie not to do. I was such a bad example.

With a reach below the dash, I released the hood, seriously dismayed when smoke billowed from beneath. My leisurely, wide open morning was ruined, and now I had no time left for the self-indulgent whine-fest I had been treating myself to. Hauling myself out the door I lifted the hood and reeled back at the burnt rubber smell. Somewhere in there was a belt in need of replacing, probably. Hands on hips and face directed to the sky, I wandered to the side of the van and leaned against it to wait for the smoke to clear so I could get a closer look.

"Hey, Willa. I thought it was you!" I jumped at the sound of my name, eyes sliding to the side to find Jennifer Winston waving at me from her car at the pumps. She must have recognized me from church back in the day, or from her bakery. Sabrina and I had consumed many slices of her banana cake together there since I'd been back in town. "You stuck? I'll call Cletus to come give you a hand. Hang on." She pulled her phone from her back pocket.

"No! No, thank you, that's okay. I can fix it myself after the smoke clears. But—uh, thank you!" I called. I didn't have the money for Cletus Winston to fix it, or even tow it to his garage in town. The Winston Brother's Auto Shop had a great reputation for being fair. But I wasn't worried about fair, I was worried about how much money this would cost me. I heaved out a sigh and tried not to freak out as everything in my life fell apart around me.

"Okay. You're sure?"

"Yes, I'm sure." She got in her car with a wave and drove off. Still hoping it was a spark plug, I went around to the engine to peek. Spark plugs were cheap, and I had some in the back. But most of the other parts in a vehicle this old, though cheap, were not readily available and had to be ordered. Which meant waiting. And I needed this van in order to go to work. I needed to work in order to—*Gah!* I needed to stop thinking in order to avoid spiraling into a panicked, crying heap in the gas station parking lot. Enough.

I poked around inside the engine, choking on the gross burnt rubber smell and growing more impatient by the minute, as I couldn't seem to find the problem.

"Need some help?" I jumped, head hitting the underside of the hood as I flew back to find Everett standing next to me. Dead sexy with his massive arms crossed over his massive chest, taunting me with his sexy forearms and his rolled-up sleeves.

"No! I mean, how did you know I was here? It hasn't even been fifteen minutes—"

"You're in Green Valley, Willard. I got three different phone calls telling me to come over here and pick you up. Jennifer called Cletus and he called Ruby to get Wyatt's number, since you told Jenn not to call him. But Ruby called me instead of Wyatt. Suzie Samuels saw you when she left her studio to get lunch, called my shop, spoke to Garrett, who called me. Then my mother spotted you as she drove by. And now here I am, ready to help. Lucky you." He winked at me and I found myself blushing just like a simpleton.

"Scoot." He nudged me over as he bent to look at the engine. "It's a mess in here, Willie Bean. I'm going to call the Winston's garage for a tow—"

"No! I don't have money for a tow!" I protested.

"We can't leave it here," he argued. "I'll have them take it to my place. We can work on it there. I have everything we'll need in the garage." He examined closer under the hood. "Probably not all the parts though. We'll have to wait on those. Guess you won't be moving out after all, huh?" His sideways grin deepened my blush as I studied his gorgeous face, eyes shining with sincerity and the desire to help me. He must have talked to Gracie, because I hadn't mentioned moving out to him.

"Uh, I guess not," I whispered.

"I don't want you to leave." He reached out to smooth my hair back, lingering at the crown of my head and coming to a stop at the back of my neck. "Does it hurt?"

"Huh?" I questioned.

"You bumped your head pretty good, Willard. Does it hurt?" With his hand on me, I felt no pain. Just a jolt of lust firing through my system warming me up from the inside.

"I've had worse. I'll live." My attempt at a joke failed as he scowled and backed away, shoving his hands into his pockets.

"You'll be safer at my place with the alarm system and fence." Did he think Tommy used to hit me? Is that why he scowled?

I opened my mouth to say something, but…what? I did not want to talk about Tommy with him, or anyone else for that matter. It was the biggest shame of my life, falling for his crap and putting up with it for so many years. "Thank you for coming." I finally said.

His eyes found mine. "Always, sweetheart." The words were more than a promise to help fix my van. Everything was *more* with him than what it appeared to be on the surface. I wanted to open my arms and take it all, everything he was offering with words unspoken. But what would I ever be able to give him in return? My life was in shambles and inside—where it really counted—I was a hopeless wreck. He held out a finger as he stepped to the side with his phone. I heard him arrange the for the tow. "Get what you need. Let's go home."

Home. I wished with all my heart I could offer him even half of what he had already given me. With a reach inside, I grabbed my purse, locked the doors and headed for his truck.

He slammed the hood to my van down then joined me in his truck. As we turned on the road toward his house, I flinched as I spotted that green truck again. Slamming my eyes shut, I said a tiny prayer that it wasn't Tommy. Everett glanced at me from the corner of his eye and took my hand in his—like he knew what I was worried about. It was on the tip of my tongue to tell him everything, just spill my guts and let the chips fall where they may. He was so strong, and I felt so weak right now.

"That was Tommy in that green truck. If that's what you were thinking." His eyes darted to mine briefly, then back to the road.

After inhaling a huge breath, I deflated into the back of the seat, sinking down until my head was as low as I could get it without actually crawling down to the floorboards. "I kind of knew it," I whispered. "I thought I saw him parked in front of your shop before—"

"It was him. He paid me a visit—warning me away from you."

"I'm so sorry—" I murmured, hopeless regret slammed into me as I took in Everett's steely expression and barely checked anger.

He cut me off. "Did you tell him to talk to me?" he asked, voice like a whip.

"Well, no—"

"Then don't you dare apologize to me. Don't even think of taking responsibility for that asshole or anything *he* chooses to do. I mean it. Just don't." His jaw ticked as anger radiated out of him and he glared at the road ahead.

My head shifted to the side and I watched the town drift by as he drove. "'Kay…" I whispered. I didn't know what to say. Or how to act, or even how to feel anymore. It was too much. Everything was just too much.

His hand slid into mine again. "Shit. I'm sorry, sweetness. I never liked him and the thought of you being with him for so long? A man like him? It drives me fucking crazy whenever I think about it."

I turned back towards him. His profile had softened but he still watched the road and avoided my eyes. "It's okay, Everett." I linked our fingers and held on. He was like an anchor holding me to the earth, keeping me tethered against the winds of my fears. And for now, at least, I decided to quit thinking I didn't deserve him and just held on.

CHAPTER SIXTEEN

EVERETT

"Love sets everything it touches free. When you're in love, Everett, holding on means letting go."

— *PAPAW JOE*

S *exy and protective from afar.*
    Fuck afar. I would be protective from right here, next to her. It was best that I stay where she needed me to be. Her hand squeezing mine in a death grip told me not to let her out of my sight until Tommy was completely out of the picture. It occurred to me that he would fight her. That he wouldn't accept anything she had to say unless she were saying words he wanted to hear. I knew his type —controlling, domineering, a bully— and I knew him. I had no respect for men like that and I would not tolerate him trying to intimidate Willa.

"We're here," I whispered. Her head had fallen to my shoulder as she leaned sideways over the console, asleep, with my hand gripped tightly in hers. When I noticed her start to drift off, I switched to the scenic route home. Obviously, she needed a nap before going to Genie's tonight.

"Everett?"

"Wake up, sweetheart." Unable to help myself, I shifted to the side so I could kiss the top of her head. She smelled of flowers and something warm, like vanilla. I could spend forever with her sweet scent in my nostrils and wished she was in my arms like the other night.

She sat up and her startled eyes grew round as she looked around, adorable in her confusion. "It's late." Her eyebrows furrowed and her big blue eyes landed on me. I grinned.

"You fell asleep, so I drove around for a while to let you rest." Glancing at the clock on the dashboard, she shifted her hair behind her back, only to have some of the wild curls shoot back around and frame her face, melting my heart in the process.

"You must have been driving for hours—it's three-thirty, Everett."

"It's no big deal, you needed the sleep. You snored the whole time," I lied. She didn't really snore, but occasionally she would let out the cutest little snort. Like a puff of air from her nose. When awake, Willa had an effortless elegance about her. She was graceful and feline in her movements, all lithe and sexy as hell. During the night we spent together, I discovered that sleeping Willa was not elegant at all. In fact, she remined me of my Papaw Joe when he'd crash out in his recliner during Monday Night Football after having a beer or two. All wide-open mouth, hair in her face, and arms and legs akimbo. I have a king-size bed and she had taken up most of the space. It worked for me because it meant she'd been all over me like I was a human body pillow and I liked that. Willa slept like an old man and, god help me, I thought it was hot.

"I do not snore, Everett! Take it back. Oh, no! I was supposed to have lunch with Sabrina," she cried while looking frantically around for her cell phone, patting her pockets then leaning over to check the floor.

I held it up with a chuckle. "No worries, she called. I answered and explained. She'll see you tonight at Genie's, with Wyatt."

"Oh. Thank you, for…thank you for everything, Everett. Today was the worst and I—"

"Always, sweetheart, anytime. Anything you need and I'm there. I already told you that and I meant it. Everything I have is yours." *Including my heart.*

"I don't know what to say. I shouldn't be here like this, with you. You could do so much better—" The empty sadness in her eyes startled me. It broke my heart that she felt this way.

"Stop it. Why do you say things like that?" She huffed out a startled breath along with a false laugh. Her eyes hit the ceiling of the truck as she turned her head toward the passenger window.

"I...I feel like...My mother always said that I—I don't know. I can't—" I captured her chin with two fingers to force her to look at me. To force her to see the truth in my eyes. I wanted her to see exactly how much she meant to me, how much I wanted her to be right here with me, and how there was no way on earth I could ever do better than her. With a dip of my head, I kissed her. Just once, a simple brush of my lips over hers, but I hoped it communicated what I couldn't adequately express with words. God, I was no good with words...

A rap at my window caused me to bump my head on the ceiling as I turned around with a curse. "Gracie!" Willa's startled voice rang out, breaking the moment we had almost shared. I lifted a chin toward Gracie, and she stepped back so I could open my door.

"I rode the bus home," she complained as I got out of the truck. "No more hitching, just like I promised." Her head tilted as her backpack slid off her shoulder.

"Do you have a driver's license?" I questioned.

"Yeah, why?" I reached into my truck and clicked the garage door opener attached to the sun visor. I had an old Ford Bronco in there. I'd bought it in high school and restored it. It ran, but I preferred my pickup because it was easier to haul stuff around. "Y'all can use that." I removed the key from my keyring and offered it to Willa who now stood at my side.

"I can't use your car! That's too much," Willa protested. She refused to take the key.

131

"Well, I can. I'll drive her to work every day when I get home from school." Gracie snatched the key with a laugh. "And I'll pick her up whenever her dopey ass needs a ride back home," she promised.

I laughed. "Deal." She rolled up to her tiptoes and smacked a kiss on my cheek, then gave one to Willa.

"Thank you, Everett. You're the best. I'm going to go call Ruby."

"You're welcome," I shouted after her as she slammed her way into the apartment.

"You're doing too much for me, Everett. I can't—"

"It's just a car. I'm not using it, so it's no big deal. Why is it so hard for you to accept help?"

Her mouth opened to answer but nothing came out. I grinned at her as she stood there clearly frustrated with my question. Willa was generous and she cared about people. Flipping the script on her would probably be effective.

"Would you help me if I needed it? Are you helping Gracie by letting her live with you?" She nodded. "How does it feel, Willard? Does it feel good to help when you know you can? Don't answer, just think about it." I tugged one of her curls, watching it straighten and then bounce back up. I held her eyes until they softened on mine and I cupped her soft cheek with my palm, lingering there while she leaned into my touch, telling me everything I needed to know without words. I wanted to kiss her again, but I'd already stolen one kiss today. More would be pushing it. For now, I'd settle for this. Soft touches to let her know how it would stay between us. Little things to show her I cared until she was ready for more again.

"I'll drive you to Genie's tonight and take you home when you're off." It wasn't an offer; it was a promise. "Have Gracie go spend time at the Logan Ranch with Ruby, or one of her other friends tonight, okay? I don't want her to be alone here. At least not until I finish the security system tomorrow."

"Okay," she whispered as she gazed at me. Why had she thought I would let her go so easily? As long her eyes reflected back what was in my own, I would stay. I would stay forever if she allowed it.

CHAPTER SEVENTEEN

WILLA

"You have everything you need here at Lavender Hill, with your momma and sisters. Don't ever count on anyone for things you can do yourself. People will always let you down."

— MOMMA

I headed to the apartment to get ready for work and contemplate this insane day. Maybe make a list or bullet journal my feelings. Thoughts swirled around like a tsunami of jumbled up doubts and fears—about money, my mother, Everett, Tommy, the entire popu-lace of Green Valley seeming to know about my business, my van breaking down, and probably some stuff I was forgetting to worry about for the moment—and I had not begun to get anywhere near sorting it out in my head.

"Gracie?" I called as I entered.

She popped her head out of the bedroom with a huge smile. "It's like you never broke up with him at all. He's kind of awesome, Willa."

"I—yeah, he is. How did that happen?" Maybe I would focus on the Everett issue first.

"I've read about guys like this," she said excitedly. "He's the good kind of alpha. I don't think you have to worry."

"What are you talking about?"

"How can you be friends with Sabrina and not know about alpha heroes?" She rolled her eyes, landed on the couch with a *plop* and patted the cushion next to her with a smile. I had time before work. With a shrug, I joined her.

"Number one, go to the library. You need better books. Get some romance novels and lose the—" She picked up my copy of *The Shining* from the coffee table and tossed it to the floor with a shake of her head. "No wonder you're so fucked up," she muttered. "At least get *Rose Madder*, or something that could actually help you right now."

"I know what alpha heroes are, okay? And I don't feel like talking anymore." I stood up.

"I bet you don't. You know what's up now, don't you?" She cracked up as she watched me grow flustered.

"Yeah, he's going to stick around whether I want him to or not," I grumbled.

"Nope. That's not it at all. We both know you still want him, right?" I looked away. "Uh-huh, well, you don't have to admit it because it's written all over you. You want him, bad. Well, Everett knows it too, and that is why he's still around. If you really *didn't* want him, he'd be gone. That's the difference between him and Tommy. And yeah, I know about the roses and Tommy being at Everett's shop, so don't bother trying to keep it from me, okay?"

"God! How, how does everybody know everything? What is it with this place?" I stormed off to the bedroom to change for work and stew over everything. After selecting my appropriately dark attire for the evening's shift—black jeans, black cowboy boots, black Genie's tank—I stuck my face in the mirror to apply my work makeup. More lashes, eye liner, and painted lips equaled more tips. And I was not above painting my face up for money. Lord knew I could use it.

Speaking of money, where was my van? Everett said he would have it towed here, but it wasn't outside. I inhaled a deep sigh. Maybe I should take up meditating, or yoga. Or maybe I needed another nap and a bubble bath. Jumping wildly from thought to thought was not working for me. I needed to get my mind focused on one track and let the other stuff float to the side. For now, work would be my focus. And Gracie, always Gracie.

"Willa! I'm going to take Everett's cool-as-shit Bronco and go to Ruby's to do homework. Bye."

"No! Wait!" I planned to take the Bronco to avoid riding with Everett to Genie's. He was dangerous to my libido. I had an out of control lady boner for him and being near him was making it worse, dammit. *Gah! Get your mind back on work. And don't let Gracie take that Bronco.*

"Oh, you want to drive it, now? Do you?" She was laughing at me. She knew too much, just like everyone else in this freaking town. Formerly homeless, teenage runaway Willa with her scandalous past and broken-down escape van started banging her landlord and is potentially being stalked by her ex-husband. What a winner.

"Yeah, I'll drop you off then go to work." I said. Her eyes drifted upward as she thought about it. As if she had a leg to stand on in this argument, or any other option.

"But I wanted—"

"I'll drive you. I'm older. I outrank you. You spend the night with Ruby, I'll arrange it with Sabrina. I don't want you to be alone here until—"

Her eyes widened. "Are we freaking out about Tommy?"

"Not freaking out. Being cautious, okay?"

"Gotcha. I'll get my clothes ready for tomorrow. Or your clothes, rather. My stuff is still at Momma's." I sighed and added gathering Gracie's things and talking to my mother to my list of stuff I did not want to do.

I shot a text to Sabrina while Gracie got ready. I hoped nothing else would come up to add to the list while making a plan to avoid Everett, Tommy, and everyone else who knew my business. I wasn't worried about people noticing me at Genie's. The pace was so fast it was easy to keep people at the small talk level of "Can I help you?" and not engage. It was everywhere else in town I had to avoid.

CHAPTER EIGHTEEN

WILLA

"I own you, Willa, and I protect what's mine."

— *TOMMY*

I dreaded my shift tonight. All the crap in my life felt like it was bearing down on me. My van was who even knew where, and it was broken down so I couldn't leave town. Taking Everett's Bronco and running off with it would be stealing. I didn't want to leave Gracie and honestly, I still had a bit of hope left for Everett and me. But I didn't want to stay either. Keeping my head down and going to work was my only option. Quelling these out of control and wildly opposing thoughts seemed like an impossible feat, but I would endeavor to soldier on.

Everett's Bronco was old but ran perfectly. His ability to repair and maintain old vehicles was just one more thing to admire about him. Not only admire, because we shared that hobby. Now I was imagining long weekends spent fixing cars together. He would be shirtless, of course, and sweaty, and covered with motor oil, while I worked by his side, maybe in a skimpy tank top perfect for peeling over my head. Then we would sink down to the garage floor and

—*Stop it. Think of literally anything else.* Scrambling through my messed-up thoughts, I landed on a memory of my father. I had learned to fix cars from my daddy before he left us. The ability to fix cars and the desire to escape my problems like he did were all he ever gave me. I guess I should be grateful I got something good from him before he left.

Scowling and squinting against the flashing neon sign in my Aunt Genie's parking lot, I pulled into an employee spot near the dumpsters on the side, toward the back of the massive lot. With a crunch of my boots, I hopped down to the gravel and did my best to abate my anger by stomping through it to the rear entrance. I was in a *mood*. Wanting things I could not have and hating the things I was stuck with.

"Willa-girl, it's beyond busy and tips are incredible! Seems like everyone in Green Valley came out tonight!" My cousin Patty hugged my neck as I stowed my stuff in Aunt Genie's office. I couldn't help but smile at her as I returned her hug and snagged one of the half aprons from the hook by the door.

"That's good to hear. We both know I could use the cash," I teased as I took a small order notebook and pen from the shelf in the corner.

"Yeah, I know! You should have let me help. I love you, you big dummy." Trailed by her lilting laughter, she ran off back out front. After tying back my hair, I joined her through the big double doors to the front and froze in front of them, taking it all in.

Immediately, I grew overwhelmed by the live music blasting from the stage at the rear of the dance floor and throughout the speaker system. Pounding bass and the twang of the country guitar charged through my system and muted my thoughts while at the microphone, the singer sang of his "Friends in Low Places" almost as well as Garth Brooks. Live music was so much louder and always attracted a huge crowd. Patty was right; this place was packed to the gills. A smile crossed my face as I began to anticipate tips galore. Quickly I washed my hands in the small sink by the door and made my way out front to wait tables with Patty and the other waitresses.

Two blonde blurs swept over, each taking one of my hands. A smile filled my face as my sisters hugged me, kissed my cheeks, then ran off to sit at the bar.

"Willa!" My head followed by my body turned toward the high-top table sitting near the corner of the dance floor at the sound of Beau Winston calling my name. "I have your van at my shop," he announced. "Everett had it towed. I was going to call you tomorrow and offer to buy it." His grin was so easy and friendly that I almost said yes without thinking.

"Oh, I can't sell her. I spent too much time getting everything right."

"I figured. Never hurts to ask, right?"

"Nope, it doesn't. Do y'all need another pitcher?" I gestured the empty pitcher on the table.

"Yes please. Hey, darlin'." My eyes rounded and I tried not to laugh as I saw Hank Weller seated alongside Beau, innocently sipping a beer while giving me a friendly, flirty chin lift, and a deftly discrete top-to-toe look. He had absolutely no idea what he might be in for if one of my sisters spotted him.

"I'll bring it right over." I imagined for a moment going to the Pink Pony and applying for a job—bet I'd be able to pay off my attorney a lot faster working for Hank at his strip club. *Yeah, no thanks.* Back at the bar, I warned my crazy sisters to stay away from Hank. They assured me they were over it and in no mood for anything but dancing and darts. I delivered the pitcher, refilled their glasses then moved on to the next table, all while making a mental note to inquire about my van and how to get it Everett's house. I sighed because I already knew I would forget all about my mental note as well as my van, until it hit me again that it wasn't in Everett's garage. I needed a nap, or a vacation. More like an extended stay in a mental hospital for "exhaustion." Basically, I needed a freaking break, dang it.

I spotted Sabrina and Wyatt with Boone and a few of the other deputies along with their wives or girlfriends. They had pushed a few of the high-top tables together and were chatting over beer and chicken wings. With a wave, I passed them to continue to my section of the bar.

Sabrina stood up to follow me, so I paused on the way. "How are you doing, Willa?"

"Oh! I'm fine. It's busy, isn't—"

"I know you're not fine." She held up a hand to quiet me. Sabrina was shy, but she certainly had her moments. Everyone did, I supposed. "I also know it's not the time to talk right now. But now *you* know that *I* know you're not fine. Got it?" I let out a giggle. Sabrina attempting to be bad ass was hilarious and adorable. But I *got* her, and since she had always *got* me, I would make time for another lunch date.

With a salute, I continued toward my section. "I got it! I'll text later!" I tossed over my shoulder. It would have to do until we could sit down and talk.

Heading to the rear of my section of booths, I spotted Drew and Ashley Runous. I knew Ashley from growing up together in Sunday school at church, but to my mother's endless chagrin—that she was more than happy to wax on about during dinner the other night—I had not been back to church since I'd gotten home. So I didn't know her husband, Drew. Sabrina had pointed him out to me the last time we were at The Donner Bakery for a banana cake fix, and I totally understood her old crush on him. He was dreamy hot. With a smile, I took their orders and the next few table's orders and made my way back to the bar.

My eyes drifted over the tables as I hustled to enter everything in the computer. Was it because I was paying closer attention tonight, or was it because of the live band that there were so many more familiar faces in the crowd this evening? Yeah, Green Valley was a small town, but it seemed as if every table was filled with people I knew. No sign of Everett yet, though. My heart fell at the thought of not seeing him tonight, and I immediately felt shame at the idea I could be leading him on and might end up giving him false hope. Then I felt confused as I realized that it wouldn't actually be false hope, because I wanted him so bad. I was such an idiot. I needed a hot-mess intervention. Someone needed to shake me and tell me to stop being such a dumbass.

From the bar, I saw Everett arrive with Jackson and Garrett. He spotted me and blew me a kiss, laughing as I blushed and twisted to the side like a girl in a movie. I wished I were a girl in a movie, because then maybe I'd get a guaranteed happy ending instead of these insane bursts of giddiness that would pop up whenever Everett was near. He made me forget who I was sometimes. But as soon as I remembered, it would go away, smashed back down by guilt and shame and the knowledge that it was an absolute fact that he could do better than me and all my piles of baggage.

I gathered my tray of drinks and held it over my head as I headed to my tables. The quicker I was, the better the tip. Making the rounds of the rest of my section, I once more headed to the bar to put in my orders. On tiptoes, I tried to catch another glimpse of Everett, but I couldn't find him in this huge crowd. "She's got it bad," I heard Sadie whisper to Clara. Yeah, I did have it, and it was so, so bad. My heart was pounding like a drum and my insides were twisted up in knots because I knew he was here, and I didn't know where. It drove me crazy that he wasn't up here at the bar where I could see him.

"You okay, honey?" My head swung to Aunt Genie, sliding my tray of drinks over the counter and looking at me with concern etched in her features. Why did everyone keep asking me that? Were my outsides reflecting my insides? If that were the case, then I'd look like a flaming dumpster right now.

"I'm totally fine. I just wish everyone would quit asking me—"

Her face turned to stone as her eyes shifted from somewhere behind me then back to meet my eyes. "Come back behind the bar, Willa. Come on, sweetie, right now."

"Okay..." I breathed then moved to do what she said. Aunt Genie wrapped her arms around me. Patty was filling a pitcher of beer behind her but suddenly she was at my other side. Flanking me, almost guarding me. What the heck was going on? The lights of the bar blurred into pulsing white spots as chills ran through my body.

One of the bouncers stood at the end of the bar with a nod. "Thank you…" I mouthed to him.

After a glance behind her to see who Aunt Genie was glaring at, Sadie whirled in her stool with an outraged shout. "That dick!"

"That motherfucking dick! Oh, hell no!" Clara shot out of her stool and stood up in front of the bar—in front of me. I flashed to the times Clara would yell back at Momma, getting in the middle of her hateful rants against me. Sadie and Clara were fighters; they always stood up to Momma, but I was a runner. I took everything inside, letting cruel words tarnish my heart. I ran away from her only to find more of the same with Tommy.

Sadie took off her high heel and brandished it like a weapon above her head. "Aren't you supposed to stay away from her? Fuck off, Tommy," she yelled as icicles replaced the blood in my body and I trembled in Aunt Genie's arms while Patty held my hand in hers. The last time I'd seen Tommy, he'd hurt me. I wasn't afraid he would do it again right now; there were too many people around. But he brought out feelings that I hadn't felt in almost two years. He made me feel small again, insignificant, *less*. Maybe I was afraid of standing up for myself. I had never done it before.

My eyes went wide as they darted blankly over the sea of customers on the other side of the bar, trying to see where he was. Trying to determine which direction I was going to run to get away from him.

I briefly spotted him, near the door before Garrett interrupted his stride with a rough hand on his shoulder. With a glare he shook Garrett off and continued toward me. But Jackson James stepped in front of him, putting a halt to his swift progression in my direction. Jackson didn't put a hand on him, but the message was the same—he was not welcome in here. But Tommy persevered in heading toward the bar, toward *me* while various Green Valley citizens intercepted him along his way. Beau, Boone, Suzie Samuels and her badass friends, even Naomi Winters from the library, holding hands with Sabrina, all stood in Tommy's path to glare at him as he walked down the length of the wooden bar, toward the rear where I stood. He shook them all off, finally made it to where I was, and sat down next to Clara with a smile.

"Dick," she repeated and flipped him off.

"Nice to see you too, Clara."

"I fucking hate you, Tommy," she shot back. "And just so you know, I'm waiting for the exact right moment to toss my drink in your stupid face." One of the bartenders slid a huge glass of beer in front of Clara with a chin lift then went back to standing next to Genie with his beefy arms crossed over his chest.

"Thank you," she said.

"Yeah, and I have a shoe just waiting to have your face imprinted on it. But I'd be happy to see you arrested instead. Why don't you just go away?" Sadie added and waved her shoe over her head.

"Classy as ever, Sadie." Tommy snickered.

"Fuck off," she replied then sat next to him, facing backward, elbows on the bar, so she could continue to glare at him while he attempted to catch my eye. Which was proving difficult since Clara had hopped on the bar to weave in front of him, actively preventing him from laying his eyes on me.

"You should leave now, while you're still free to go on your own." Everett's voice was low and full of anger. I gasped as he took Clara's seat, leaning a big forearm onto the bar to sit sideways in the stool and hover menacingly over Tommy with a ferocious glare.

"Willa, I'm sorry. You know I didn't mean to hurt you—" Tommy's voice echoed in my ears. I hadn't felt this kind of paralyzed anger in almost two years. Not since the last time I'd seen him, handcuffed and being shoved into the back of Wyatt's police cruiser, screaming my name. I flinched and tried to take a step to leave, but Aunt Genie held me firm.

"I got you," she whispered in my ear as she held me close. "*You* belong here, Willa. Not him."

"You don't get to talk to her," Everett stated.

"Make that hell no you don't get to fucking talk to her," Clara yelled in his face.

"She doesn't want you here. She doesn't want you at all. Not anymore," Wyatt said as Sadie got up to let him have her seat, still brandishing that shoe like she was just waiting for a shot.

"Big sister has your back." She winked at me and I choked on a sob that turned into a strangled laugh after she snatched Clara's huge beer and tossed it in Tommy's face. Tears filled my eyes spilling over, and I knew for certain I was having an emotional breakdown.

"It's time to go, Ferris." Jackson said from behind Tommy.

"Let's take a walk outside. It can be easy, or we could just arrest you," Boone added from Everett's side.

"I need to talk to my wife," he stated while swiping beer from his cheeks, stubborn as always. Only this time I would not be playing peacemaker at his side. This time I was *not* his wife.

"Don't listen to him, Willa," Patty whispered in my ear.

"I won't." I shifted my gaze to her while she squeezed my hand and my eyes slammed shut.

"Open your eyes, honey, and look," Aunt Genie ordered. I opened my eyes to look beyond Tommy, where she pointed.

The customers were more than just a sea of nameless faces, they were people I knew—from Momma's farm stand growing up, from church, from the Piggly Wiggly, and from right here in this bar. I knew them, and *they knew me.* Many of them had stopped their drinking and dancing and fun to join Wyatt, the other deputies, my sisters, and my… Everett, in the attempt to get Tommy to go away. They stood behind Tommy with glares aimed at his back while offering supportive and understanding smiles to me. Some of them even told him to leave. I wasn't the outsider here, Tommy was.

"You belong here. Not him." Before I could reject it, Patty had reiterated the thought that had just darted through my mind. Maybe it was something about the repetition. Or maybe I was just finally seeing clearly for the first time since I came back.

"Tell him, Willa," Wyatt encouraged with a soft smile.

"I don't want to talk to you, Tommy," I stated. I barely made a sound, but I said it.

"She said it. She doesn't want to talk to you. Time to go, Tommy." Wyatt stood up.

A smarmy grin crossed Tommy's face. How had I ever found him handsome? "This is a public place—"

"Well, I own this public place," Aunt Genie said, cutting him off. "Would you fine officers please escort him out of my bar?"

"Yes, ma'am," Jackson answered with a huge grin.

"And I don't want you coming back here, Tommy. You hear?" she added.

"I hear you, Genie," Tommy grumbled and stood up. "Willa, honey, this isn't over. We need to talk." He held his hands out, placatingly, his eyes doing that puppy dog thing he used to do whenever he knew he'd pushed me too far. I ignored his pleading look and shook my head side to side. He turned to leave, shaking off Jackson and Boone on the way. "I'm going."

I drooped in Aunt Genie's arms as a huge sigh left my body— along with most of my energy. I couldn't talk to him alone, not ever. I could barely talk to him in a bar full of people even when most of them had stuck up for me. *Were they here just to stick up for me?*

"How did this happen? Did you know he was coming?" I tugged Aunt Genie to the back counter to whisper my question.

"No, not for sure. But I knew it was a possibility. And honey, you need to get a restraining order against him—"

"Did you arrange for all these people—"

"Shoot, Willa. You always did come up with the craziest ways to deny that people actually like you," Patty said, incredulous. "How would Momma arrange for something like this? People noticed what was going on and they care about you. Plus, this is a small town and he's a known asshole. No one wants a jerk like him around." I let my eyes wander over the crowd as people slowly moved back to their evening, going back to their drinks and their dancing.

Aunt Genie laughed. "The only ones I called were your two crazy sisters."

"We'll take any opportunity to cuss out that dumbass," Sadie butted into our whispered conversation.

"Truth. I hate that guy. Always have," Clara added from her perch on top of the bar.

"I'm going to take her home, Genie," Everett said.

"Good. I don't want her driving alone," Genie agreed.

"Hey! I'm working—"

"You're off the rest of the night. With pay. No lip," she stated.

"But—"

"No but. No lip. Goodnight, honey," Aunt Genie's eyes softened on me as she pulled me close. "Take some time. Rest tonight and gather your strength. This place will be here tomorrow," she whispered in my ear.

"Okay, I will. Thank you." After hugs from Aunt Genie and Patty, I cashed out my apron, hung it up, and headed out front. Clara and Sadie kissed me goodbye. Then it was all Everett—hand on my waist, protective, hovering Everett—guiding me through the crowd like he'd murder anyone who dared step into my space to give me a problem. I must admit, it was hot. I loved this protective streak from Everett. With Tommy it had never been about being concerned for me and my feelings. It had been about me being a piece of his property, a plaything he didn't want to share.

I caught Sabrina's eye as we passed their table. She grinned and shot me two enthusiastic thumbs up, making me laugh through my— I didn't know what I was feeling—something indefinable that I'd never felt before. Acceptance?

"Yo! Give me the Bronco keys, Willa. I'll drive it home when Boone and I leave." Garrett slid up to my side with a smile. Pulling them from my pocket, I passed them over to him.

"Thanks, Garrett."

"Let's go home, Willa," Everett's voice was deep as he bent his head to mine, so only I could hear.

Home.

I knew what I felt.

What I felt was—at home.

CHAPTER NINETEEN

EVERETT

"If a man's any kind of man at all he knows the difference between love and lust. Lust is in a hurry, but love is already there."

— *PAPAW JOE*

She trembled beneath my palm as I guided her to my truck. The lights, high on the poles in Genie's lot, illuminated her tear-streaked cheeks making her freckles stand out against the pale alabaster of her face. That bastard had scared her so bad she'd lost her color. And her trembling was not from the chill in the air. I slid out of my flannel shirt and draped it around her shoulders. She was without a jacket tonight and the brisk breeze raised goosebumps over her skin. I wanted to pull her into me, warm her up, and give her the comfort she so clearly needed. But her posture was stiff, as if she was unsure of how to act around me. Tugging the flannel tight around herself she thanked me. I stayed near, but not touching.

"You're welcome, Willard. Let's get you home. I'll make you some hot chocolate and warm you right up." Her eyes darted to the side, briefly meeting mine as she smiled at me.

"You're good at this," she murmured and looked away.

"Good at what?"

"Taking care of people, of me. I mentioned it the other night. But it's worth repeating. You're—I've never met anyone like you, Everett. You make me feel—"

We made it to my truck, in the dark back of the parking lot. She turned to face me while I placed a hand on the roof and stepped closer to her. "How do I make you feel? Tell me, sweetheart."

"Safe. I never feel safe like this, except when I'm with you. How do you do that?" Her eyes were shiny and so big and blue in the moonlight as I studied her. Her lips were deep, dark pink, eyes lined in black, slightly smudged from her tears. She was heartbreak; she was strength. She was my dream not-yet-come-true.

"I'm glad I make you feel that way. I'd never hurt you. Not ever," I promised.

"I know you won't, Everett. Don't let me hurt you." Her soft smile turned sad as she turned to open her door and got in. Shutting the door behind her, I inhaled a deep breath and ran around to the driver's side. She could hurt me. She could end me, and it wouldn't stop my feelings for her. Being with her was like being in the ocean. Under water, the pounding of your heartbeat combined with the rush of the waves to feel almost deafening in your ears. Then when you surface, you realize it's the rest of the world that was too loud, all the noise unnecessary. When I was with her, she consumed me. All I could hear—or see, or feel—was her.

The drive home was torture. I wanted so much to reach out and put my hand on her thigh as if she were mine, to tug her close and steal a kiss. I wished I could show her how beautiful she was and make her believe it, to show her how much love the right man could give her. She was killing me, yet she gave me life with every second I sat beside her.

My arm on the console was tense as I held myself back. Until her hand slipped across my skin to rest her palm against mine, fingers interlocked. She held on and it gave me hope. With a soft squeeze I brought our hands to my lips and pressed a soft kiss to the back of hers. Her soft sigh was the answer to a question I didn't yet have the nerve to ask. I pulled into the driveway and shut the engine off.

She would be coming with me, to my part of the house. Whether or not she ended up with me in my bed was up to her. No way would I let her be alone without the alarm system in place. If necessary, she could have my bed and I would take the couch. "Let's go," I said. Confused anticipation flooded my veins as I hopped out and darted around to her door.

"Do we need to wait for Garrett and the Bronco?" She murmured after I opened the passenger door and helped her down.

"No. He knows where to park it, and he'll probably have a late night. Let's get inside. It's cold out here." Taking her hand, I led her toward the back porch, to my part of the house.

"I should go home—" her hand fell out of my grasp as she turned away.

"You should come with me." I grinned at her. "I have cookies, and marshmallows to go with the hot chocolate. We could watch *Firefly* again. Gracie is with Ruby for the night, right?"

"You really are an old man, Everett," she teased. The easy smile that crossed her face reminded me of when I first met her. Except now that I knew some of what that easy smile had hidden, I realized it was just smile-armor. Something she used to hide her secrets behind.

"It's true. Inside this body lies the heart of a senior citizen. Come on, Willard, I want to show off my cocoa skills. The marshmallows are homemade—my mother brought them by earlier—and the cookies are, too," I confessed. With her, I didn't need to hide my real self. I was determined to make her feel the same way.

"Your mother's food is irresistible." She acknowledged with a grin, and preceded me through the back door into the kitchen as I held it open.

"So, I have my mother to thank for my good company tonight. I accept that. Her chocolate chip cookies have won prizes."

She leaned back, hips against the counter, looking adorable in my flannel shirt. "I know! That used to piss my momma off so much! All we would hear about after the judging was her ranting about your mother and how she always won first place in the cookie category. *Gah!* She would get so mad. She'd be in a horrible mood for weeks." She let out a wistful sigh. "I wish I'd known you when we were kids, like my sisters did."

"I'm four years older. We probably wouldn't have run in the same circles." I grabbed the milk and measured it into a pan to heat.

"You're probably right. It was just a silly thought. I'm stuck in wishful thinking…"

I set the whisk on the counter. This required my full attention. "What else are you wishing for?"

Her eyes darted to the side as she bit her lip. "That I'd never met Tommy. That I had met you instead." Her hands gripped her elbows as she hugged herself and studied the floor. With my flannel shirt wrapped around her body, it was almost like an extension of me. But it wasn't good enough. With a soft slide, I ran my hands up her arms to her shoulders and pulled her into my chest. Her soft cheek pressed against my collarbone as she sighed against me, relaxing into my body.

"I wish that too." My whispered words rustled the loose curls on the top of her head before I placed a kiss there. But unlike Tommy, I wouldn't have taken advantage of an innocent, heart-broken young girl, no matter how beautiful and grown up she appeared to be. Rumors about her mother's harsh ways had been floating around Green Valley for years. But the front she put on in her business—as an earthy, wholesome, mother-earth farmer—kept them as merely rumors instead of fact. The more I gleaned of Willa's past, the more I believed the rumors about her mother were true. It explained so much about her. She had gone from her mother to Tommy, to alone, wandering aimlessly. She was lost. "Every-thing will be okay. I promise," I soothed as I pulled her tighter against me.

Her nod was slight as she leaned away. "I'm sorry," she whispered.

"Don't be sorry for having feelings, Willard." My smile was soft as I cupped her cheek to brush away an errant tear that she had not managed to hold back.

With a glance at the ceiling she laughed almost artificially then shook her head as if to shake her emotions away. "Okay, don't let the milk scald. I want to taste your famous hot chocolate," she teased. Her small smile was tremulous.

"Sure thing, sweetness." I winked, and to my satisfaction, she blushed. "Grab the cookies from the pantry," I instructed as I stirred the milk with the whisk.

"Yes sir." She saluted. A real smile crossed her face this time, bright and beautiful. "And where are the marshmallows?"

"In the fridge." I added the cocoa and sugar mixture along with a splash of vanilla to the milk and watched her bustle around my kitchen, gathering mugs and a plate for the cookies. Seeing her so comfortable here made my thoughts run out of control. I wanted her safe, happy, in my home, with me. *Mine.* My heart was a wild thing in my chest and my eyes grew hot with emotion. She was so close, within my grasp, but I didn't have her, not the way I needed her. Not yet. "*Firefly* marathon?"

"Of course." Her smile was quick and easy as she piled marshmallows and cookies on the plate.

"After you, Willard." My head tilted toward the living room as I gathered our filled mugs and some napkins.

After placing our sweet bounty on the coffee table, I dug out the remote and started the show. "We left off on episode twelve, right?"

"Yeah, 'The Message.' This is a good one."

"You say that as if they're not all masterpieces," I chided.

"Whatever was I thinking?" With a bump of her shoulder to mine, she settled against me on the couch to watch. Almost an hour went by in affable silence while we lingered over our mugs of hot chocolate and snacked on the cookies. My arm slipped around her shoulders and she cuddled into my side. We sank into each other, relaxed and comfortable as the next episode started up on the DVD.

"This is one of the three episodes that never aired when *Firefly* was originally broadcast, episode thirteen," I murmured.

"I know, I haven't seen it in years. 'Heart of Gold'..." she breathed as she stiffened against me.

"You okay?"

"Yeah, fine. It's been a day, you know?" Her false smile had returned but I had no idea what put it there. I passed her another cookie then settled back in the couch to watch the show—and to keep an eye on her too. She nibbled at the cookie and only half paid attention as the episode began. During the last episode and our previous *Firefly* marathon, she'd been all in...

My eyes narrowed on the screen as the crew of *The Serenity* arrived to help an old friend after the town bully threatened to take the baby away from the prostitute he had impregnated.

Abruptly, Willa stood up and stalked to the window. With a sweep of the drapes, she stared outside. "Let's watch a different one."

"Okay. Is something wrong? Do you need to talk?"

"No, I just don't like this one. I can ask for another episode without talking about it, right?"

"You can do anything you like, sweetheart."

"Maybe I want to do you." My flannel shirt slid off her shoulders and hit the floor to pool at her feet as she turned around, leaving her in her tiny Genie's tank top and skintight jeans. I gulped as she prowled toward me, whipping her tank over her head and tossing it behind herself. With two big steps forward she was at the couch, sinking her knees into the cushions to straddle my lap.

"Willa..." I murmured as her lips covered mine and her fingers sank into my hair. My hands slid across her back and down, gripping her hips then drifting around to squeeze her perfect ass in my palms. I wanted her. I was so ready for her that every other thought flew out of my head.

"I want you to kiss me, Everett. Kiss me hard and make me forget—"

"Look at me," I ordered. Her eyes sparked with need as she met my gaze. *No more looking away from me.* "I'll do anything you ask, sweetheart, give you whatever you need." The promise was as dark as my hidden fantasies of her. The ones I only let out at night when I was alone. I kept them locked up tight, waiting for a moment like this when I could feel her close to me again and unleash them.

Her fingers tightened in my hair as she pulled my head back, crashing her lips to mine once more. She said she wanted me to kiss her, but this seemed to still be her show. Slanting her mouth over mine, she kissed the breath right out of me. Like a riptide, she caught me, no escape, overwhelmed. *Hers.* "Everett," she moaned against my lips, letting her body sink down into mine and covering me with the warmth between her thighs while she arched against me.

Hands at her waist, I shifted her to her back on the couch, yanked my shirt over my head and covered her with my body. "Wait," she gasped, shoving me gently at my shoulder. I moved back while she reached between her breasts to unclasp her bra before pulling me roughly back with a hand behind my neck until we were pressed tight again. Mouth to mouth we breathed each other in. We were so close I could feel her heart beating against mine.

Her eyes shimmered in the dim lamplight of my living room as the TV sounded in the background. I watched as tears formed on her lashes to flow like a river down her temples and into her hair. "Sweetheart, tell me." I moved to the side and gathered her trembling body into my arms, her head to my chest.

"I'm so sorry," she choked on the words as she cried. "We can finish. I know you're hard, I feel it against me. I didn't mean to get you all worked up—"

"Stop that right now. You don't have to—"

"But I practically attacked you and now I'm crying all over you—"

"So what? That doesn't mean we can't stop. You don't have to do anything but know that I'm here for you. To listen to you, to hold you, to do whatever you need me to do."

"Can you just hold me?" I pulled away enough to see her face, her eyes rounded with a surprised expression that shattered my heart.

"I'll hold you forever if you'll let me. And I'll listen to whatever you have to say," I hinted.

"Why aren't you mad at me?" Her whispered question pierced a hole in my soul, while somewhere in the back of my mind a murderous rage built against Tommy Ferris.

"Oh, baby, no. I'm not mad at you. Tell me what has you so upset. Please let me help you."

"I—I was pregnant." My arms convulsed at the possible implications of that statement. "That episode made me think of it and I couldn't get it out of my head. Tommy hated the idea. He wanted me all to himself. He told me to get an abortion. But I wanted my baby, Everett. It's all I ever wanted. Someone I could just love who would love me back..." Her voice trailed off as she buried her face in my chest.

"What happened?" Softly, I brushed her hair back and tilted her face to mine. I wanted her to see that I meant what I said. "You can tell me anything," I murmured.

Her chin brushed my chest as she nodded, eyes filled with unshed tears. "Tommy never hit me or hurt me until the end. But he would say terrible things and punch holes in the walls, or throw things, or get into fights in bars, stuff like that. And he always got so mad at me—just like my mother." The last part trailed off to a whisper and her head dropped to my chest once more. "Once I had my baby to think about, I knew I had to get away from him. I couldn't let her grow up like I did, and I couldn't get rid of her. Tommy lost his mind when I told him I was leaving him. He slapped me, shook me by my arms, then threw me to the side. I crashed through our front window—he didn't mean to do it; he was as shocked as I was, I saw it on his face. Wyatt showed up right as it happened. He called for an ambulance and arrested Tommy."

"You never told anyone you were pregnant? Not even Wyatt?"

"No. But I told Wyatt I wanted to leave Tommy. He was going to meet me at the house. He wanted to be there just in case. I thought that was silly, that Tommy would never hurt me. Wyatt had talked to me a few times—he knew what kind of person Tommy was, what his temper was like. Wyatt planted the first seeds in my mind that I could leave, that I didn't deserve the way Tommy spoke to me, and I didn't have to take it."

"And the baby?"

"Nobody knows. Tommy doesn't even know that I didn't get the abortion. I went to a clinic for prenatal care, the kind where battered women go, so it was all a secret. The window wasn't high, I didn't fall far, and I landed on my hands and knees. But the glass cut my arm. I got stitches at the hospital, but I didn't tell them about the pregnancy. As soon as the doctor finished stitching up my arm, I went to the clinic. Everything looked fine. Her heartbeat was strong, she was moving; she was okay. Then about a week later I started cramping and miscarried. My doctor said it was unlikely the fall caused it, but there was no way to be sure since I was so early in my pregnancy. I was barely four months along, hardly showing at all. I named her Mia. Nobody knows her but me. It's like she was never even real…"

"Hey, she was real. She was yours and she was real. You knew it when you named her, didn't you? Mia means mine."

Tipping her head back, she met my eyes. "Are you for real right now?"

"Yeah, I'm real," I chuckled in surprise.

"Don't let me hurt you, Everett. Don't let me mess this up."

"Don't let me go and you won't," I pressed a soft kiss to her forehead.

"I think need time. I spent two years driving around in a safe, quiet little bubble with only Wyatt to talk to. I came back to Green Valley. Physically, I'm home. But inside, I'm still running away. It was so quiet on the road. All the noise in my head from Momma and Tommy was gone. I had no one telling me how stupid I was, or pointing out every little mistake I made, or how everything I did was wrong. It was peaceful, you know? I enjoyed the silence and when I didn't, I filled it with music or a podcast or I would call Wyatt and talk to him. I feel like I need to learn how to be in the world again. And I need to take control of my life without running away. I need to learn how to stand up for myself, and I need to learn how to stay."

"I'll give you time. I'll give you everything. Just don't let me go."

"I don't want to let you go. I want to be with you, Everett. But I want to—I want to be whole."

"I understand. And I think it's a great idea. How can I help you?"

"Don't give up on me?" she whispered.

"Never," I promised. Her lips parted as she gazed at me. I kissed her, just once, before I pulled her closer and tugged the quilt from the back of the couch to cover us. "We'll skip this episode, yeah?"

Her chest expanded with a huge sigh before she relaxed against me. "Yeah."

We kicked off our jeans and shoes to settle in in. Eventually, we fell asleep on the couch, wrapped up in each other until morning.

CHAPTER TWENTY

WILLA

"Sometimes the best part of building something new is tearing down what stood in its place."

— *EVERETT MONROE*

I sat in Everett's Bronco, parked at the curb across from Green Valley High school watching Gracie apply layer after layer of black eyeliner until she resembled a raccoon. Or maybe Courtney Love during her Hole days. "Don't you think that's enough, Gracie?" I was not an every-day makeup person. I wore lip gloss and sometimes mascara, but only because my eyelashes were blonde. Gracie was on another level. She smirked in the mirror as she applied burgundy lipstick. "I don't get it," I finally said.

"I'm not trying to be pretty, Willa."

"You don't have to try, you just are."

Her head tipped to the side, followed by her eyes as she looked at me like I was an idiot. "I can't believe I have to explain this to you. Jeez. When you look like us, the reputation precedes itself, doesn't it? Tall, blond, pretty, dumb as a pile of rocks, and probably a slut too. Am I right?"

My eyes shifted to the side. That sounded about right. I nodded to acknowledge her observation. "I guess so. I never really thought about it."

"So, what does the way I look right now tell you about me?" Her hand waved across her face. "All this eyeliner, boots perfect for stomping, ripped jeans—it says don't fuck with me. If you grab my ass in the cafeteria, you'll end up with a broken toe. There will always be guys who don't take hints, like your ex-husband. Clara used him as an example whenever she lectured me about older guys who like taking advantage of high school girls. Tommy was a predator, Willa. And you need to get that restraining order."

"*Gah!* If one more person tells me that—I called my attorney this morning, okay. Everyone was right. I did the thing. I'm going to have a restraining order; it is imminent. Maybe even by the end of the day since my attorney is like a dog with a bone and she hates Tommy as much as I do."

"Well, that's good."

It made me uncomfortable to think of my life this way. Like I had been a victim of something; like Tommy had preyed on me. But it was true. I'd been young and stupid and hurting over so many things, and he'd been there to seduce and distract me for every second of it. "You're right. Clara is right. Tommy was a bad person. I don't want you to end up with someone like that. I'll never go back to him. I want you to know that, Gracie." I was thankful that I'd had two years away from Tommy before I needed to face the possibility of seeing him again. "And who grabbed your ass in the cafeteria? I'll go in the school right now and yell at someone. Just point me in a direction."

"I know you're not going back to him. But he's in town, and you need to get strong, Willa. Sometimes you have to let the inside and the outside match. Want to borrow my lipstick? And don't worry about the ass-grabber. Clara and Sadie came down here and raised hell. He's gonna be scarred for life and probably live with his momma forever. They scared the shit out of him. It was hilarious."

"Good. And you also have me now to come to for help, Gracie. Don't forget it." I wiped my soft pink lip balm off with the back of my hand, took the lipstick from Gracie, and used the rearview mirror to apply it. Gracie nodded with approval.

"You look like a bad ass. Let's change the subject, because I have to get to school. I'll explain exactly how I do it. Don't be nervous."

"Are you sure I won't get into trouble? It's not an official job."

"Look, they don't care. They make money off the pizza regardless. All you have to do is stay in the car. Only go into the restaurant and get a table when you have an order. I updated my website to add your number. The money goes straight to Pay-Pal—*bing, bang, boom,* you're done. It's easy." Gracie was instructing me in the ways of opportunistic pizza delivering at Pizza Hut. "It doesn't matter how early it is either. Weird, right? I once delivered a pizza to Sienna Diaz-Winston at nine o'clock on a Saturday morning. She was pregnant, but still. People want their pizza, and they don't want to put on their pants to get it. Know what I mean?" I nodded. I felt the same way about pizza and pants.

"Hey, wait a second! You weren't even sixteen when she had her last baby. How did you deliver pizzas?" I didn't need to live in Green Valley to know about Sienna Diaz-Winston's business because she was also *Sienna Diaz*, movie-star, filmmaker extraordinaire, and the idol of my best friend, Sabrina.

"God, you're such a newb at life." With an exasperated sigh, she slammed her hand over her mouth. "I'm sorry. That was mean. You've been under thumbs for a long time, Willa, and I'm glad you're out. But seriously, I do what I want, and you should too. I've been driving since I was fourteen. Uncle Keen showed me how. And don't tell Momma I've been talking to Daddy's side of the family, okay?" I nodded my agreement. "You're all about taking control of your life, right? Making that money, paying your attorney, being the boss of you. Don't let rules stop you from getting what you want. Don't let anything stop you. And no more running."

"Okay. Eff the rules!"

"That's the spirit! And take this. It's my extra stun gun. If Tommy tries to mess with you, shock his ass, then kick him in the balls a few times and call the police. He can't make you talk to him if you don't want to. Oh! The grocery lists for the old people are on the coffee table at home. You can do a few of them today. Since I'm working for Everett after school, I have to cut back on my hours. I don't want to burn out, right?"

"Oh yeah, totally." I took the stun gun delicately. I didn't want to shock myself.

"Don't be scared of it, Willa. It's easy to use. Just push that button, then *zap!* I tested it on myself." She shook her head. "I don't recommend that, by the way."

Fighting back laughter, I put the stun gun in my purse. "Can I please wipe that racoon eye liner off?"

She shook her head. "Nope. I'm not ready to be strong without it. Like Dumbo's feather, you know? Plus, it looks cool. Every time I catch a glimpse of myself, I remember I'm brave, and I can to anything I want. Do whatever it takes, Willa. You're strong inside. Let it out, okay? When I first got here, you seemed like such a smart-ass, tough girl. But you're really not. You just pretend you are to keep people away. Like Everett."

I was taken aback. "How did you get so observant?"

"Clara's had me going to therapy since I was ten. I learned a lot from my shrink. Plus, I think it's innate. I'm just nosy." She shrugged.

"I love you, Gracie."

"I love you, too. But I have to tell you one more thing. I'm sorry, Willa."

"What for? You haven't done anything wrong. At least not so far today," I teased.

"Sometimes the way I say things is mean. It's not always about something specific I've said, it's my tone. My therapist said I need to apologize every time I realize I've done it. I have anger, Willa. Loads of it—at Daddy for leavin', at Momma, and I used to be angry with you too. But I'm not anymore. I know you now. You aren't like Sadie, Clara, and me. You don't close your heart and ignore all the shit Momma says. All her words go inside of you and you keep them there. The hurt feelings stay with you, and they never turn to anger so you can let them go. The only way you knew how to get away from it was to leave. You should really learn to get pissed, instead of letting her hurt you, or letting Tommy. And it's okay to cry while being pissed off, even I do it sometimes. You should see Sadie yellin' at Momma, tears and snot flying everywhere. But the point is, she doesn't take her shit. Also, I'm sorry about last night when I said your head was up your butt about Everett. That was uncalled for."

"It's okay, Gracie, I forgive you. Because I know you now too. Maybe I should go to your therapist. Maybe it would help me figure out why I can stand up for myself if it's someone I don't know, like when I'm at Genie's working and some dumbass hits on me, but I couldn't with Momma or Tommy."

"Well, at Genie's they're mostly strangers. You don't have to care what they think. You want Momma to love you. Same with Tommy, before the divorce. My therapist helps me. He lets me drone on and on and then he'll say one thing and then all of a sudden, I understand my feelings." She studied my face. "I'll text Clara about it from school. I don't want you to change your mind."

"Okay, that's probably a good idea." I laughed. "Bye, Gracie." I could use therapy. I was at least five kinds of crazy.

"Bye." With a huge smile, she got out of Everett's Bronco and headed toward the Green Valley High entrance to start her day. I was off to Daisy's Nut House for doughnuts, then to Everett's shop to give him breakfast for a change before I made my way to deliver groceries to senior citizens and hang around the Pizza Hut parking lot for delivery requests. I had money to make, a divorce attorney to pay off, and a life to reclaim—to reclaim by staying and fighting for it, not by running away. I took a glance at myself in the rearview mirror before I drove off. Burgundy lips, huh? Outside reminders of courage before I had them on the inside. Maybe Gracie was onto something. Maybe I really would make an appointment with her therapist.

I remembered last night with Everett. And the things I had told him about Momma and Tommy. Gracie had a point about how I never let their words go. I never let *anything* go, and the burden was heavy.

Telling Everett about my baby last night was the best thing I had ever done. It lightened my heart. I never realized how much my grief had been weighing me down, too heavy to carry on my own. I wasn't ready to tell anyone else, and I might never be, but sharing her with Everett made her feel real again. It made all the difference in my perspective. I felt like I could grieve for her properly now. I would never stop wondering "What if?" and I would never forget her. But I finally felt like my heart could start to heal enough for her to live there with less pain.

* * *

I stood in the entrance to Everett's shop, box of doughnuts in hand. I had stopped there at the sound of clattering dice dropping onto the huge gaming table in the rear of the shop. Everett sat at the table's head in a heavy wooden chair with his back to the propped open door. He was DMing a game of *Dungeons and Dragons*. Silently, I stepped inside and slipped into a chair near the front so I could listen. Garrett, Weston—Sabrina's nephew, who should be in school with Gracie right now—along with what looked like a few of Weston's friends, were the players. As DM, or dungeon master, Everett would set the scene, and act as the lead storyteller, as well as make sure everyone followed the rules.

"You are Ashe Redgrove," Everett began, addressing Garrett. "A young wood-elf paladin, tasked with scouting the location of Faye, the lost queen of the mermaids. She is marked by scars and tattooed on one arm to designate her station. If the rumors are true, she now resides in hiding from her king, near the rocky cliffs of the Emerald Sea. She bides her time, waiting to reclaim her power and her throne. Everyone in your village knows she is dangerous, wily, and intelligent. But she is also delicate and untrusting; she is a broken creature, and beyond beautiful. With long winding pale blond locks, eyes as blue as the sky and deeper than the sea she inhabits, you will find it hard to do anything other than her bidding. Once you have secured her location, a party will be dispatched to rescue her and return her to her people for a great reward—" I let out a loud sigh as he spoke and as I leaned forward over the table to rest my chin in my hands, my chair squeaked out a huge fart sound over the wood floor. But I didn't even flipping care. He made me a mermaid. I was a freaking fantasy mermaid queen for crap's sake. Is this what a swoon felt like?

Garrett's head shifted to mine and a wide grin crossed his face. "Well, hello there, mermaid queen."

Everett almost fell out of his chair and I almost swooned for real when he turned around to look at me. A blush rose over his cheeks above his beard as he grinned. He was sexy—adorable and hot—and so sweet I couldn't stand it. Then his head dipped forward as he looked at me through the fall of his hair, with raised eyebrows, and hot eyes, and I swear, my heart stopped.

"Hey, Willa!" Weston greeted me with a huge smile. He was always such a good little boy. I couldn't believe how much he had grown. He'd gone from the sweet-faced boy I knew to Green Valley High's star quarterback. "Let's go, guys. Game is over for now, right Everett?" The boys got up and followed Weston, who clearly knew what was up. I offered them doughnuts as they left.

"Well, this paladin is clearly not the one to do the rescuing today. Later." Garrett snagged a doughnut on his way out. I stood up and joined Everett at his table.

"I brought doughnuts," I said. My eyes were full of sparkles and glorious dreams and I didn't know who I was anymore because for the moment, I had lost my angsty edge.

"Thank you, Willard." He took the outstretched box from my hands and set it on the table.

"You're welcome." My eyes drifted away from his to the carved wooden mini figures distributed over the game map spread across the table. The mermaid caught my attention. My eyes darted to Everett as he swept it into his hand before I could get a good look. "Let me see?" I reached out to take his closed fist with both hands. With a sheepish grin, he relaxed his palm in my grip, sending shivers up and down my spine at the feel of our fingers brushing against each other. The mermaid was delicate, painted with white blond hair and blue eyes. Her tiny tattoo was identical to mine and she had my face. My eyes slid to his as my heart melted in my chest and the shivers turned into a burning need. This man—how was he real?

"You've been on my mind—" His voice came out in a soft growl as his eyes blazed into mine.

Goodness gracious, holy crap, he did all kinds of things to me. Dirty things, sweet things, easy things, and things that got my mind filled with so many complicated thoughts that I was constantly spinning from one to another. I couldn't speak. I couldn't think. My mouth opened but nothing came out but a soft, short moan.

"I wanted to ask you something." He interrupted my embarrassing moan with what would probably be an irresistible question. *Yes.*

"Okay," I murmured, lost in whatever it was he was about to say. He was totally dreamy right now, and me asking for time last night was stupid, stupid, stupid. I mean, we could be having sex on this gaming table right now if I hadn't asked for time, dammit.

"Can I take you to dinner sometime? To the Front Porch, maybe?"

"Like, on a date?" A huge grin formed on my face before I could even attempt to hide my delight or play it cool.

"Yeah, a date." He chuckled.

"You know what? I've never—" The pathetic truth stuck in my throat before I could get the words out. I was sorry I brought it up in the first place and shut my mouth.

"What?" he murmured with a sweet smile.

"I've never actually been on a real date—uh, me and Tommy just snuck around when I was young and then we got married. We didn't really have date nights or anything like that. I should stop talking now." I clammed up and stared at the table.

"You should always talk to me. I want to know about you, Willard."

"There's not much to know. And what there is to know is kind of pathetic." I spoke to the top of the table because I couldn't look at him.

"That's not true. Here's the thing with you—yes, you were dealt a shitty hand. But you're about to play the hell out of it, aren't you?"

My eyes shot to his. "What do you mean?"

"You're taking your life back, is what I mean. And I'm glad. But I'm a selfish man. I want you too much to let you go while you do it. So, I've decided to go slow. And I think you need wooing."

"Wooing?" My voice was a high squeak.

"You haven't been properly wooed." He smirked and leaned back in his chair. Flexing that huge bicep as he bent his arm to run a hand through that sexy long hair. I was fighting the urge to—basically, I was fighting whole bunch of urges right now. Number one being to crawl up that broad chest of his and kiss the hell out of him.

"I don't know, Everett. I think you properly wooed me the other night. And who says wooing anymore?" The laugh that burst out of him was loud and the grin that crossed his face could light up the room. All this sexy goodness *and* he wanted to woo me? Yes, please. He could woo me all night long…

"So, do we have a date, sweetness?" he drawled.

Heck yes, we have a freaking date. "I think that can be arranged."

"Perfect. We'll make plans. Maybe I'll call you tonight." He winked at me and with that, I knew our date would be something I'd want to remember forever. "What's on the agenda for today?"

My cheeks heated at my lame career trajectory. "Well, I'm going to park at the Pizza Hut for a few hours—"

His eyebrows shot up. "Gracie is giving it up? I saw it on her website. She gave me her card when I hired her."

"For now. I'm also taking over her senior citizen grocery delivery thing, maybe mow a few lawns. She swears that I can make a few hundred a week doing her odd jobs. I want to pay off my attorney, Everett. It's step two. The first step was getting the restraining order. I've also requested more hours from Aunt Genie at the bar. All of Gracie's side gigs are something I can do immediately while I apply for a second job. I'm also considering working for my mother part time since Sadie will be leaving to work for your dad."

His eyes crinkle smiled as he gazed at me. "I'm—is it condescending if I tell you I'm proud of you?"

"No, not all." An involuntary smile crossed my face. "I'll take it as a compliment. I have to get going. I'll see you tonight?" I stood up to leave but turned back at the sound of his boots hitting the floor as he sat forward.

"Uh, uh, not yet. I'm going to kiss you goodbye." He reached for me as he spoke. Big hands spanned my waist, giving me a tug. My knees landed between his legs on the chair, while my hands slid up his hard chest to drift into his hair. His lips brushed against mine as he whispered, "I'm gonna make you mine, sweetheart. But the difference from what you knew before and now is that you'll be yours first." His eyes held mine and I couldn't look away. Just then I realized that when Everett looked at me, I didn't lose myself in him. When I was with him, I was free to *be* myself. I could say whatever I needed to say, and he would listen. And wasn't that just like a dream come true?

He kissed me goodbye—softly, slowly, sweetly. It was a kiss that didn't claim; it gave, and I wanted to be strong enough to give it back.

CHAPTER TWENTY-ONE

EVERETT

"Absence is to love what wind is to fire. If it isn't love, the flame dies.

If it is love, get ready for an inferno".

— PAPAW JOE

Willa was now in the business of self-improvement. She wanted to heal, grow and be independent. And since all I wanted was her, I was now in the business of waiting. Time trudged on as I took a giant step back to give her the distance she had asked for. I never let on that I was dying to touch her, or kiss her, or just hold her. I had the feeling that it would be easy to convince her to drop everything and be with me. Our chemistry was still there every time we were near each other. Half of me wanted to just take what I wanted, but the better half wanted to give her what she needed.

We had gone back to dine and dash breakfasts, complete with subtext filled small talk and flirty looks. Back to her checking me out with hot eyes when she thought I wasn't looking—but the trouble for her was that I was *always* looking. She took every available hour she could get at Genie's; and since Gracie had started working for me after school, Willa had taken her place hanging out at the Pizza Hut in town, delivering pizzas to whoever shot her a text, mowing lawns, babysitting, and delivering groceries to some of the home-bound senior citizens. All that plus working part time for her mother almost every morning and appointments with Gracie's therapist every week meant that I hardly ever saw her. The positive aspect of her change in routine was that she seemed to feel better about herself. Her smiles were easy and genuine. And sometimes *she* was the one to make our morning coffee. I was happy for her, and proud, even though I was lonely. The only things to keep me going of late, were the quick goodbye pecks and soft smiles she'd give me whenever I happened to be around as she was leaving. It had been weeks of this. We hadn't yet gone on our date, and I missed her. I worried constantly if she was getting enough sleep and taking care of herself. Her schedule was insane, and I feared she would burn out.

Taking control over her life was important to her. I let go of what I wanted so she could fly. Sure, this was Green Valley, Tennessee, and not some big fancy city, but independence was independence no matter where you were. Willa needed to see she could make it on her own. I could wait. For her, I would wait forever. Sure, there were a lot of other women in the world, but none of them were *her*.

The sun rose in the sky with bursts of orange and pink as I stood in Daisy's Nut House, a box of doughnuts in my hand. My eyebrows raised in surprise when I spotted Tommy through the window. He had been staying away from Willa; maybe the restraining order was actually a deterrent. Plus, from what Wyatt found out, Tommy's father had put him to work and on a tight leash. He was working as a salesman, selling cars at one of his father's lots in Maryville. It had to burn that he couldn't be a cop anymore.

"Monroe," he addressed me. I lifted my chin then turned to leave. He followed me to the parking lot. "I need to talk to you." He stopped me with a hand on my arm. I shook him off with a glare. "I want you to give Willa a message. I can't talk to her myself right now. I wrote her a letter—"

"Are you crazy? Take a hint, Ferris. The divorce and a restraining order are hint one and two."

"I finally have some time off work and I need to talk to her." That smarmy, slick smile was back on his face and I wanted to knock it through the back of his skull.

"Because talking to her worked so well for you last time? Why don't you just give up? She doesn't want you." This fucking guy. He was the kind of guy who couldn't take "no" for an answer and gave the rest of us a bad rap.

"I know you want her, Monroe," he accused, as if he had a right to make a claim on her, as if they hadn't been divorced for over two years. "I know you're trying to take her away from me. We were married for almost a decade, man. One mistake isn't enough to throw away an entire rela—"

"Are you serious?" I shouted, incredulous. "One mistake? You threw her through a god-damn window! And that doesn't even begin to get into what you've—look, none of that matters. What *I* want doesn't matter." My fist pounded against my chest and I wished I could pound some sense into his thick skull instead. "What *you* want does not matter. But you're too selfish to see that. I'm done. Stay away from her, Ferris. Don't make me step in any more than I already am. You won't like it."

"She's *my* wife. She'll come around. As soon as I can make her listen, she'll forgive me. She always forgives me." Pushing past him with a glare, I got into my truck, made a quick call to Wyatt to report the Tommy sighting, and took off to bring Willa breakfast at her mother's farm.

During the drive I gained control of my temper. There was no sense in acting like an angry fool and scaring her. I didn't need to tell her to watch out for Tommy with anger clouding the message. The news should be matter of fact and logical, even if my feelings about him being in town and wanting her back were the exact opposite of logical. When it came to Tommy Ferris, I felt like punching first and asking questions later. He spoke of her so possessively that I was sure I would get the chance—the bad side of me looked forward to it.

I parked next to my Bronco with a grin and got out to go find her. With a look around I remembered how beautiful it always was up here, and today was no different. Except for the vibrant lavender, everything was colored in shades of green, from the trees blanketing the mist covered mountains to the herb gardens across the way. My mother often visited this place to shop. Sometimes I drove her, and we always had to take a moment just to stare in awe at the sight. It was something straight out of a landscape painting.

My work boots crunched over the gravel as I passed through the parking lot to the whitewashed farm stand. It looked like a small stable with bushels of lavender lining the area beneath the huge windows on either side of the entrance beneath the overhang.

"Boys, come back here!" I quickly jumped back as two blond little boys raced out of the front door followed by Willa's sister, Sadie. None of them were watching where they were going.

"Sorry. I'm so sorry," she yelled over her shoulder as she raced after the boys up the road to what I assumed was the family house. The sign on the fence said, "private".

With a hand on the door I paused to listen. "She's wasting a whole day's pay. I warned her about this very thing. She can't afford to mess up like she's so prone to doing, while working for someone as prominent as Bill Monroe. Our reputation in town is bad enough after your daddy left. And let's not forget all the crap you've pulled in your lifetime, missy. Someone as gullible and easily led as Sadie should have never had children. Those boys are no sicker than I am, and they should be in school. Willa Faye, I want you to refill the lavender bushels from the stock out back. Then I want you take stock of the honey and rotate it this time as you fill the shelves. Don't mess up like you did yesterday. I had to redo everything because you were too stupid to check the dates on the bottom of the jars. I don't have that kind of time around here. Be careful this time, you hear?"

"Yes, Momma. I won't mess up this time." I hated the way her voice sounded. Resigned, accepting. I opened the door and stepped inside, determined to put a stop to it.

Her mother turned to me with a huge smile. "Welcome to

Lavender Hills. Willa will be glad to help you. I'm on my way out to tend the bees. Bye, now." She flitted around me before I could say anything. My mind battled with my heart. Should I say something? Or should I let it go for now. My mind said I should maybe let it go, while my heart demanded I address the situation.

"Everett! What are you doing out here?" A quick swipe under her eyes with her hand told me to address it. My heart won. I couldn't let it go.

"Is that how she always talks to you?"

She shrugged. "I'm used to it. It's no big deal and I need the money. I'm so close to being able to pay my attorney off, Everett. I'll be free of everything after that. Then I can go back to just working for Aunt Genie and quit all the other stuff. Besides, she's my mother and she's never going to change. Unless I want to cut her out of my life, I need to learn to handle it, right?"

"Don't let it set you back. Promise to quit if it gets too much and it's okay to cut her out if she won't make an effort to change."

"I promise. I might cry about it, but I don't let it sink in and stay like before. It's her problem, not mine. I'm sad for her. Nothing is going to set me back. I have goals." Her soft smile beckoned me to her.

My bootsteps fell heavy on the wooden floor as I walked toward her behind the cash register. "What goals?"

Twinkling blue eyes smiled into mine. "You mentioned something about a date awhile back. I'm ready to let the whole pizza delivery thing go, and I'm off from Genie's tomorrow night. So…"

"Ah, does this mean we're back to the wooing and I can take you to the Front Porch?" I grinned.

"If you still want to—"

"I want to. Don't doubt that, sweetheart. Since I first saw you with Sabrina in Genie's, I've wanted you. But, you're more to me now. I don't just want you. I need you."

"I've missed you, Everett, so much. Being this busy is—"

"It's what you needed to do, and I understand. But now—"

"I'm ready for more. And I think I have something to give."

"You've always had something to give. You just know it now. You've found you."

"I did. I'm right here," she breathed.

"And you're beautiful." I brought my hand to the nape of her neck, to rest beneath her blond curls. Smiling at the way her neck arched and her lips parted, I dropped my head low to steal a kiss. Her eyes crinkled at the corners before drifting closed as she stepped out from behind the counter and into my body.

"More," she whispered, hands sifting into my hair, tugging, demanding.

I kissed her hard, wanting to get us back to where we were before she started working so hard. Back to before I'd missed her, her body, the taste of her mouth on mine and the way she felt in my arms. The ache in my heart eased as she melted into me.

CHAPTER TWENTY-TWO

WILLA

"She bides her time, waiting to reclaim her power and her throne."

— *EVERETT*

Everett's kiss lingered on my lips for hours after he left, leaving me in a dreamy love haze. The only thing to dim it was the idea of going to the Front Porch. Fancy and Willa did not mix. In other words, I had nothing to wear. And since shopping and Willa also did not mix, I shot a quick text to Sabrina asking to borrow something. She said, yes, along with expressing her excitement, and that settled that.

Hours drifted by as I rang up customers and tidied the farm stand while at the same time trying to tune out my mother's harsh words whenever she popped in to check on things. Sadie was here as well, but she had her hands full with Flynn and Rider who pretended to be sick this morning in order to stay home from school.

Finally, the hour was nigh. Lunchtime meant I was off for the day. At least at this job. As the clock slowly drifted toward noon, I swept the farm stand and tried to push all the mean shit my mother said out of my head.

It meant nothing.

It couldn't hurt me.

Except that it did and it would never stop as long as I kept in contact with her.

It was clear I couldn't work for my mother anymore. I was so close to paying off my attorney, but this wasn't worth it. Every day I left with Momma's words ringing in my ears. The more I was around her the longer it took to let them go. Those two years of silence on the road taught me that I needed peace, quiet, and kindness. Working here was the opposite.

"Hey, Willa. I took Flynn and Rider to school, the little boogers. I can take over for you. Momma's still out with the bees, probably yelling at them and criticizing their honey, as she does."

"Sadie, how do you do it? How do you live with her and not lose your mind?"

"I have no other choice at the moment, unfortunately. I don't get child support since I don't know where my loser husband is to even serve him with papers. I'm married to a dead-beat, and I can't even afford a divorce. I didn't even know we were broke until the foreclosure sign went up in the front yard." She plopped onto the wicker couch in the corner and stared at the wall.

"I'm so sorry," I commiserated.

"I want to be like you, Willa," she said.

I laughed, so hard that I had to flop down next to her. "That's crazy," I finally said.

"It's not. You're straightening out your life. One step at a time. I envy you. I'm a hot mess—living up here with Momma, trying to save up first and last month's rent just to get into a shitty apartment in town. Bill Monroe pays well, but I have two growing boys so I'm stuck working here too. I can't quit. I had to buy new shoes and jeans yesterday because they've already grown out of the stuff I got at the beginning of the school year." Her head drifted back to lean against the wall.

"Is Momma mean to the boys?" I had to ask. Maybe I could keep coming around until Sadie was able to move out, to support her and the kids. That would fit in with my whole not-running-away thing. Plus, I loved my sister and I wanted her to be happy.

She shook her head and a tear slid down her cheek from beneath her closed eyes. "No," she whispered. "She loves the boys. She's great with them. It makes me—I'm jealous of my own kids, Willa."

"I'm so sorry." I let my head fall against her shoulder.

She gave my hand a squeeze. "It is what it is. I'll be okay. I'm always okay, one way or another. This won't last forever."

"Well, I'm not going anywhere. I'm back for good and always here to talk."

"Except right now, since it's noon and you're off." With a grin, she stood up to go behind the counter. "Go home and take a nap. You look tired. Your dark circles have dark circles."

"That's a good idea. I'm out of the pizza delivery business, so I have time for a nap before Genie's tonight."

"If you have time, swing by Everett's shop when school is out. Check out what's going on over there with Gracie. Little miss has some secrets. The good kind for a change." Sadie waggled her thumb and pinky near her ear for me to call her later.

"I've just added that to my list for the day. I'll call you."

As I drove home, the idea of taking a nap infiltrated my thoughts until it was the only thing left in my head. I had been working at least ninety hours a week lately and I was beyond exhausted. Everett's house loomed in the distance up the road as my eyesight blurred around the edges. I was about to take a nap so hard. No more pizzas, no more lawn mowing, or old people grocery shopping. I was burnt out. From now on I would stick to my job at Genie's, no more side gigs. My bed called to me and I could not wait to climb inside and shut my eyes.

With a frown, I maneuvered around a huge potted rose bush sitting smack dab in the middle of the driveway. Everett wouldn't have left something in the way like that. I hopped out of his Bronco for a closer look. The tiny buds on the bush were white. My heart dropped to my stomach and I spun around to peer up and down the street. *White roses*—were these from Tommy? A card fluttered to the driveway as a light breeze kicked up. I bent to retrieve it.

I'm sorry.
   Willa, I love you. Give me a chance to make it up to you.
   Please call me.
   Tommy

Balling the note up in my fist, I threw it toward the street with a low scream. Then I ran around to the side of the garage to wheel the huge green garbage tote down the driveway and with a grunting heave, I chucked the pot into the trash. With a huge sigh I stomped down to the street to collect the note and throw that away too, because litterbugs were the worst. Tommy was the worst. I hadn't heard from him in so long that, stupidly, I'd thought he'd given up and moved on. This day had turned into the worst. *Boo. Hiss.*

A smile crossed my face once I realized I was more angry than scared. Sure, it was a rose bush and a stupid note I was handling, and not the actual Tommy. But I still counted it as progress. A call to the Sheriff Department was in order instead of a nap. I was too wound up for a nap now anyway, thanks to Tommy and his freaking roses

"Willa!" *Dammit.*

"Momma?" I spun away from my door to find my mother headed up the driveway. Her old Ford pick-up truck was idling on the curb. I guess she wasn't planning on staying...

"I have something to tell you and I don't have your number. Tommy was just up at the house, asking about you."

"What did you tell him?"

"I told him to leave you be. That boy is trash, Willa. I tried so hard to get you to leave him alone back then. You have a restraining order, dontcha? Gracie told me you did. Do you want to come get one of your daddy's old shotguns to use in case the sheriff department doesn't arrive in time to get him?"

I collapsed to the porch, head in my hands. "Yeah, but I don't want a shotgun. I have Gracie's stun gun though."

Momma sat next to me and patted my leg. "That will work, I guess. Do you want to come and stay with me? I'm not afraid to just shoot him," she offered.

"No thanks. Everett installed an alarm system. And see the fence? He slides it closed and locks it at night, my front door is behind it. And I'm not convinced that he'd actually do anything to hurt me anyway. Maybe I just need to tell him to leave me alone. You know, be firm about it."

Her eyes were full of doubt as she looked at me. "Maybe. Well, I'm leaving. Get in the house. I won't leave until your door locks. Go on now, don't sit outside on the porch like an idiot."

I stood up to go inside, marveling at the fact that she was almost nice to me. But *almost* was not good enough. Not anymore. I hesitated before spinning away from the door. "Momma!" She turned at the sound of my voice.

"What is it?"

"I won't be working at the farm anymore."

An annoyed sigh huffed out as she rolled her eyes. "I didn't expect you'd stick around for long anyway. Now, go on inside."

I crossed my arms over my chest. "Gracie will stay here with me."

"Fine. I can't say I'm surprised. She's a lot like you were back then—a pain in my behind. Now, go on inside so I can leave. I have work to do up at the farm."

"Bye, Momma." This was more than a *see you later* kind of goodbye. This was a forever kind of goodbye. She watched me go into the apartment. I heard her truck start not long after I turned the lock on the door.

My mother's words were still ringing in my ears as I called Wyatt and told him about the roses. I'd made the right decision; she would never change, and it was best to just keep her out my life.

I took a quick shower, dressed in my Genie's work clothes, and left. Being here by myself hurt, but the hurt was making me mad instead of making me want to run away. All this getting mad was making me hungry. I needed something gross from a drive through and a huge Diet Coke to help me process my feelings.

By the time I finally made it to Everett's shop, the dice were rolling on the tables and Gracie was behind the counter flirting her ass off with Sabrina's nephew, Weston. I backed out before they saw me and hopped in the Bronco, parked at the curb, to call Sadie.

"She likes Weston?" I hissed into the phone. I wanted to yell it, but I also didn't want Gracie to hear.

"Yes!" Sadie shrieked into the phone. "Isn't it awesome! He's a good boy! Everyone in town always says it—Weston Adams is a good boy! One of us finally has a decent picker! I mean, you like Everett now, but not until after years of being with a total fucking dick. You had to learn the hard way like me and Clara. Momma too, for that matter. Gracie is breaking the cycle, Willa. No more high school heartache with sexy, asshole bad boys for the Hill women!"

Her enthusiasm was infectious. My mood improved, and a huge smile filled my face. "Maybe it's all the therapy?"

"I don't know! I just know I'm happy. It gives me hope, which is kind of sad, but I still feel it."

"It's not sad. I kind of want to be more like her," I confessed.

"Girl, don't we all. Shit, I have to go. The boys are fighting upstairs. Last time I left them unsupervised this long they had a water balloon fight with a box of condoms they found in Clara's old room. Boys—!" Her phone clattered to the floor, or a table. Either way, she was no longer there.

"Willa, come here." Gracie had her head popped out of the shop's doorway as she beckoned me inside. Hurrying out of the Bronco, I ran to the door. I spied Weston driving away in his Jeep, so I felt free to *squee*, and hug Gracie with obnoxious glee.

"*Ew*, Willa, stop it! Gracie doesn't squee, okay?" She backed away, brushing off the front of her shirt as if I gave her squee cooties or something.

"Well, Willa does and she's happy for you. Weston is a good boy!"

"God, you sound just like Sadie. She told you to come here and spy on me, didn't she?"

I shrugged. "Maybe she did. So what?"

"Ugh, fine. Get it out of your system. Ask me one question."

"Only one?"

Gracie shook her head at me in disappointment before a slow smile crossed her face. "Yes. Only one. Asked and answered. We're moving on now."

"Crap! Dammit. You tricked me!"

"Yeah, and it was sadly easy," she teased.

"Whatever. Rudy McRuderson."

"Move on, Willard. I already have. You should come inside. Everett will be here during his dinner break to balance the drawer and check on everything. Maybe you can make out with him in the corner."

"Again, I say, whatever." She turned around to laugh in my face, the little stinker. I decided to move on. "Do you like working here?" I asked as I followed her inside.

"Yeah, Everett's so nice. Don't screw it up, Willa. It would be good for you to be with him. Good for all of us to have someone like that in the family." She grabbed a broom and started sweeping. "No pressure or anything." She smirked.

"Oh yeah. It sounds like you'd keep him over me if we—broke up? I mean, we're not exactly *together* together. I don't know. Never mind." I sat at a table with my Diet Coke and sipped it while she swept the now empty shop.

"You're together. It's just not, like... You haven't said the words, is all. You haven't declared it officially. Like, updating your Facebook status, or getting a tattoo together, or a big fat diamond ring. Though, you do have his Netflix password. Don't forget about that."

"*Ew.* No diamond ring for me. Tommy and his trust fund gave me a huge one, so no thanks. I'd rather have something different. And if I ever have another wedding, it will be all about the cake. Tommy hates cake. That should have been clue number one that he was a huge moron." I laughed.

"Who hates cake? What a tool." She held out her fist and I bumped it. "Y'all have a date tomorrow, right?"

"How do you already know about that?"

Her eyes rolled into mine. "From Ruby, of course. You texted Sabrina to borrow a dress. Ruby texted me. We're doing a find-a-dress-for-Willa party tomorrow morning. You'll have to get up early. Sorry."

"Oh, okay. *Oooooh*, maybe Weston will be there," I teased in my best girly girl voice.

"Shut up. And, no, he won't be there. He has football camp practice going on, or whatever. He applied to UT. He wants to play football there like Wyatt did."

"That's awesome!"

"I know—"

"Ladies," Everett greeted as he walked through the door.

"You're early. Awesome. I have a test tomorrow I need to study for. Can I leave?" Gracie hopped up and ran around the counter to grab her backpack.

"Go ahead. I'm off early too, I'll close tonight."

"You're the best, Everett! Bye, y'all."

"We need to talk," I stated.

"Ominous." He smirked as he sat down across from me.

"It could be. Tommy left a huge potted rose bush in the driveway today. I called the Sheriff Department. Do you think that's okay, even though it was just a potted plant and a note, and I didn't actually see him?"

"Absolutely. He's not allowed to contact you at all."

"I—don't you think I should talk to him and tell him to his face to leave me alone—"

"No way. Wyatt and the Sheriff's Department, along with a cop buddy of Wyatt's in Maryville, are all keeping an eye on him. He's been there the whole time. Until today, anyway, when he visited your mother. It's under control. Eyes are on him all the time and this will definitely be enough to have picked him up."

"Oh. Okay. Uh, thank you." I still felt weird. Growing up, me and my sisters had taken care of each other, but that was different because we'd all been in the same boat. Everett was not in my boat. Everett was the captain of his own ship, and I envied that.

"What's that look on your face for, Willard? I can almost see the smoke coming out of your ears."

"I'm just thinking." His eyebrows raised. "I mean, I'm getting used to the idea of being taken care of." My eyes drifted down to the table. "And I'm tryin' to think of ways to take care of you." I mumbled the last part under my breath, but he heard me.

"No worries, sweetheart. When the time comes, I have no doubt you'll take care of me."

My cell phone alarm went off. "I have to get to Genie's," I said on a huge sigh.

"Drive straight to Genie's and text Patty when you get there. One of the bouncers will meet you at your car."

"Have y'all thought of everything?"

"Everything but how to get him to go away," he answered with a frown. "Maybe I should just beat the shit out of him."

"No, don't do that. He's petty enough to have you arrested and sue you. You'd think divorcing him would have done the trick, but I guess not."

He chuckled and reached for me as he stood up. "This won't last forever. Try not to worry."

"I'll try." His eyes crinkle-smiled into mine, making me all melty inside.

"Good. Until tomorrow night." With a sweet kiss to my forehead he walked me to his Bronco and helped me inside.

CHAPTER TWENTY-THREE

WILLA

"You haven't been properly wooed."

— *EVERETT*

The Logan Ranch was bustling with activity at way-too-early o'clock in the morning. Sabrina's dad and her newly adopted son, Harry, had provided me with a blueberry muffin and cup of coffee after they'd answered the door. Now I was sprawled across Sabrina's bed listening to her, Ruby, and Gracie trying to guess what type of dress Everett would like best. Who cared about crap like that? I just wanted a dress, not hours of speculation.

"This is way better than homecoming dress shopping was." Ruby was sprawled on Sabrina's bed, sipping a glass of orange juice while Sabrina pulled dress after dress out of her closet for me to try on.

"This is just like a girly rom-com movie," Gracie added. "We need big glasses of wine, and a cheesy pop song to montage it. Oh! And Willa, you need to pout and be cute. You know, act all harried and frazzled."

"*Ugh*, that's too many dresses." I flopped onto my stomach, burying my head under Sabrina's pillow. "Pick your top three, and make them all black," my muffled voice instructed. There was no way I was going to try that many dresses on. I was not a dress kind of girl—I was jeans and cowboy boots, tank tops and leather jackets —and fancy dresses were way out of my comfort zone. Thus, the reason why I was here, borrowing a dress for my date with Everett tonight.

"That was awesome, Willa!" Ruby exclaimed.

"I'm being serious. It's too many. I'm not doing it."

"Shut up, Willa. Don't be such a poop. You missed this experience, the whole getting-ready-for-a-date-with-your-girlfriends thing. I'm going to check it off the list." Gracie lifted the pillow from my head then hit me with it.

"What list?"

"We made you a list of stuff you missed out on because of Tommy." I looked at her out of the corner of my eye as she held her cell phone out to show me.

"Y'all did what now?" I sat up. These girls were nuts.

"We made a list of the most important things a woman should experience before she dies," Ruby explained. "Some of this applies to you too, Sabrina, so pay attention."

"Girls, we don't need a check off list," Sabrina protested, giving me a wide eyed—a.k.a. WTF?—look.

"No list. I'm barely into this whole dress thing as it is," I protested.

"I got it. This one." Sabrina held out a tiny piece of black fabric. My jaw dropped as I sat there and stared at her. With a laugh, she threw it at me.

"I can't believe you own this dress, Sabrina." I said as I draped it down my body and looked in her mirror. It had spaghetti straps, was cut in the center almost to the navel, and it was short with a flippy little skirt.

"Uh, well, since I married Wyatt I've been—"

"She's been dressing like a sex kitten on date night. She's giving new meaning to the whole sexy-librarian thing." Ruby finished for her.

"Ruby!" Sabrina blushed, and I laughed and tossed the dress at her head. She caught it with a sheepish smile.

"What? You know it's true, Sabrina. I mean, that's why you do it, right? To drive Wyatt nuts. Date night comes around and Sabrina lets her hair down and takes those glasses off." She looked at Gracie and they rolled their eyes together. "Anyway, you should see his face every other Friday night. It's priceless. Oh wait, here you go." She tapped on her phone then held it out to me.

"You made a YouTube page of Wyatt?" I asked as I scrolled through.

"Heck yeah, I did. It's monetized now. #StopAndGoSuperman for life. I made six-hundred bucks off my page last month."

"We should add Everett and split the money. If we filmed him working on his house, we could retire at age eighteen. He never wears a shirt," Gracie whispered to Ruby.

"No. No way," I protested. But then all the times I'd watched him through the window as he worked outside ran through my mind as I scrolled through the thumbnail images of Wyatt on Ruby's YouTube page and I reconsidered. *Six hundred bucks? No, it would be wrong...*

"Yeah, don't worry. I would never do that," Ruby scoffed. "Wyatt lives here. It's like, no effort involved to just aim my phone at him."

"Delete it, Ruby. All of it. I mean it this time." Sabrina turned to me. "Here, go try this on." I caught the silky slip of a dress with a smirk as she tossed it back to me.

"Yes, ma'am." I headed into her bathroom, slipping off my boots on the way. I quickly changed and then threw open the door.

"Hubba hubba, look at your legs." The wolf whistle from Ruby almost sent me back to the bathroom.

"It's too short, isn't it? I'm taller than you, Sabrina. And I can't fill out the top part of the dress like you."

"No, no, it's perfect. With Sabrina, it's all about the boobs," Ruby explained. "You're all leg. He's going to flip, especially if you wear heels—" I watched as she and Gracie had what had to be an entire conversation with their eyes. I would have to be on the lookout for rogue teenage girls and hidden cell phone cameras tonight.

* * *

I had to borrow heels from Sabrina. They told me I couldn't wear my cowboy boots, even though they were high heeled. Whatever. I was dressed and ready, hair down in wild curls, wearing heels—platform, four-inch, with one strap across the toes and one around my ankles—that would make me almost as tall as Everett. The idea excited me. These shoes were not made for walking—or pacing as the case may be—and I was wearing a path in the carpet in front of my door as I waited for him. With a glance at the clock I determined that I was ridiculously early. I had no concept of proper getting-ready-for-a-date timing.

I blew out a sigh and contemplated adding more lip gloss. Or maybe some eyeliner? I should have made up my face like I did for work. *Gah!* A knock on the door startled me. With a laugh, I shook it off. It had to be Everett. I paced back to the door and opened it, almost falling on my ass when I took a huge step back to slam it in Tommy's face. I locked every lock and stood there with my heart in my throat.

"Go away!" I yelled.

Bang. Boom. Crash.

This was not the sound of Everett working outside. This was the sound of Tommy about to break my freaking door down with his foot. I ran for my back door, threw it open and darted up the stairs to Everett's kitchen. With a twist of the knob, I was inside, locking the door behind me and freaking the eff out.

"Everett!" I shrieked. His footsteps pounded down the stairs as he ran down. I ran across the kitchen to meet him only to freeze slack-jawed at the sight of him in nothing but a pair of tight black boxer briefs. Whoa. Holy crap, whoa.

"What! What is it? What's wrong?" He froze in alarm. His eyes grew wide as they moved up and down my body, while a flush spread up his chest to heat his cheeks.

"Tommy. It's Tommy. I ran up here."

"He's here?"

"At my door. I slammed it and locked it."

"Stay here and lock the door behind me." He raced through the kitchen and down the basement steps. I locked the door and ran to the window overlooking the driveway to watch. I couldn't see my porch because of the overhang, but I saw Tommy's truck idling at the curb. No sign of Tommy though.

I tried to quiet my breathing so I could hear. Then I tried to reason with myself. There was no need to be scared like this. In all the years I had been with him he had only hurt me once—physically, anyway. He wouldn't do it again, right? I had already left him. I'd done my worst to him. Maybe I should just go down there and tell him to leave me alone for good.

I gulped in a huge breath of air, which did nothing to calm my racing heart or my panicked imagination.

Why was I panicking?

No, I could do this. Everett would be down there. I wouldn't be alone with Tommy. After descending the stairs, I made my way through my apartment to the closed door where I heard muffled voices on the other side. I threw open the door to see what was happening.

"You can't just stun gun people, Gracie!" Everett's voice filled the air as I watched him throw his arms out to the sides in frustration.

"But, he's a dick! Clara told me to shock first, ask questions later whenever it came to him," she shouted back.

I stepped onto the porch to see Tommy sitting off to the side, propped up against the house.

Ruby knelt at his side, waving her hand in front of his face. "How many fingers am I holding up?" She stood up as he hefted himself to his feet with a murderous scowl on his face.

"I should have you arrested," he shouted at Gracie, who flipped him off in response. I wished I had even half of her nerve.

"For what?" Everett growled. "You're on my property. You dented my fucking door with your boots, and you wouldn't leave when Willa told you to. *I* should have *you* arrested."

"I don't need this shit. Go on and call the Sheriff Department.

Tell them to meet me at home. I'll be waiting with my father's attorney. I'm leaving. I'll call you, Willa. We're gonna have that talk." He stalked off to his truck and left. As if my slamming the door in his face and running away was not enough of a hint that I didn't want to have a talk with him.

"I want you to delete those pictures, Gracie." Everett pointed a finger at Gracie.

"I didn't take any pictures." She shrugged, the face of innocence.

"Delete the *video*, Gracie," I said.

Her lips pursed and her eyes shifted to the side. "Fine, sure, okay. Come on, Ruby. We're going to Daisy's. This was stressful. We need pie." She hugged me and whispered in my ear, "I got video of him in his underwear, Willa. Think of the money we could make."

I tugged her to the side. "He's in his underwear. That is hugely different than Ruby filming Wyatt reacting to Sabrina and you know it."

She thought for a second. "*Gah!* You're totally right. I'm a jerk. I'll delete it right now, from the cloud too." After a few swipes, she held her phone out. "It's gone!" She called over her shoulder as she ran to join Ruby.

"Thank you, Gracie," Everett called out to her retreating back.

"I'm really sorry. I didn't think it through," she yelled from the passenger side of Ruby's Jeep as they pulled away.

"Well, that was interesting," he said with a chuckle.

"Yeah, at least this time he left without having to get half the town involved." My attempt at a joke fell flat; he didn't laugh.

"Let me borrow your phone to call Wyatt. I'm pressing charges about my damn door. And they can pick him up for violating the restraining order."

I tried to listen as he spoke to Wyatt, but I was distracted by the way he was checking me out as he talked. The heat in his eyes burned away any fear I had felt from seeing Tommy. Everett ended the call and passed my phone back to me.

"They put out the call. He'll be arrested on sight." His eyes roved over my body, smiling as they roamed. "You look fucking beautiful,

Willard. That dress is uh…I, uh... And those shoes. You are stunning. And here I am. Standing in the driveway. In my underwear. This isn't what I had in mind when I said I wanted to woo you properly." His head shook side to side as he stood there grinning sheepishly at me.

"I don't know about that. You? In those underwear? Pretty freaking woo if you ask me."

"Pretty freaking woo?" That smile, big and white, combined with those dimples? He was so insanely dreamy and ridiculously hot standing there that I wanted to just skip dinner and eat him instead.

"Totally." I grinned. "I wouldn't mind getting the whole woo right now, in fact."

"Oh yeah? Maybe I'll give you a woo, just for you, then take you to dinner. How about that?"

"Just for me?" I almost backed away as he stalked toward me, like maybe he was the one getting the snack before dinner instead of me. I squealed as he put a shoulder to my stomach and picked me up in a fireman's hold to carry me around the side of the house to the back porch. He opened the back door, slammed it shut with a kick and took me to the living room. As I slid down his body, he grabbed the hem of my dress to lift it over my head and toss it to the floor, leaving me in nothing but my heels and a pair of black lace bikini panties.

"Now," he said.

"Now?" I breathed, my eyes wide with curious amazement. *What was he up to?* He nodded and chest to chest, eye to eye, walked me backward to the couch while his hands slid over my bottom to push my panties down. I kicked them aside as I walked.

"Sit." I sat. He knelt in front of me, nudging my legs apart with his shoulders. With his hands behind my knees, he lifted until my feet were on the couch, my legs spread wide, him in between.

"Ready?" His blazing eyes roved over my body, up and down coming to rest between my legs. *Holy crap.*

I nodded enthusiastically. "Yes, please," I breathed. I was soooo ready for this. Words failed me as he lowered his head then stopped. He was right *there*, but not quite touching me.

"Do you remember what I said when I was inside you all those nights ago?" His fingers traced lazy circles over the insides of my thighs, tickling my skin, holding me open, driving me crazy with anticipation.

I remembered everything about that night. I nodded again as my eyes found his.

"Tell me what I said." I could feel his hot breath on my slick skin, so close. "Tell me, sweetness, and I'll give you what you need."

"You said…um, you said you wanted to taste me." I murmured as I watched his eyes smile into mine with a satisfied gleam. How was he able to be as sweet as he was, while also being so absolutely, gloriously naughty?

"Good girl. Now show me where." My chest heaved as my hand drifted over my breasts, trailing lightly down my stomach to show him. As soon as my fingertips touched my clit, he shoved them aside with his tongue. My head fell back to the cushion as my body arched toward his mouth.

"God, Everett," I squealed.

"Mmmm," he growled against me, sucking me into his mouth. My hands hit the couch as my hips thrust into his face. Two big palms grabbed my writhing hips to hold me still. "Relax. Just let it happen," he murmured against me. "I'm in no hurry, sweetheart. I could do this all night, as long as it takes."

Trembles shot through my whole body at his words as I tried to relax. His hands eased their grip and started to caress lazy patterns across my body, up to my breasts, down my thighs, then up again to cup my cheek as his eyes glinted with pleasure and he winked at me.

He liked this.

I turned malleable, boneless, into absolute putty beneath his generous mouth and seeking hands. My mind drifted into nothing as I watched his face. His beautiful honey brown eyes smiled into mine then grew hot as he entered me with one finger, then two, thrusting gently until he found the spot he was looking for and pressed up. Delicious pressure, sensations I never knew were possible, arced through me. The soft scratch of his beard against my most sensitive skin, his fingers oh-so-gently stroking inside me, and his blazing eyes holding mine kept me anchored amidst this overwhelming, swirling, tidal wave of need as my hips bucked once, twice, and I let go of everything and flew apart. How would anything ever feel this good again?

He placed a soft kiss to the inside of my thigh and then stood, sweeping me into his arms to sit on his lap. With one of his long legs on the floor and the other bent on the couch he cradled me in his arms. I curled sideways against him with my bottom between his legs to tuck my knees to my chin. With feather light strokes down my spine, he soothed my racing heart.

"Listen sweetness," he whispered in my ear. "Last time we were together we got out of control. We didn't use any birth control, or even talk about it. It all happened so fast and I wasn't careful with you. I want you to know that no matter what happens it will be okay. I'm here for you, no matter what, and I'm not going anywhere. Ever. Do you understand what I'm saying?" I nodded. "Are you okay?" His lips brushed the top of my head as he pushed my hair over my shoulder. The whispered question. A kiss sweetly given. Was I ready to feel like this? But then, how could I refuse him? My body had melted for him before. But now it was my heart.

"Yes, I'm perfect." I was not perfect. My mind was still a little bit blown and I was not operating on all cylinders, kind of like my van, wherever it was. *Where the heck was it?*

"Ready to go to dinner?" I tipped my head back to get a look at his face. Well, didn't he look smug? Whatever, he'd earned it.

"Sure," I let out a huge sigh, making him laugh. "I need to clean up first. Maybe fix my hair or something." I flipped my legs over his and stood up to stretch. He steadied me at my waist when I wobbled on these ridiculous heels. I turned in his arms. "What about you?" I reached between us to maybe return the favor, but he moved out of my grasp.

"I'm not worried about me. That was my appetizer. I'm ready for dinner." I was kind of disappointed I wouldn't be enjoying an appetizer as well, but I consoled myself with thoughts of dessert later tonight. His fingers smoothed through my hair, pushing it back over my shoulders as he drew me in for a kiss. "We have all night. There's no rush and no pressure. But just in case, there are condoms distributed all throughout this house," he whispered against my lips as he pulled away with a grin.

"All night…" I agreed on a breathy sigh. "I don't think I can actually wear that dress in public, Everett. Not after what we just did. I won't be able to even think of anything else."

He chuckled. "You can wear whatever you want, Willard."

"But you really seemed to like that dress—"

"What I like is *you*. The dress was a stunner, but you don't need it to be gorgeous. Maybe keep the heels on?" he asked with an adorable grin. "I like being eye to eye with you." He drew me close and rubbed his nose against mine as he kissed me softly.

"You've got a deal." I knew my smile was huge as I gazed into his eyes. This was the kind of smile that warmed me up straight to my soul. My cheeks were cramping, and my heart was about to burst out of my chest to fly into his.

"I'll meet you in the kitchen." With a kiss to my nose, he darted back upstairs. I gathered my dress and undies and went down to my apartment to get ready.

CHAPTER TWENTY-FOUR

EVERETT

"Everett, always defend your woman. But never lose control."

— *PAPAW JOE*

With my hips against the counter in the kitchen, I waited to hear the click of those high, sexy-as-hell heels coming up the stairs. I had grown used to waiting for Willa. Every morning I woke up hard for her, aching for her, missing her. We'd spent only two nights together, but those two nights were transformative for me. With her down in the basement in her own bed for these past weeks, I was stuck staring at the ceiling all night, wondering if she were sleeping okay. Hoping she missed me even half as much as I missed her.

I was nervous. I was more nervous for this date than I'd been in years, maybe ever. Staring out the kitchen window into the dusky sunset in the backyard, I tried to remember if I'd ever laid it out there for another woman the way I had for Willa—if I'd ever been as vulnerable, honest, *myself*—only to come to the conclusion that no woman I had ever dated had ever made me feel as if I could. Wyatt had been right when he told me Willa was not the type to judge. I felt at home with her; I wanted to keep that feeling and I wanted her to feel it too.

My eyes darted to the basement door as the *click, click, click* of her shoes announced her presence. I hadn't felt anticipation like this since senior year, right before prom. That night began and ended with disaster, starting when my date got pissed that my bowtie looked like Darth Vader's "TIE Fighter" from *Star Wars*. My mother had made it for me. The center of the tie was the cockpit and the sides were the wings. It was *awesome*. I still had it. But my date was not thrilled. Prom ended with her breaking up with me and calling me "immature". The clicking grew louder, so I stood up straight and smoothed down my tie, quickly removing my Death Star tie clip with a grimace and stuffing it into my back pocket. I adjusted my shirt-sleeves and stood there fidgeting like a nervous kid. I blew out a breath and took a step toward the door to open it for her.

Black sequins sparkled beneath the light of the stairwell as she looked up at me with a smile. Her body—clad in the sexiest halter top I had ever seen, tight black dress slacks, and those fuck-me heels —filled my vision as she walked up the last few stairs. Being above her as I was, I had a perfect view of a long gold chain dotted with tiny stars nestled between her breasts and it was all I could do not to groan out loud. She was like a different Willa again. In the dress she was sex-bomb hot. Now she was back to the easy elegance I had grown used to. I was also in black—slacks, shirt, tie, and shoes—and realized we had inadvertently matched our clothes.

Her smile lit up my kitchen. Her lips were like burgundy wine, and I wanted to taste them. I also wanted to take her out on the town and set the tone for how I wanted us to be. She was more than someone I wanted to sleep with or hang around at home with. She was more than just *a* girl. She was *the* girl. I wanted not only her, but everyone, everywhere, to know what she meant to me. And I knew if I got even just one taste of her lips, I'd never be able to tear myself away to leave the house. So, I reached for her hand and said, "Let's go."

* * *

The Front Porch was upscale, the fanciest restaurant Green Valley had to offer. The night was beautiful, starry, and clear, so I'd reserved a table on the porch of the old Victorian building.

I helped her out of my truck, fighting back a groan when my hand met the smooth, bare skin of her back. She was not making this easy on me, that was for sure. But her smile came easy as she met my eyes and it warmed my heart. "Thank you, Everett." After a peck on the lips, we headed to the restaurant.

I slipped my arm around her waist. "Cold?"

"No, I'm fine." Her arm drifted around my lower back, hand coming to rest in my back pocket. *Oh shit.*

"What's this?" She pulled out the tie clip and examined it under the beam from the light of the high pole next to us. "It's the Death Star! Why aren't you wearing it on your tie?"

"I, uh—" With a smirk, she slipped it into the hair at her temple, using it to hold the long, curly locks to the side. She grabbed my hand and continued walking, tugging me along behind her as I enjoyed the wiggle in her walk from the heels and the alabaster glow of her bared back.

The resurgence of my nerves was inevitable as I watched the reactions of the other customers—mostly men—as they stopped and stared. Some tried to be subtle and some were blatant as they tracked Willa's movements while we followed the hostess across the porch to our table. Willa was a showstopper. Her platinum curls, tossed over one shoulder, shone in the glow of the moonlight. I pulled back her chair and she gave me a smile.

"Everyone's staring at me, Everett," she hissed after the hostess left with our drink orders. "We shouldn't have come here. It's too fancy for a waitress from Genie's—" Her panicked eyes darted around the porch and I leaned to the side to block her view.

"They're staring because you're beautiful, Willard. Not for any other reason. You've been working hard on yourself. Don't let your mother's words get back into your head."

195

"You're right. I mean, about my mother." She twisted her napkin into a tight spiral, then lowered it to her lap. "Sometimes I just need a reminder, I guess. You think I'm beautiful?" How could she not know she was stunning?

"You look absolutely gorgeous. You belong here, just as much as anyone else does."

"You're sweet. It's just, sometimes I don't understand what you see in me. I don't know if I ever will. I—"

"Stop it. No. We need to address this before it goes—"

We were interrupted by the waitress. We both ordered, but I couldn't tell you what we were going to get—something about steaks and vegetable medleys, maybe a potato? After handing her menu to the waitress, Willa had pressed her leg against mine and kept it there, occasionally shifting it up and down to rub against mine. If she took her shoe off and shoved her foot up my pant leg, I might bust through my zipper. I had been testing the strength of it off and on ever since my parking lot discovery of her backless halter top. Seeing my Death Star tie clip catch the light as it held her hair back made my heart melt and my dick get hard—a perfect example of why my relationships always failed. *Immature. Geek. More into your toys than you are into me.*

The smell of flowers and vanilla hit me as she smoothed her hair behind her shoulders and leaned forward to take my hand into hers. "You were going to say something?"

"Yeah. Where have you been all my life?" I blurted it out before I could stop myself or even think about it.

A rosy blush slid up her neck as her face dropped forward. I could only see her eyes because my tie clip held her hair back. "Waiting," she whispered.

"I have been waiting for someone like you forever." We laughed in unison as our waitress arrived with our drinks and a basket of rolls. We watched her slide them onto the table then our eyes snapped back to each other. "Relationships should be easy," I said. "I take care of you. You take care of me. Easy. I feel that with you, and I like it."

"But I haven't taken care of you, not really. I'm always the one who needs—"

With a shake of my head I explained. "You get that I'm a huge nerd, right? My mother brings me spaghetti sauce and bakes me cookies. I have lunch with her almost every Sunday." She was nodding, like *so what?* "Do you think many women, once they see my collection of *Star Wars* action figures, or—" I gestured to my tie clip in her hair. "All the stuff I like repels most women. None of them ever wanted to stick around after they got a glimpse of my living room. Do you think any woman other than you has ever watched *Firefly* with me? Or even acknowledged that it is the best show in the world?" Her mouth had dropped open a little bit, but I kept going. "Do you know how many times I've been called immature because I collect *X-Men* comics and can quote *Lord of the Rings* almost verbatim? Too many times to count, Willard. I am *me* when I am with you, and it is priceless."

"Are you serious? I mean—really? All that stuff is part of what makes me like you so much." She was incredulous and outraged on my behalf. My heart filled, and I fell just a little bit more for her.

"Well, you're the only woman I've been with who has ever felt that way," I stated and took a sip of my iced tea.

"But, look at you! You're so hot. And I'm pretty sure your six-pack is actually an eight-pack. They couldn't even let that geek stuff slide to get piece of you?" Her nose wrinkled, and her head tilted as she checked me out.

"Come on," I chuckled as my cheeks heated. I'd had my fair share of *fun* in my life. But over the last couple of years I'd found myself wanting more, so I'd cut back on dating and kept to myself.

"Willa!" The color left her face and she sank in her seat as Tommy's voice rang out. I stood and moved in front of the table to block her. I waved away our waitress, who was coming to check on us.

"Tommy is here. I thought he would have been arrested by now," she whispered.

"Don't worry. Call 911 and stay right here. Don't say a word.

I've got it." She nodded frantically as she stood behind me straining to look over my shoulder.

Tommy stepped onto the porch, carrying a take-out bag like nothing out of the ordinary was going on and glaring at me with murder in his eyes. "I knew you were after her! You're on a fucking date. All that talk about what you want not mattering was complete bullshit. I knew it. That's my wife you're with!"

"She's not your wife—"

"Willa, honey, I need to talk to you." He tried to go around me to get to her, but I intercepted him. We kept up this bizarre two-step until he tossed his bag onto a table and attempted to shove me. I didn't budge. I'm six foot six, built solid, and I have a physical job. Not to mention the fact that I have three brothers; I spent my youth wrestling, fake fighting, and driving my mother insane with them. There was no way in hell I would allow a prick like Tommy to knock me down. He took a step back and glared at me while I took a quick glance back at Willa who was frantically tapping her phone to call 911.

"I'm calling the police, Tommy. Please leave Everett alone," she begged as she stood pressed back against the front window of the restaurant. The fear in her eyes and the defeat in her expression fueled my temper but I managed to beat it back and keep a level head.

"I just want to talk to you! Willa, put that fucking phone down," Tommy shouted.

Our waitress showed up along with the manager. "The Sheriff Department has been called. Tommy, you need to leave now. Try to think of how your father will feel about this and go home before you get into trouble, son." The manager was attempting to use logic, but it wasn't going to work. Tommy was working himself up to a rage; I could see it coming just as easily as I could when we used to play basketball against each other back in high school.

"I will not! That's my wife he's with. Come on, Willa honey. We can talk this through just like we always used to do. Come with me so we can just talk. Please, baby, I miss you." He took a step back, holding out a hand placatingly in her direction.

I answered for her. "She's not going anywhere with you."

"It's not up to you, Monroe, now is it?" He fired back.

"I'm staying here with Everett, Tommy. Why don't you just go home?" Willa's soft plea snapped something in him, and he took a swing at me. I dodged it as the manager herded Willa and our waitress back toward the porch railing and out of the way. Luckily, we were at the edge of the outdoor dining area so there was no real risk of anyone else getting in the middle of our scuffle.

Tommy took another swing; I ducked and came back with an uppercut to his jaw. His teeth cracked together as he stumbled back a few steps before regaining his balance. "She doesn't want you anymore. Let it sink in," I growled through the tight clench of my jaw.

"Fuck you, Monroe," he grunted. Sirens sounded in the distance. Tommy turned, vaulted over the porch rail, and darted to his truck. His tires skidded over the paved surface as he peeled out of the parking lot and sped off toward the highway.

My eyes darted across the crowded porch where most of the diners sat gaping as two sheriff cruisers pulled to a stop—Wyatt in one, Boone in the other.

"What happened?" Wyatt called as he made his way up the porch steps.

With a huge inhale, I stood up straight. My eyes found Willa, standing stock-still at the railing with our waitress. She moved to approach, but I shook my head, so she headed back to our table and sat down instead.

"He was at my house, trying to kick my door down. That's why we called the first time. Then he was here picking up takeout—"

"I saw the whole thing." Devron Stokes, one of the waiters sidled over. "Tommy started all of this. And he refused to leave when the big boss asked him to—"

"He headed north out of the parking lot. Toward the highway," I interrupted.

"You on shift tomorrow if we have questions?" Wyatt asked.

"Yeah, man." Stokes answered.

"We'll call you tomorrow, Ev. You can come down and make a statement then. Let's head out, Wyatt." Boone ordered.

Wyatt slapped me on the shoulder as he passed. "We'll get him. Take care of Willa."

"I will." I started back toward our table, passing curious faces as I went. I shook my head as I walked; I wasn't stopping to talk to anyone.

Willa saw me coming and stood up to meet me. "Obviously we can't do this," she said as soon as I made it back. I pulled her chair out, but she continued to stand, wringing her hands, and staring at me with those big, blue eyes. I placed my palm on the back of her neck and pulled her to me to kiss her forehead.

"Obviously, that's a bunch of crap," I murmured, putting my forehead to hers. "He's a pest. A bully. He's used to getting his own way, and he can't stand it that he's not going to get you back. He'll burn out and if he doesn't, he can go back to prison and rot."

"You don't know him like I do," she argued.

"Then we'll deal with whatever comes up. Don't worry."

Her eyes squeezed tight in frustration as her chin dropped to her chest. "I can't help it. I should just talk to him. Why can't I bring myself to stand up to him? I feel so stupid. I mean, I can tell anyone else off. Why not him? Will you teach me to hit like that? You knocked him back with one punch."

"I'll teach you. It's good to know how to defend yourself."

"I don't want to stay here anymore. People are looking at us. Can we go home, Everett?"

With a fingertip, I lifted her face so I could see her eyes. "Anything you need. Let's get out of here. We can take our dinner to go."

"I don't even want dinner. What I want is your couch, a hug, and some *Firefly*. I want to go inside, lock the door, turn on the alarm, and stop thinking about this. I want him out of my mind." I pulled her into a hug, dropping a soft kiss to her cheek.

"I do too. Try not to worry. They'll get him." I took a breath in as I gave her one more squeeze. Let's go home, sweetness."

CHAPTER TWENTY-FIVE

EVERETT

"You can't force love, or deny it, or hide it. When two people are meant to be, it just happens. Like death and taxes, but more fun."

— *PAPAW JOE*

The drive home was quiet. Silence descended between us like a warm blanket. We didn't need words. Our feelings were finally the same and that was enough. She held my hand and smiled. I dropped her hand to squeeze her thigh and keep her close until we made it home. I pulled into the garage and rolled to a stop. Hurriedly, I darted around to open the door for her.

She stepped out of my truck and into my arms, looking wild in the eyes. Latching onto my hair she pulled me into a hot kiss. She was so much taller in these heels, and I liked her this way. Not only were we at eye level, the heels made her wobbly and a little off balance. In a moment like this, she was dependent on me to keep her on her feet and more than anything, I wanted her to need me. I gripped her hips and yanked her into my body to run my hands over her ass and back up. The warmth of her skin beneath the flimsy ties of the halter top was as necessary to me as oxygen. I needed the feel of her skin under my hands. I untied the strings at her waist and let my fingertips drift up over the smooth skin of her back. With the other hand I caged her against my truck and urged her to kiss me again. With another rough tug of my hair, she slanted her mouth against mine and touched the tip of her tongue to my lips. I opened for her; I would do anything for her.

This kiss wasn't about her trying to forget something, it was about me and her. The difference was clear now that I'd experienced her both ways. She was completely in this moment with me, not somewhere in her head fighting against memories of her past.

She was delicious, and mine, and I never wanted to let her go. I was almost sure I wouldn't have to.

A startled giggle burst out of her when her back slid against the cold door of my truck. I put my arm around her to keep her warm.

"Sorry, Willard. We should go in the house." My voice was guttural against her mouth as I tried to speak through the kisses she was peppering over my lips and neck as she loosened my tie and started unbuttoning my shirt.

"Yeah," she whispered. But she didn't follow me as I stepped back. Instead, she reached for my belt buckle and with deft fingers, undid it. "I want you like you had me before dinner." Her grin was wicked, and nothing like I'd ever seen from her as she unbuttoned my pants and reached inside. My stomach dropped and I was abruptly hard.

"I'll give you anything you want, sweetheart. I'll give you everything," I hissed as she found me, giving me a soft stroke, leaving her thumb against the tip. "But let's get inside. Now." Taking her hands, I pulled her along after me, across the back porch where I fumbled in my pocket for the key, then threw open the door, kicking it shut, and twisting the lock behind us.

We crashed into the kitchen, her arms around my neck, me tripping on my lowered pants to end up a little off-balance with my hips against the corner of the counter. She grabbed the end of my unknotted tie, pulling until it slid to the floor. "I like how you make me feel, Everett. I'll always be safe with you." She panted as she pushed my pants all the way to the floor, following them down my body until she was on her knees in front of me. "I've never wanted to do this before. But right now, I can't imagine doing anything else." One second she was speaking to me, and the next I was in her mouth. Her hot, silky, sucking mouth. Her tongue lapped and swirled while my mind emptied of almost all thoughts, yet became laser focused on her. Her blue eyes, her full burgundy lips wrapped around my cock, and her gorgeous blond hair filled my gaze as she rapidly undid me.

I gritted my teeth and clenched my jaw as my cock throbbed in her mouth and I tried to keep from losing my mind. Crazily, I wished she would stop so I could take her to bed and get inside of her. At the same time, I never wanted this tortuous pleasure to end. Stuck in this moment, paralyzed by her sweet eyes gazing into mine and her hot mouth devouring me, I stood still, as pulsing bolts of rapture gathered at the base of my spine to shoot throughout my body.

"Oh god." I groaned and tried to pull away from her. "Baby, please come up here. I'm gonna..." I issued a warning. But she didn't stop. With a slight nod, she sucked harder while her hands joined her mouth to drive me over the edge. My head fell back between my shoulders as I sagged against the counter. *Damn.*

"You're mine now, Everett," she whispered, licking her lips and smiling as she looked up at me. Her eyes held mine and I couldn't look away. Why would I? Everything I had ever wanted was kneeling at my feet, and in this moment, I knew I would love her forever. I was hers, without a doubt.

"Come up here, sweetheart." I reached for her hand to help her up. Eye to eye we stood, and with a light tug I untied the remaining string behind her neck. The sequined bit of fabric floated to the floor, baring her breasts to my hungry gaze. "How are you this beautiful?"

Her soft laughter floated over the air. She ran her hands around my shoulders to push my shirt down my arms to join hers on the floor. I kicked off my shoes and toed off my socks as her lips quirked to the side and she grinned at me with no answer. I noticed the dark burgundy lipstick she had become fond of lately hadn't budged. And *fuck me* it was hot. Only this time I could take her mouth and have a taste of it. That lipstick took her from pretty to sexy, from gorgeous to a little bit dangerous, and it mesmerized me. It had kept me in thrall for weeks, watching her as she had worked and changed and grew. Her feisty spirit was still there, but she wasn't using it to hide behind anymore. Now, it was just perfectly *her* and I loved it.

I kissed her hard, slamming my mouth to hers. I'd been going crazy all these weeks, not being able to kiss her sweet lips. Now that I had the chance again, I had to fight against moving too fast. Her hands threaded into my hair, pulling me close as her breasts flattened against my chest. With a moan, she opened her mouth and sought me with her sweet little tongue. I had been thinking of this for weeks— her soft curves, silky skin, that gorgeous blond hair wound around my hand.

"I want something from you, Everett," her breathy whisper against my lips sent shivers down my spine.

"Anything. Name it and it's yours," I growled.

"I want you to call me Willa again. Say my name." I pulled back to kiss a long line up her graceful neck, using my hand in her hair to tilt her head to the side.

"What else do you want me to say, Willa?" I whispered in her ear, gently biting the lobe before continuing. "Do you want me to tell you how much I ache for you? Not having you tears me up inside, Willa. I hurt. Do you want to know that I dream of you? Ever since our night together, I have felt you in my arms. You haunt me, Willa, you make me burn for you." I gripped her waist, steadying her while she melted against me. Her head lolled back on her neck and a sexy little moan was the only answer I got. "Tell me what you want to hear, Willa, and I'll say anything. I'll do anything to have you again."

"Everett..." she murmured, mostly breath instead of sound.

Switching our positions, I urged her to lean against the counter. Once she was steady, I bent low to remove her shoes. As I looked up at her, the tiny pulse in her throat fluttered almost as fast as the wings of that tiny Calliope hummingbird I had spotted the other day at the feeder. I dropped to my knees to press my ear between her breasts. I wanted to hear that her heartbeat raced like mine did. "Can I touch you, Willa? Are you mine?"

"Yes." Her baby blue eyes rounded as she gazed at me. "I have always been yours, Everett. Yes," she breathed. With quick fingers, I unhooked her pants and lowered the zipper to tug them over her hips. With a shimmy, she shook them off and kicked them aside. She wore red lace this time, with a little bow on the waistband, just like a present.

Images of us, tangled together, loving each other, spun through my mind like the twisting wheel of a kaleidoscope, bursting bright with hope. My thoughts raced out of control like wildfire as she become inevitable instead of unobtainable. The beautiful torture of waiting for her was at an end and I needed her naked right now. I dropped a kiss to her stomach before sliding her panties down her legs. I stood up to lift her to the counter. Her little panting breaths against my neck drove me crazy as she wrapped her legs around my waist and held on. I could feel her against me, so warm and wet with need.

Moonlight filtered in through the uncovered windows, bathing us in light. I leaned forward to capture a pebbled nipple in my mouth. Her hands flew to the sides to grip the edge of the counter as I ran the flat of my tongue over her breast. Her taste had become as necessary as air.

"Take me to bed," she whispered against the top of my head.

"Anything you want." I traced nibbling kisses up her chest, across the delicate line of her collarbone, then up to her lips where I took her mouth in a kiss that I hoped gave as much as it took.

Those long, sexy legs wrapped me up tighter as I gripped her hips in my hands and lifted. She wrapped herself around me, letting her head drop to bury her face in the crook of my neck, licking and sucking and kissing me as I walked us upstairs to my bedroom.

With knees to the bed, I moved us until she was pressed up tight to me with her back up against the headboard. After rolling on a condom, I let her slide down my stomach until the head of my cock was poised at her entrance. Deep, deep inside, I felt that pressure, that need, to just slam inside of her and unleash. But I held it back. This woman deserved to be cherished. She needed the love I felt for her to be expressed slowly. And I needed to give her that love more than I needed to fuck her.

"I want you inside of me, Everett. Please..." Blazing blue eyes and softly writhing hips tested my will as I slowly lowered her, filling her up inch by inch, watching as the heat in her gaze increased as she bit her lip and let out a soft groan.

"Willa, right here, me and you, this is everything. This is how I make you mine. Every inch, every squeeze, all your kisses and sexy little moans. Everything you need is mine to give. Tell me what you want."

"More, Ev. I need more—" I pulled out and thrust back in, harder this time. "Yes, please..." Gripping her curvy hips in my palms I braced her against the headboard and increased my tempo, harder, faster, *more*. The lovely arch of her neck beckoned my mouth and with biting kisses, I tasted her skin, smiling as goosebumps filled the path my mouth had traveled.

Letting one hip go, I slid my hand between our bodies. I was about to lose my mind. She felt so good, so hot, like I was wrapped up in silk. Her breath hitched as I pressed my thumb against her, swirling it in a small circle until those small breathy hitches became moaning pants in my ear and she let go for me. All the longing, all the worry, all the fear that this would never happen again flew away as fiery pleasure ran through my veins. I clutched her tighter and fell into her, letting myself go as she had just done.

She wrapped me in her arms and legs as I slid my hands from her hips to gather her close, still inside her, connected by more than our bodies this time. Something else had passed between us, primal and essential.

I started to move us so I could lie down with her, but she stopped me. "Don't leave me, Everett. Stay inside, I like you here."

"I love you," I whispered. "I've been in love with you for so long, Willa. I don't expect you to say it back. But I can't be here like this with you, inside you, feeling so much, and not say it." Her head lifted from my shoulder. Her eyes darted to mine and I froze, still as a statue beneath her. A glorious smile lit up her face as those gorgeous blue eyes of hers sparkled with unshed tears.

"I love you, too," she murmured. "I'm not afraid to let myself love you anymore. We deserve this, Everett. You take care of me. I take care of you. That's the way it's gonna be with us. Easy, just like you said." The tears sparkling on her lashes fell, flowing like a crystal river down her cheeks.

"Always," I promised, brushing her tears away with my thumbs as she nodded. "Why are you crying, sweetness?" I cupped her cheeks and placed a kiss on her forehead.

"You told me you love me. But you have been *loving* me the whole time I've known you. What you say is what you do, Everett. How could this be real?"

"It's real. I'll show you every day."

"I'll show you the same. I swear it," as soon as the promise left her mouth, I sealed it with a kiss.

"I have to work at the shop all day tomorrow. Spend the day with me?" Realizing that this could be our life together and thrilling to the prospect, I smiled at her.

Her eyes softened on mine. "Yes. I need a day off, and I would love to spend it with you."

"Those are words I've been waiting to hear. Let's go to sleep, sweetheart." I shifted us to lie down, flicking the covers up, tucking us in.

After more whispered I love yous, she fell asleep. With her sleepy head on my chest, and her hand held in mine, I was in heaven. The starlight from the window illuminated her face, soft in sleep, lips pursed in a perfect cupid's bow. She was the loveliest thing I had ever seen, almost too beautiful to be real. I pulled the blanket higher to cover her shoulder, then with a soft kiss to her sweet cheek, I relaxed against the pillows and drifted off into my dream come true.

CHAPTER TWENTY-SIX

WILLA

"Girls, there is something I know for an absolute fact. Ain't one thing in the world a man won't do for you if you yell loud enough."

— *MOMMA*

The words were red and bold, painted on my front door when I finally made it outside after getting ready for the day. "Whore," written in huge block letters just waiting for the neighbors to see. Just waiting for my heart to rip out, and for me to cry like I used to whenever he called me names. But not this time. This time, instead of capitulating to his cruelty and groveling for his approval, I found myself lost in a strange euphoria where I felt happy and completely pissed off at the same time. Or maybe I was happy *because* I was pissed off, instead of off crying in a corner somewhere. Rolling with it, I stalked over to the garage to gather cleaning supplies. Bizarrely, I was glad he did this. A smile, wide and pure filled my face, joining the ice-cold rage in my heart, as I searched in Everett's cupboards for something to scrub away Tommy's extremely misguided attempt to cow me.

"God, Willa. I just saw the door. Are you okay? Wyatt just called;

they haven't found him yet." Everett rushed in, taking me in his arms from behind.

"I'm totally fucking fine. I'm about to clean that mess up." I spun to face him, not able to resist placing a kiss on his gorgeous, generous, magically oh-so-capable mouth. "It's a beautiful day, isn't it?"

"Yeah, it is. You're all right?" His eyes were wide and speculative on my face as a small smile traced across his lips

"I'm serious. In the weirdest way ever, I am happy he did this. I'm kind of scared, but I'm mostly mad, and that is a first for me—" I gestured wildly to my front door. "This is classic Tommy manipulation. He's trying to knock me off balance, make me try to win back his approval. It took me a long time to see what he had been doing to me, that gaslighting bastard. And after all this? Kicking the door, spray painting your house, fighting with you at dinner—he's going back to prison. Once they catch him, he's gone."

"Yeah, you're right about that. It's just a matter of time. I'll help you clean up and then we'll head to the shop for the day." He took the bucket from my hand similarly to how someone would take a live nuclear warhead from a psychopath—gingerly, with extreme caution. I grabbed scrub brushes and the container of cleanser from the work bench to hurl them inside the bucket.

"It's a mother-flipping plan, man." I stuck out my hand for a high-five. With lips quirked to the side and a wide-eyed head shake, he smacked palms with me.

"I've never seen you like this," he said cautiously.

"You and me both! I've never felt like this. I'm free, Everett! This proves it. I feel nothing for him. Not. One. Thing. Except for an extreme amount of anger that I even need to deal with his dumb ass after spending so much time and money getting that divorce. Something clicked for me last night. He can't *make* me do anything I don't want to do. I have a stun gun, Everett, and I have you. Plus, once they catch him, he'll be back in prison where he belongs. And I'm so mad right now that I could probably kick his ass all by myself."

"You're not just putting on a brave face? You don't have to pretend with me."

"I'm really okay. And I love you for making sure. I just love you, Everett." The bucket fell to the driveway as he yanked me into his arms.

"I love you too, Willa," his deep voice sounded in my ear as he kissed a hot trail down my neck and back up. "I waited a long time to say your name like this." Pulling me closer, he took my mouth in a hot kiss. He turned to back us up into the garage where he pressed me up against the wall, grinding himself against me. I breathed him in and let some of the anger out. Everett consumed me in the best way. With one arm he caged me against the wall, pulling back with a sexy, lip biting man pout as he caught my gaze and held it.

"We should stop before we get carried away," I whispered. "We'll be late to open the shop. Everyone will be waiting for us."

He shook his head and kissed me again, groaning against my lips in protest. "It's hard to let you go, sweetness."

"You never have to let me go," I promised, sliding out of his arms to pick up the bucket.

* * *

"My mother is here," Everett said with a grimace, as we pulled up to the curb.

"Why does that bother you? She's always been nice to me."

"Oh, she'll be nice to you. Don't worry about that, Willa. She's going to smother the crap out of you." His eyes slid to mine as he shut off the engine. "I'm surprised Sabrina hasn't mentioned anything—"

"Yoo hoo! I see one of my favorite boys in that truck! Come out here and hug your mother, Everett. You too, sugar pie." Her smile was huge as she waved me over. I looked back at Everett with a sideways grin.

"I told you. She has a sixth sense about shit like this. Prepare yourself, she probably has dinner planned for tonight and already knows we're officially together—"

"That's crazy!" I scoffed and hopped out of the truck. Only to turn around and step into one of the warmest hugs I'd ever received.

"*Eeeeeep*! I'm so happy!" Mrs. Monroe gave me a squeeze then stepped back to pat my cheeks with a huge smile on her face.

"Oh!" Was all I could think of to say. I'd met her a few times and she was always friendly, but this was on another level. There were expectations and, I swear I could see *plans* in her eyes.

"No more of that Mrs. Monroe nonsense. You call me Becky Lee now, honey. Later, after y'all get married, we can move to Mom, or Momma, whatever you prefer. Just—don't call me 'Ma.' Garrett insists upon addressing me as such, and it drives me batty."

"Oh-kay…" I jumped, startled when Everett slipped his arm around my waist.

"Dial it down a notch, Mom. You'll scare her off," he warned her with a smile. My eyes were huge as I looked up at him. I wasn't scared, just kind of overwhelmed. And, how in the heck did she already know? *I* barely even knew, for goodness sake.

"Oh, hush, you. Don't tell your momma what to do," she admonished him with a sparkling smile. Her rings glittered in the early morning sunlight as she reached up to pat his cheek. The gentleness of her touch and tone of her voice belied her words, and I gulped back a sob. In my experience being told to *hush* was never this pleasant. The beautiful burn of this moment settled into my soul like a balm as I snuggled into Everett's side.

"Yes, ma'am," Everett grinned. "So, who was it? Who told you?"

"Well, I really wouldn't know what you are talking about," she huffed with a dainty giggle. Her eyes landed on mine with a conspiratorial glimmer and I couldn't help but grin at her, even though I did not know what we were conspiring about. "Us girls stick together," she announced and took my hand, pulling me from Everett and into her side. "Sabrina told me she loaned you the dress I bought her," she whispered in my ear as my eyes grew huge. *She* bought that slinky, sexy, barely-even-a-dress dress? *Holy crap.* "I knew that could only mean one thing, and I was right. Look at you two! Finally! I called it when I first set eyes on you last Halloween. I said, 'Becky Lee, that girl is the one for your Everett. She's sweet, she's funny, the kids love her, and she's pretty as a picture.' Of course, I was right. I am always right about my boys! Yay!"

"Yay!" I repeated as she gathered me into another hug. She smelled like chocolate chip cookies and rosewater, her sprayed blond bob tickled me beneath my chin, and I got the sense that when Becky Lee Monroe gave a hug, she meant it. She patted my cheek, then returned to her car to grab two large cooler bags out of the trunk.

Gracie was standing in front of the counter, hand in hand with Weston, when we finally made it to the door. "When are you going to make me the manager, Everett?" she yelled once she spotted us.

"Never," he teased with a laugh. "Or maybe after you graduate high school. Being the manager is a lot of work."

"That's fair. And probably a sound business decision. Ruby is on her way. Is Garrett going to be here for the game?"

"Yup. Wyatt and Sabrina should be here any minute too," he answered.

"What's going on?" Holding a finger up to Gracie and Weston, I tugged Everett aside. "I thought it would be me and you here today. Maybe a customer or two." I whispered to him while Becky Lee winked at me with a knowing look as she passed us to head inside.

"I brought munchies for your tournament!" she announced, bustling around the tables to distribute little wrapped trays to each one.

"It's tournament day. I thought you could play your rogue. You know, show me what you got, Ceto." He winked.

"Or I could play the mermaid queen instead," I suggested with a wink of my own.

"You could be the mermaid queen tonight. I have a huge bathtub you haven't seen yet." He nipped at my ear after whispering that tantalizing possibility into it. And with that, images whirred through the dirty projector screen in my mind. Everett was a D&D roleplay nerd, which meant our sex life had limitless potential and I was set for life.

"Don't gross me out. We're all still here, you know." Gracie's

215

eyebrows were in her hairline, while Weston chuckled to his Converse, refusing to look up.

With a wicked grin, Everett swept me up and carried me through the doorway. Giggles flew out of my mouth as I wrapped my arms around his neck with visions of the future running through my mind as he kissed me.

"Oh, barf. You're going to be one of *those* couples, aren't you?" Gracie snarked.

"What's wrong with that?" Weston slid his arm around her shoulders. I laughed as she blushed. Maybe she would be part of one of *those couples* too someday.

"Get your hands off my wife!" Tommy shouted, slamming the door of his truck and stalking up the sidewalk. "Put her down." Everett set me down inside the shop, stepping in front of me to block the entrance with his body.

I shook my head side to side to side while bursts of panic edged into my thoughts, coloring the periphery of my vision white. Fighting the panic, gasping for breath, I remembered how I'd felt in the driveway: angry, strong. I remembered what Gracie's therapist taught me and counted backward from ten in my mind as I recalled how I felt over the two years I spent away from him. I'd found peace on the road and I wanted my freaking peace back, dammit. "I'm not your wife anymore," I shouted from behind Everett. "We're divorced. How could you forget? You spent enough time fighting it." I took a step back, right into Gracie and Weston. She gripped my shoulders, while Weston held my hand. Was it wrong to borrow a little bit of Gracie's strength? I whirled to the side as Becky Lee slipped her arm around my waist.

"You'll be just fine, sugar pie. Everett won't let him get anywhere near you," she whispered in my ear. "Go on now, Gracie, call the police." Gracie's warmth left my back as she turned to make the call.

"The divorce is bullshit and you know it," Tommy shouted. "We took vows in front of God, Willa. You will always be my wife." He weaved side to side on tiptoes, trying to catch my eye around Everett. Perfect, wonderful Everett who stood like an unmovable sentry in front of me.

"We were in Las Vegas, Tommy. God had nothing to do with it. We took our vows in front of Elvis, and he'd probably agree with me that you're an asshole," I yelled over Everett's shoulder.

"I'll let that slide, honey. I'm still willing to forgive you for going out with this loser last night. I'll still take you back. I love you."

"But I don't want you back, Tommy. And I don't love you anymore. In fact, I don't think I ever really loved you. You were nothing but empty promises and lies. A pretty face and a nice body, but you're dead inside. You're selfish and cruel and I'm finished putting up with you."

Becky Lee's arm around my waist tightened as she shouted at Tommy. "Willa is right. You are nothing but a bad seed, Tommy Ferris. I've been calling your momma every day to make sure she and your daddy keep you busy and out of Green Valley. And you can bet your bippy I'm going to call her today. You're breaking your mother's heart, Thomas Daniel Ferris. Shame on you." He didn't seem to care what we said. His eyes were wild with anger, glinting with barely leashed rage. I steeled myself. His expression told me he was about to erupt. But we were in public, not in our house in Nashville where he could punch the walls and throw things to his heart's content. Maybe he figured he didn't have anything else to lose.

He stopped weaving around and let his eyes land on Everett with a sly look. "Come back to me, Willa. I'll give you the baby you always wanted."

"Liar!" I screamed, shaking out of Becky Lee's hold and surging forward to lean around Everett's shoulder. From the second Tommy had stepped foot near the shop I had been teetering on a precarious edge between anger and fear. Red filled my vision as rage sent me over the side, consuming me. I rushed around Everett to shove Tommy. Fists to chest, pounding, pushing him back along the sidewalk toward his truck. I needed him gone. I wanted to hurt him like he had hurt me so many times before with his words. "You wanted me to abort our baby, Tommy. When you knew it was all I'd ever wanted." I shrieked in his face as I pummeled his chest with my closed fists.

"Well, you did it. That proves what kind of mother you'd be now doesn't it?" That same cold cruelty that always glinted beneath the surface shone from his eyes as he shook me off. I stumbled back into Everett. I hadn't realized he was so close behind me. My eyes darted to the side as Everett stepped in front of me and Becky Lee gently pulled me back.

That cruel look on Tommy's face used to make me crazy. At one time I would have done anything to make him look at me with tenderness again. I used to believe I had to earn his love. I've since learned that love doesn't come at a price. Love doesn't make you bleed inside, dying a little bit every day until you forgot who you were.

Tommy reached out to shove Everett. He sidestepped it and I broke away from Becky Lee as my temper got the best of me. "I did no such thing. I chose my baby. I left you." My voice was an unrecognizable screech, as if it came from somewhere near the bottom of my soul. Rage and grief battled for dominance in my heart. Once more rage won, and I slapped Tommy across the face. The impact of it vibrated through my hand, stinging, and burning a throbbing trail of pain up my arm. His head whipped to the side, red blossoming over his cheek. Before I could react, he shoved me; the past flew through my mind as my body flew sideways to land hard, my hip crashing to the sidewalk as my hand skidded across the cement. I looked up to see Everett shoving Tommy toward the hood of his truck and Becky Lee leaning over to help me up. She pulled me toward the doorway of the shop. My head spun as sirens filled the air in the distance.

"You're not worth all this trouble, you bitch! I can't believe I wasted all this time on you." Tommy's voice was muffled. Everett had him pinned down with his cheek pressed to the hood of the truck.

"Good! I don't want to hear from you. I want you out of Green Valley and I never want to see you again! Do you understand me?" My heart raced in my chest as I finally uttered the words I should have said from the beginning of this whole mess.

"You were a shit wife anyway. Always crying over something. You can have her. I'm through with this." The more he spoke, the less I felt, until I was numb and trembling at Becky Lee's side.

I watched blankly as Jackson James pulled up in his cruiser to arrest Tommy. Once more the past filtered through my thoughts as I recalled Wyatt arresting Tommy years ago. I couldn't seem to hold onto a thought. The sound of Jackson's voice reciting Tommy's rights filtered through my mind like it was coming from underwater as I blankly watched him put cuffs on Tommy's wrists and fold him into the back of his cruiser. The lights from Jackson's cruiser faded into the distance as I slowly returned to reality. Would this finally be over? "My hand hurts," was all I could think to say.

"You'll be fine, honey. We'll get you all taken care of," Becky Lee whispered soothingly as she pulled me into her arms.

"You did it," Everett said from over her shoulder. Becky Lee stepped aside, and Everett cradled my face in his palms. "You stood up for yourself," he whispered.

"I should have done it a long time ago."

"Bravery is bravery. It doesn't have a timetable. I'm proud of you." He tipped my head back for a quick kiss.

"I'm proud of you, too!" Gracie shouted from the doorway. "Weston wouldn't let me come out. We did call the police though, so there's that."

"I got a Coke from the machine. Put your hand around it." I took it from Weston. It eased the burn in my palm.

"Thank you, Weston."

"Sabrina is going to be mad that she missed it." Weston stated. "She hates that guy."

"She won't miss it." Gracie held up her phone. "Once I saw that the Incredible Everett Hulk and Momma Bear Miss Becky Lee were glued to your side, I relaxed. I also recorded the whole thing for evidence. No one will ever be able to say he didn't start it. Plus, check you out, Willa. You were so brave and you didn't let him run you down." She tugged me inside the shop and pulled me into a hug. "A baby?" she whispered. "You miscarried, right?" I nodded against her shoulder and she whispered in my ear. "I'm so sorry. You'll be a great mother someday, Willa. Look what you've already done for me. I'm at least fifty percent less angry since you came back to town and let me live with you. You make me feel like I have somewhere to come home to. Just like a good mother would."

"Listen to Gracie. You're going to be a wonderful mother, Willa. I lost a baby—my only girl—between Wyatt and Garrett. Breaks my heart to this day. My cup runneth over with my boys, it's true. But she's in my heart, and I miss her." She looked me dead in the eye. "My Everett will take care of you. He's a good boy. But when you get that longing in your heart, you come to me. Because I *know*." My shoulders shook as she wrapped her arms around Gracie and me.

"You're making me cry," I choked as tears fell down my cheeks, soaking into Gracie's shirt. I stepped back to find they were both crying too.

"Come on." Everett opened his arms and we all stepped inside. "Grab the Kleenex from the counter, Weston."

"On it," he called back and passed us the box.

A few minutes later, Wyatt and Sabrina rushed in with Ruby. Garrett showed up, followed close behind by Boone and Barrett. And following that, the day was spent relaxing in Everett's shop, talking with friends, chatting with customers, and playing Dungeons and Dragons. There was a lot of hugging, some crying, and the day ended with all of us eating pizza from Pizza Hut, which Wyatt had to pick up, because unfortunately, Gracie and I were too busy to deliver today.

CHAPTER TWENTY-SEVEN

EVERETT

"To my grandson, Everett. I leave my house in town. Fix her up, son; I know you can do it. I also leave you my building on Main Street. Make your dreams come true. Seize every day, take every chance, and live without fear. Papaw loves you."

— *PAPAW JOE*

"How were you sure you wanted to propose to Sabrina?" I asked Wyatt. We were fishing at Sky Lake; his stepson Harry was with us on the small aluminum fishing boat.

"I couldn't think of any other way I wanted to spend the rest of my life, other than with her," Wyatt answered. As if it really were that simple. Could it be?

"Yeah, I mean, how did you know it was the right time? You know, not too soon? I don't want to rush her."

"You think too much, Everett." He grinned at me. "How do you know anything? How do you know when you are hungry, thirsty…? You just know. When there is no other option than to keep her with you forever, then you know."

"I think you should marry her, Uncle Everett. If you do, then she will be my aunt. I don't have an aunt anymore, since Riri is my mom now. And I like Willa."

"I like her too, Harry," I agreed.

"No, you don't. You love her. That's why you want to marry her." He mumbled as he cast his line in the water.

Their words distilled all my swirling thoughts down to one simple fact. "Okay. I need a ring."

"I knew this would happen." Wyatt elbowed me with a chuckle.

"You're such a romantic, Wyatt." I couldn't help but rib him a bit. It's what we do.

"Nothing wrong with being a romantic." He gestured to Harry. "Look what it's brought me. A little fishing buddy, right Harry?"

"Yes, we are fishing buddies. Riri hates fishing. But my Pop likes to fish. Sometimes he comes with me and Wyatt. Sometimes Weston does too. Mel hates fish. They make her scream. I left one in her room one time. It had pretty eyes, but she didn't like it." Sabrina was "Riri" to Harry and Wyatt's girls. Her adoption of Harry went through right before Wyatt and Sabrina married. And now plans were in the works for Wyatt and Sabrina to adopt each other's kids and make one big, blended, legally-binding family.

"I can't get her a diamond. I overheard her say she doesn't want another diamond ring. What else is there?"

"I know," Harry announced. "I like gemstones. I just learned about sapphires yesterday at the library from Miss Naomi. Get a mermaid sapphire. It is also called a Montana sapphire, a peacock sapphire, and a sea-garden sapphire. Mermaid sapphires can be all of the blue colors, sky blue, greenish blue, turquoise blue, aquamarine blue. Why are there so many blues? Oh! Willa likes mermaids! She has one on her arm. And she said she is a mermaid queen. I heard her tell that to Riri."

Wyatt smirked as he drew his arm back to cast his own line, which told me he'd heard the mermaid queen story. "Who told you?" I asked.

"Garrett called me right after it happened," he admitted.

"Of course. Nothing is secret around here. Which works for me, I guess. Now I know what kind of ring to buy. Thank you, Harry."

"You're welcome, Uncle Everett." He shrugged. "Thanks for the aunt."

* * *

When you knew something was right, the idea of waiting for it was crazy. I couldn't be with her, knowing we were meant for each other, and not do something to make it happen. Over the past few weeks, I'd been making plans. And now, burning a hole in my pocket, was one round mermaid sapphire in sky-blue, exactly like her eyes, set on a twisted platinum band. Tonight, would definitely be the night.

I pulled Willa's van into the driveway and hopped out. I had already packed everything we would need to camp overnight at Sky Lake. The familiar sound of my Bronco pulling into the driveway put a smile on my face. With a turn I saw Willa waving at me wildly from the driver's seat with that gorgeous smile lighting up her face.

"Everett! Oh, my van!" Willa hopped out of my Bronco and raced past me up the driveway to run her hands over the van. "Where has she been? I kept forgetting to ask!" I chuckled. I swear, she was about to spread her arms out and give it a hug.

"I just picked it up from the Winston Brother's garage. She's all fixed up. It took forever for some of the parts to come in. Cletus said something about catastrophic engine failure, but I knew how much you loved her, so I had them fix it anyway."

"I'm not even mad that I don't get to fix her myself. Thank you!" I laughed as she pressed her cheek to the hood and grinned at me.

"You're welcome, sweetness. How about a test run to Sky Lake? Feel like going camping tonight?"

"Uh! Yes! I'm off. I'll go pack."

"Already done. I just got back from the Piggly Wiggly with food. We are all set to go."

"Best day ever!" With a run and a hop, she was in my arms. She was wrapped around my body and tied up in my heart. I knew I'd never let her go.

"Let's get on the road." She covered my face with kisses as I walked us the few steps to the van. "Get in."

"Okay." With a huge grin she opened the door and sat in the driver's seat. "This was a school bus, so you'll have to sit in the back, Everett. Bummer." She giggled and started it up.

"That's all right. I'll test that big bed you've got back there. Make sure it's comfortable for later tonight." I plopped onto the mattress, which was surprisingly soft.

"Solid plan." Her laugh filled the van as she pulled out of the driveway.

The drive to Sky Lake gave me the time I needed to get my thoughts in order. I had been so caught up in choosing the stone, designing the ring, making sure everything about it would be perfect for her, that I didn't bother to think of what to say. I was meticulous about reserving a campsite, shopping for groceries, and getting the van fixed, but apparently, I was about to leave the words to chance. Maybe it would be better that way.

"We're almost there. Are you sleeping? You've been so quiet," she said as she pulled to a stop and turned around in her seat.

"I'm awake." I crossed the van to sit on the bench behind her chair and direct her to our spot near the lake. I'd been guaranteed it would be picturesque and beautiful, exactly right for my plans. "Back up into the spot."

"'Kay," she said as she turned the van around.

It was going on twilight hour, and soon the sky would catch fire, turning from shades of blue to burn out into pinks and golds. "Come back here with me, sweetheart." I crossed through to the back of the camper van to open the back doors, letting the warm late spring breeze filter through. The doorway acted like a frame for this perfect view. She sat next to me on the mattress with our legs dangling over the side.

"Look at the trees, Everett. You can see them in the lake, just like a mirror." I slipped my arm around her waist to tug her into me. "It's beautiful out here," she murmured and turned her face to mine. I watched the sunset reflected in her eyes as the light turned her hair to gold.

"You're beautiful," I whispered. "I know we haven't been together for very long, but I can't imagine ever being without you, Willa."

"I feel like I've known you forever. Time doesn't matter when you feel this way." Her soft, smiling eyes glowed as the fire of the sun's light diminished.

"I don't know what the future holds, but what I know for sure is, everything I've never done I want to do with you." I hopped from the edge of the van to stand before her.

"I love that, Everett. Yes." Her huge smile lit me up with more joy than I'd ever felt in my life.

"Yes, what?" I chuckled.

Her head tipped back, and her cheeks colored red as she answered. "Uh, you have a bulge in your pocket. I mean, I can tell it isn't the usual package. When you're happy to see me, it isn't shaped like a little box."

I threw my head back with a laugh. "My god, I love you, Willa."

"I love you too, Everett. More than I ever knew it was possible to love another person. So, my answer is yes. You've done enough waiting for me. I don't want you to wait for my answer. Ask."

I dropped to a knee and pulled out the box, removed the ring, and tossed the box into the van. "Willa, will you marry me?"

"Yes, I will marry you." Tears glinted on her lashes after I slipped the ring on her finger. As she held her hand out to admire it, her eyes darted to mine and she gasped. "This is the prettiest thing I have ever seen. What is it?" I took her hand in mine and smiled.

"It's a mermaid sapphire, for my mermaid queen, Willa Faye," I said with a kiss to her palm.

"Get up here with me right now," she demanded while reaching for my shirt to pull me to her. I obliged, standing up to seize her cheeks in my palms and kiss her sweet pink lips. I couldn't get enough of her. Gently, I urged her back. She scooted while I climbed up to cover her body with mine. Turning to the side, we kissed to seal this deal. We belonged to each other now and nothing would ever tear us apart.

"I'll make you happy, I promise," I vowed between kisses.

"I know you will. You have been showing me what happiness is ever since I met you. I'm a lucky girl to get to be your wife, Everett Monroe," she declared as she buried her face in the center of my chest.

Bathed in the warmth of the soft evening breeze, we made promises and love. We filled each other up with kisses and dreams of our future, and we held each other until the sun came up.

EPILOGUE

EVERETT

"I feel like I've known you forever, Everett. Time doesn't matter when you feel this way."

— *WILLA*

I took the nail from between my teeth to hammer in the last piece of trim to the window of the new downstairs bathroom. After my first strike of the hammer, the blinds in the window shot up and I stumbled a bit at the sight of Willa's face peering back at me. "Sorry if I startled you," I shouted. She shook her head and smiled before hastily lowering the blinds and turning away. I caught a glimpse of the counter behind her as the blinds fell and she stepped away from the window. Instructions were spread out over the counter with her phone on top, the timer set, counting down the seconds. A chill shot through me. *Is that what I think it is?* Shamelessly, I bent low to look through the narrow triangle that the blinds left exposed. She was pacing back and forth with what looked like a white stick in her hand.

My hammer fell to the ground forgotten, as I ran through the kitchen door, across the house, to the bathroom to pound on the door.

Bang. Crash. Boom.

"Everett! I thought you were outside!" she cried, throwing open the door just as the timer went off on her phone. I made it, thank god.

"Well, are you? Let me see it." I demanded as she laughed nervously, and her eyes filled with tears. She passed the stick to me with a tremulous smile.

"I don't know," she whispered. I took it with a nod and flipped it over.

Two pink lines.

Both of her hands flew to her belly as she gasped. With a tilt of her head, her eyes were on mine. The smile that lit up her face was beyond beautiful, beyond joyful. She was ethereal.

"Sweetness..." I breathed as I sank to my knees, wrapping my arms around her hips and kissing her stomach. The love, holy shit, *the love* I felt for her. I didn't know I could feel more than I already did.

A baby. Our baby.

"Our wedding day just got moved way up," I mumbled into her stomach. A laugh full of joy spilled from her as she melted to the floor in my arms and I kissed her tears away.

"Everett, how can I be this happy?"

"It's just us, Willa. You and me. The way it was meant to be. You take care of me."

"And I take care of you. I love you so much, Everett. Let's get married tomorrow."

"Anything you want, sweetheart. I'll call my mother." We laughed as we picked up the test to look at it again.

The next evening...

"Yeah, Ma. The pastor will be here any minute." Garrett hollered from the kitchen of my parent's house as I dashed in through the garage door. "She's doing my head in, man," he griped. "Why couldn't you wait until the weekend?"

"Willa wanted to do it tonight."

"You are whipped. Can't say I blame you though." He shrugged and stuffed a mini quiche from a silver tray on the counter into his mouth.

"Garrett William! Get away from that hors d'oeuvres tray! I am not happy that I had to order food last minute from the Front Porch instead of making everything myself, but I'll live. That is, I'll live unless you eat it all, mister. Now scat! Get out of my kitchen." He all but ran out of the kitchen, shooting me an amused look on his way out.

"You got the cake?" I asked her.

"Yes. Of course, I got the cake. Who are you talking to, Everett William?" She sighed with indignance, then rolled her eyes at me. My mother had been in—as my father liked to call it—*a state,* ever since I called her yesterday, asking if she could plan my wedding. "It is huge. Three tiers, chocolate on the inside, vanilla buttercream on the outside. And the topper is *to die for.* That Jennifer Winston is a goddess! An absolute angel! The little mermaid king and queen toppers are the absolute cutest thing I have ever seen! Willa is going to fall in love with you all over again when she sees it. That sweet little Joy will bring it over in about half an hour." She clapped her hands together with glee then leaned around me to shout up the kitchen stairs, "Garrett William, get your behind down here and wait at the door for the cake."

"Well, okay. I'm going to head upstairs to change," I said and headed to the staircase.

"Okay, honey…" she absentmindedly mumbled as I hugged her and headed up. We didn't have time for tuxedo rentals or anything fancy, so I would wear my best suit. This might be the only time I would ever get to see Willa wear something other than black. My mother was letting her wear her own wedding dress and I was dying to see Willa in white lace.

"Uncle Everett!" I spun, midway up the stairs, to see my little nieces. Mel stood at the base of the stairs with Mak, her big sister, behind her. "Look! I brought my flower girl basket, just in case you changed your mind." She waved the basket over her head while rose petals floated to the floor at her feet. Mel had been the flower girl at Wyatt and Sabrina's wedding. Due to the short notice, Willa and I weren't going to have attendants at our wedding.

"Well, I hope no one is going to throw rice at this wedding." Flynn stood next to Mel. "It's bad for the birds, you know," he said.

"I don't want to throw rice, Flynn. I have rose petals," Mel patiently explained as she gathered the fallen petals from the floor.

"That is false. We can throw rice. Ornithologists have concluded that it doesn't harm the birds. But Grandma already bought bird seed anyway." Harry entered the kitchen, with some facts about birds, a shrug, and a smile for me.

"Hey, Harry," I greeted.

"Uncle Everett! I'm so happy!" he exclaimed.

"You and me both, kid."

"I'm in the living room and I'm not touching your *Millennium Falcon*, Everett," Flynn yelled.

"I know you're not, bud," I yelled back. He was a boy after my own heart.

"Hey, hey, hey, go on upstairs, Everett." Clara entered the kitchen from the living room, arms waving dramatically over her head. "Here comes the bride and all that jazz. Go on, scoot. We need to get Willa into the secret location, a.k.a. the dining room. No peeking! The Hill sisters' luck is finally changing, and we are not doing anything to mess it up."

With a salute, I turned and darted up the stairs to go change. Barrett was at the top of the stairs waiting, with Wyatt, Garrett, and my father behind him. "We have something for you," Barrett said, hand extended with a tiny box in his palm.

"It's Grandma's wedding band," Wyatt said.

"But that was supposed to be for Barrett to use," I protested. I turned to him in disbelief. "You're the oldest."

"I'll never get married again. I failed spectacularly at it. Once was enough. I want you to give it to Willa. We all do. Wyatt got her bracelet to give to Sabrina. Garrett has her earrings. You're getting this ring, and you should have it regardless of my marriage woes. You and Papaw Joe were the closest." He thrust it into my hand with a smile. "Take it, Ev. Be happy with her. Y'all both deserve this."

I pulled him into a hug. "Thank you. And this is perfect. I thought I'd have more time to buy a wedding band." He let me go with a chuckle.

"Ten minutes, boys." My father warned. "You mother just texted me. Go change, Everett."

"Yeah, Dad's phone is about to vibrate out of his pocket. Change fast, Ev. Meet you down there." Garrett smacked my shoulder and pulled me into a hug as he darted around me to head to the backyard.

We were getting married in the gazebo. My mother had The Weather Channel blaring in the living room all morning, so even if I couldn't look out the window and see for myself, I could listen to the broadcaster tell me what a beautiful day it was. But it could have been storming and snowing, we could be getting pelted with hail, or caught in a blizzard. None of it would have mattered because today, Willa Faye Hill would become my wife, and nothing would get in the way of me becoming the happiest man who ever was.

I didn't skip down the stairs, but it was close. My heart lightened with every step to the French doors that led to the back yard. Throwing them open, I looked out at the yard. The gazebo was covered in Christmas lights, wound up with sheer white ribbon, and it appeared my mother had cleared out the floral department of the Piggly Wiggly because flowers of every type imaginable were all over the back yard. Willa's sisters, Sadie's boys, and my family were the only guests. Small was the only way to go when you only had sixteen hours' notice.

My mother came around from the garage entrance, carrying a basket of flowers. "I did my best," she said with a hesitant smile. "It's almost dusk, so those lights should start to look twinkly and the flowers—it was all they had, and—"

"Mom, every single thing is perfect. I love it. Thank you for doing this for me." I pulled her in for a hug. "I love you," I whispered.

"I love you too, honey." She stepped away and dabbed at her eyes with a handkerchief. "I'll go out and sit down. Press play on the surround sound before you come out and the music will start. Wyatt will walk her down the aisle. She asked him to a few minutes ago."

"Okay." She would be in good hands with Wyatt. I hit play and crossed the lawn to stand by the pastor in the gazebo. We were lucky we'd already obtained our wedding license.

I didn't get nervous as I stood there, but a laser focus drove through me as I watched the door and waited for her to come through. *Good things come to those who wait, but the best things come to those who fight.* Papaw Joe used to say that. Funny that the way I won Willa over was by waiting for her. But I guess you could say we both fought. I fought myself—my wants, needs, desires—and she fought her past. Now our future together was about to begin.

I inhaled a sharp breath at the first glimpse of her in the doorway. There she was, all white lace and Willa. My breath caught in my throat. She was gorgeous and beaming at me from Wyatt's side as he led her up the makeshift aisle, which was dotted with multicolored flower petals and lined on either side by our families.

"You're beautiful," I murmured as Wyatt placed her hand in mine and took his seat.

"Everett, I love you so much," she whispered.

"I love you, Willa. More than anything." Our vows went by in a blur; everything did. The world spun by, and time marched on. But not with her—we were in our own space and time. With Willa, I was at peace, I was still. I felt *right*, and so loved. All I could see was her sweet face smiling at me, her gorgeous eyes glowing with love, and that beautiful heart which had finally unfurled to let her spirit shine.

ABOUT THE AUTHOR

Nora Everly is a life long reader, writer, and happily ever after junkie. She is a wife and stay-at-home mom to two tiny humans and one fat cat. She lives in Oregon with her family and her overactive imagination.

* * *

Newsletter: https://www.noraeverly.com/newsletter-1
Website: https://www.noraeverly.com/
Facebook: https://www.facebook.com/authornoraeverly
Goodreads: https://www.goodreads.com/author/show/
19302304.Nora_Everly
Twitter: https://twitter.com/NoraEverly
Instagram: https://www.instagram.com/nora.everly/

Find Smartypants Romance online:
Website: www.smartypantsromance.com
Facebook: www.facebook.com/smartypantsromance/
Goodreads: www.goodreads.com/smartypantsromance
Twitter: @smartypantsrom
Instagram: @smartypantsromance

Read on for:
1. Nora's Booklist
2. Smartypants Romance's Booklist

ALSO BY NORA EVERLY

Sweetbriar Hearts

In My Heart

Heart Words

Monroe Brothers

Crime and Periodicals

CPSIA information can be obtained
at www.ICGtesting.com
Printed in the USA
LVHW011805070820
662641LV00004B/598